THE WATERS OF ETERNAL YOUTH

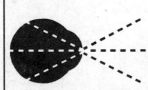

This Large Print Book carries the
Seal of Approval of N.A.V.H.

THE WATERS OF ETERNAL YOUTH

DONNA LEON

THORNDIKE PRESS

A part of Gale, Cengage Learning

GALE
CENGAGE Learning·

Farmington Hills, Mich • San Francisco • New York • Waterville, Maine
Meriden, Conn • Mason, Ohio • Chicago

GALE
CENGAGE Learning·

LIBRARY OF CONGRESS CATALOGING-IN-PUBLICATION DATA

Names: Leon, Donna, author.
Title: The waters of eternal youth / Donna Leon.
Description: Large print edition. | Waterville, Maine : Thorndike Press Large Print,
    2016. | © 2016 | Series: A Commissario Guido Brunetti mystery | Series:
    Thorndike Press large print mystery
Identifiers: LCCN 2016001160 | ISBN 9781410486936 (hardback) | ISBN 1410486931
    (hardcover)
Subjects: LCSH: Brunetti, Guido (Fictitious character)—Fiction. |
    Police—Italy—Venice—Fiction. | Large type books. | BISAC: FICTION / Mystery &
    Detective / General. | GSAFD: Mystery fiction.
Classification: LCC PS3562.E534 W38 2016 | DDC 813/.54—dc23
LC record available at http://lccn.loc.gov/2016001160

Published in 2016 by arrangement with Grove/Atlantic, Inc.

Printed in the United States of America
1 2 3 4 5 6 7 20 19 18 17 16

For Megan and Martin Meyer

Ah, perché, oh Dio,
Perché non mi lasciasti
crudel, morir nell'acque, e mi salvasti?

Ah, why, oh God,
Did you not leave me, oh cruel One,
to drown in the waters, but saved me?
                                        Radamisto
                                        Handel

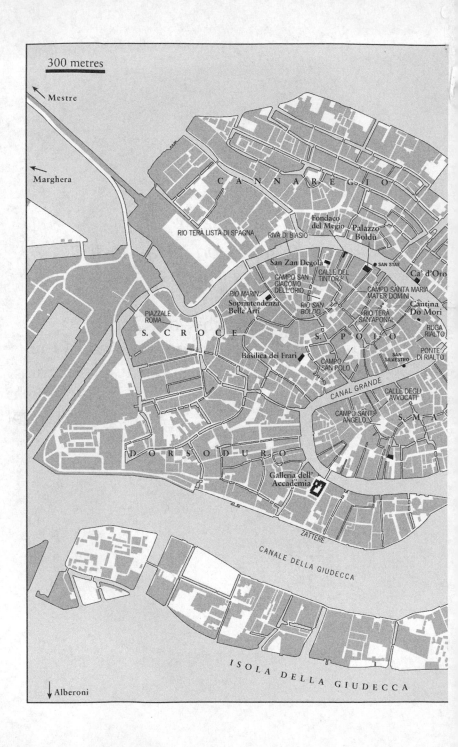

300 metres

Mestre

Marghera

CANNAREGIO

Fondaco del Megio
Palazzo Boldù

RIO TERÀ LISTA DI SPAGNA

RIVA DI BIASIO

San Zan Degolà

SAN STAE

Ca' d'Oro

CALLE DEL TINTOR

CAMPO SAN GIACOMO DELL'ORIO

CAMPO SANTA MARIA MATER DOMINI

RIO MARIN

Soprintendenza Belle Arti

RIO SAN BOLDO

Cantina Do Mori

RIO TERÀ SAN'APONAL

PIAZZALE ROMA

S. CROCE

S. POLO

RUGA RIALTO

Basilica dei Frari

SAN SILVESTRO

PONTE DI RIALTO

CAMPO SAN POLO

CANAL GRANDE

CALLE DEGLI AVVOCATI

CAMPO SANT' ANGELO

S M A

DORSODURO

Galleria dell' Accademia

ZATTERE

CANALE DELLA GIUDECCA

ISOLA DELLA GIUDECCA

Alberoni

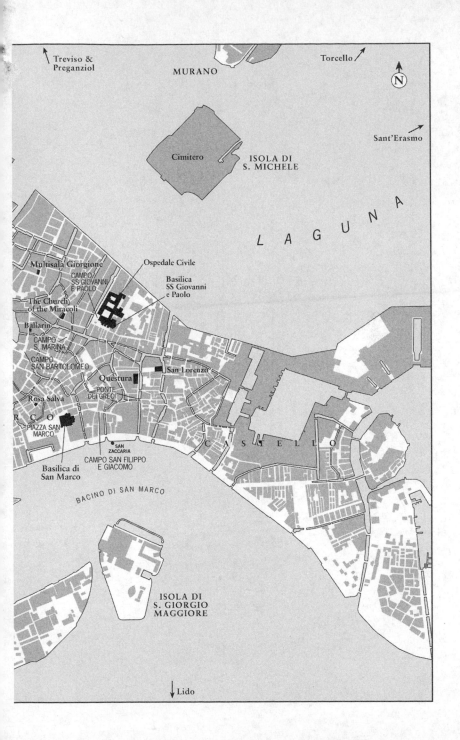

Treviso &
Preganziol

MURANO

Torcello

N

ISOLA DI
S. MICHELE

Cimitero

Sant'Erasmo

L A G U N A

Multisala Giorgione

Ospedale Civile

CAMPO
SS GIOVANNI
E PAOLO

Basilica
SS Giovanni
e Paolo

The Church
of the Miracoli

Ballarin

CAMPO
S. MARINA

CAMPO
SAN BARTOLOMEO

Questura

San Lorenzo

PONTE
DEI GRECI

Rosa Salva

R C O

PIAZZA SAN
MARCO

SAN
ZACCARIA

C A S T E L L O

CAMPO SAN FILIPPO
E GIACOMO

Basilica di
San Marco

BACINO DI SAN MARCO

ISOLA DI
S. GIORGIO
MAGGIORE

Lido

1

He had always hated formal dinners, and he hated being at this one. It made no difference to Brunetti that he knew some of the people at the long table, nor was his irritation lessened by the fact that the dinner was being held in the home of his parents-in-law and, because of that, in one of the most beautiful *palazzi* in the city. He had been dragooned into coming by his wife and his mother-in-law, who had claimed that his position in the city would add lustre to the evening.

Brunetti had insisted that his 'position' as a commissario di polizia was hardly one that would add lustre to a dinner held for wealthy foreigners. His mother-in-law, however, using the Border Collie tactics he had observed in her for a quarter of a century, had circled his heels, yipping and yapping, until she had finally herded him to the place where she wanted him to be.

Then, sensing his weakness, she had added, 'Besides, Demetriana wants to see you, and it would be a great favour to me if you'd talk to her, Guido.'

Brunetti had conceded and thus found himself at dinner with Contessa Demetriana Lando-Continui, who sat perfectly at ease at the end of a long table that was not her own. Facing her at the other end was the friend of her heart, Contessa Donatella Falier, the use of whose home she had requested in order to host this dinner. A burst pipe in the room above her own dining room, which had managed to bring down a good portion of the ceiling, had rendered the room unusable for the foreseeable future, and she had turned to her friend for help. Contessa Falier, although not involved in the foundation for which this benefit dinner was being given, was happy to oblige her friend, and thus they sat, two contessas, a bit like bookends, at either end of the table at which were seated eight other people.

A small woman, Contessa Lando-Continui spoke lightly accented English in a voice she had to strain to make carry down the entire table but seemed at ease speaking in public. She had taken care with her appearance: her hair was a cap of dull gold curls, cut short in a youthful style that seemed entirely natural to someone as small as she. She wore a dark green dress with long sleeves that allowed attention to be paid to her hands, long-fingered and thin and entirely unblemished by the spots of age. Her eyes were almost the same colour as the dress and complemented her choice of hair colour. As he studied her, Brunetti renewed his conviction that she must have been a very attractive woman a half-century before.

Tuning back into her conversation, Brunetti heard her say, 'I had the good fortune to grow up in a different Venice, not this stage set that's been created for tourists to remind them of a city where, in a certain sense, they've never been.' Brunetti nodded and continued eating his spaghetti with shellfish, thinking of how much like Paola's it was, probably because the cook who had prepared it was the same woman who had helped Paola learn to cook.

'It is a cause of great sadness that the city administration does everything it can to bring more and more of them here. At the same time,' the Contessa began and raised her eyes in a quick sweep of the faces before her, 'Venetian families, especially young ones, are driven out because they cannot af-

13

ford to rent or buy a home.' Her distress was so palpable that Brunetti glanced across the table at his wife, Paola, and met her eyes. She nodded.

To the Contessa's left sat a pale-haired young Englishman who had been introduced as Lord Something or Other. On his other side sat a famous English historian whose book about the Savoia family Brunetti had read, and liked. Professor Moore's invitation had perhaps been prompted by her having made no mention in her book of the involvement of her hostess' late husband's family, the Lando-Continui, with Mussolini's regime. On her left sat another Englishman who had been introduced to Brunetti as a banker and then, just opposite Brunetti, his own wife, sitting at her mother's right hand.

Brunetti thus sat next to his mother-in-law and opposite his wife. He suspected this placement was somehow in violation of the rules of etiquette, but his relief at being near them put paid to his concern for *politesse*. On his left sat the banker's companion, a woman who turned out to be a Professor of Law at Oxford, then a man Brunetti had seen on the streets over the years, and last, a German journalist who had lived in the city for years and who had arrived at a point of such cynicism as almost to make him an Italian.

Brunetti glanced back and forth between the two contessas and was struck, as he ever was when seeing them together, by what odd pairings life makes for us. Contessa Falier had inherited the other Contessa when the latter became a widow. Although they had been friends for years, the bond between them had grown stronger upon the death of Conte Lando-Continui, and they had passed from being fast friends to being true friends, a fact Brunetti pondered each time he met the second Contessa, so different was the sobriety of her person from that of his mother-in-law. Contessa Lando-Continui had always been polite to him, at times even warm, but he had always wondered if he were being treated as an appendage of his wife and mother-in-law. Did most wives feel this way? he wondered.

'I repeat,' Contessa Lando-Continui resumed, and Brunetti returned his full attention to her. While she was gathering her breath to fulfil that promise, she was interrupted by a flourish of the hand of the second man to her right, the one Brunetti had vaguely recognized. Dark-haired, somewhere close to forty, and with a beard and moustache much influenced by the style of the last Russian Tsar, he interjected, speaking loudly into the pause his gesture had created.

'My dear Contessa,' he said, getting slowly to his feet, 'we're all guilty of encouraging the tourists to come, even you.' The Contessa turned towards him, apparently confused by this rare conjunction of the words 'guilty' and 'you', and perhaps nervous that this person might know some way they might legitimately be conjoined. She placed both hands, palms down and beginning to tighten, on either side of her plate, as if prepared to pull the tablecloth to the floor should the conversation veer towards that conjunction.

A confused hush fell on the table. The man smiled in her direction and entered the gap created by her silence. He was speaking in English in deference to the majority of the people at the table, over whom he swept his eyes. 'For, as you all know, the *largesse* of our hostess in aiding the restoration of many monuments in the city has preserved much of the beauty of Venice and thus added without measure to its desirability as a destination for those who love it and appreciate its wonders.' He looked around and smiled at his audience.

Because he was standing near to her and

16

spoke clearly, the Contessa could not have missed the word *'largesse'*, at the sound of which her expression softened and she released her death grip on the tablecloth. She raised one hand, palm forward, in his direction, as if hoping to stop all and any praise. But, Brunetti reflected, the voice of truth was not to be gainsaid, and so the man took his glass and raised it in the air. Had he memorized his speech, Brunetti wondered, so easily had it flowed.

Then, leaning forward and seeing that the man was thick of body, Brunetti remembered he'd been introduced to him at a meeting of the Circolo Italo-Britannico some years ago. That would explain his ease with English. A small photo of his bearded face had appeared in an article in the *Gazzettino* a few weeks ago, reporting that he'd been appointed by the Fine Arts Commission to lead a survey of the carved marble wall plaques in the city. Brunetti had read the article because there were five such plaques over the door of Palazzo Falier.

'My friends, and friends of La Serenissima,' he went on, his smile growing warmer, 'I would like to take the liberty to toast our hostess, Contessa Demetriana Lando-Continui, and I would like to thank her, personally as a Venetian and profes-

17

sionally as someone working to preserve the city, for what she has done to protect the future of my city.' He looked towards the Contessa, smiled and added, 'Our city.' Then, raising his free hand to encompass the others and forestall any feeling that he had excluded the non-Venetians, he broadened his smile. 'Your city. For you have taken Venice into your hearts and into your dreams and thus have become, along with us, *Veneziani.*' This last was followed by applause that went on so long he finally had to set down his glass in order to raise both hands to push back the fervour of their response.

Brunetti wished he'd been seated beside Paola, for he wanted to ask her if they were in danger of being propelled into charm-shock; a quick glance in her direction showed him that she shared his concern.

When silence returned, the man went on, now speaking directly to the Contessa, 'Please know that we members of Salva Serenissima are deeply grateful for your leadership in our efforts to see that the living fabric of this city that we love can remain an integral, inspiring part of our lives and hopes.' He raised his glass again, but this time he waved it in an all-inclusive circle of praise.

The banker and his companion rose to their feet, as at the end of a particularly moving performance, but when they noticed that the others at the table remained in their chairs, the banker smoothed out a wrinkle in the knee of his trousers and sat down, while she carefully tucked her skirt under her, as if that were why she had risen to her feet.

Salva Serenissima, Brunetti thought, understanding the man's connection to the Contessa. But before he could try to work out just what the speaker might be doing for the organization, a deep male voice boomed out in English, 'Hear, hear,' quite as if this were the House of Lords and His Lordship needed to express his approval. Brunetti put on a smile and joined the others in toasting, though he did not follow through by drinking. His eyes went back to Paola, now in three-quarter profile as she stared down the table to her mother's friend. As if sensing his attention, Paola turned her head towards him and allowed her eyes to close and then open slowly, as though she'd been told that the Crucifixion had only just begun and there still remained a number of nails.

The man who had spoken, apparently having exhausted his store of praise, sat down and returned to his now-cold dinner. Contessa Lando-Continui did the same. The others attempted to resume their varied conversations. Within minutes the dinner continued to the tinkle of silver voices and silver cutlery.

Brunetti turned to his mother-in-law and found that the Border Collie had been called off, leaving behind a somnolent poodle, highly decorative but bored and inattentive. Contessa Falier, seeing that Paola was busy talking to the banker, set down her fork and moved back in her chair. Brunetti noticed that the woman on his left was busy speaking to the man who had proposed a toast to Contessa Lando-Continui, so he returned his attention to his mother-in-law, a woman whose opinions often surprised him, as did the far-flung sources she consulted in forming them.

Their talk veered to that week's stories about the vast MOSE engineering project that was meant to protect the city from the danger of the advancing tides. Like many residents of the city, both of them had thought from the very beginning that the whole thing stank: everything that had happened in the last three decades had only increased the odour. Brunetti had heard and read too much to have any hope that the

20

elaborate and pharaonically expensive system of enormous metal barriers intended to block the waters of the sea from entering the *laguna* would ever actually work. The only certainty was that the maintenance costs would increase every year. The ongoing investigation of the missing millions, perhaps wildly more, was chiefly in the hands of the Guardia di Finanza: the local police knew little more than what was printed in the papers.

At the first revelations of the depth and breadth of the pillaging of European money, the city authorities had grown red-faced with outrage that quickly turned to embarrassment as one high official first claimed his innocence, only to concede that perhaps some of the money intended for the MOSE project had indeed found its way to his election campaign. But, he insisted, he had never touched a euro of it for his personal use, apparently of the belief that buying an election was less reprehensible than buying a Brioni suit.

After a brief flirtation with indignation, Brunetti's native good sense had asserted itself and he had dismissed disgust as an inappropriate response. Better to think like a Neapolitan and view it all as theatre, as farce, as our leaders at play, doing what they do best.

He felt the moment when both of them tired of the subject. 'You've known her for ever, haven't you?' Brunetti asked, giving a quick glance to the head of the table, where Contessa Lando-Continui was speaking to the German journalist.

'Since I got to Venice,' she said. 'Years ago.' Brunetti wasn't sure how pleased she sounded at that; she had never, in all these years, revealed very much about her feelings for the city for which she had left her native Florence, beyond her love of her family.

'She can be the worst sort of battleaxe, I know, but she can also be generous and kind.' Contessa Falier nodded in affirmation of what she had just said and added, 'I'm afraid most people don't see it. But then, poor thing, she doesn't see many people.'

Contessa Falier glanced around the table before adding, in a quiet voice, 'This is an exception. She'll host these dinners with potential sponsors, but she doesn't like to do it.'

'Then why do it? Surely they must have an office for fund-raising.'

'Because everyone loves a lord,' she answered, lapsing into English.

'Meaning?'

'She's a contessa, so people want to say they've eaten at her table.'

'In this case,' he said, glancing around the familiar dining room, 'it's not even her table, is it?'

The Contessa laughed.

'So she invites them here and you feed them, and in return they contribute to Salva Serenissima?' Brunetti asked.

'Something like that,' the Contessa admitted. 'She's dedicated to the work they do, and as she's grown older, she's become more and more intent on seeing that young Venetians can continue to live here and raise their families here. No one else bothers with that.' She glanced around the table, then at Brunetti, and finally said, 'I'm not sure the work Salva Serenissima did on the smaller mosaics on Torcello was all that good. In places, you can see which are the new *tesserae*. But they did some structural work, too, so it's more good than bad.'

Because he had not been inside the church in years and had no more than a vague memory of sinners being sent to Hell and a great deal of pink flesh, Brunetti could only shrug and sigh, something he had taken to doing often in recent years.

Lowering his voice and moving away from

the thought of sinners going to Hell, Brunetti asked, 'The man who spoke? Who is he?'

Before she replied, Contessa Falier picked up her napkin and wiped at her lips, replaced it and took a sip of water. Both of them glanced at the man near the end of the table and saw that he was now speaking across the table to the historian, who appeared to be taking notes on a small piece of paper as she listened to him. Contessa Lando-Continui and the English lord were engaged in amiable conversation, he speaking in loud, heavily accented Italian.

Apparently feeling protected by the deep boom of his voice, his mother-in-law leaned towards Brunetti and said, 'Sandro Vittori-Ricciardi. He's a protégé of Demetriana's.'

'And he does what?'

'He's an interior designer and a restorer of stone and marble; he works for her foundation.'

'So he's involved in the things she's doing for the city?' Brunetti asked.

Her tone sharpened. 'These *things* save the city about three million euros a year, please remember, Guido. As well as the money to restore the apartments that are rented to young families.' Then, to emphasize the importance, she added, 'It replaces money the government won't give any more.'

Brunetti sensed a presence behind him and sat up straighter to allow a waiter to remove his plate. He paused until the Contessa's had been removed, and said in a conciliatory voice, 'Of course, you're right.'

He knew that tonight's dinner was meant to bring together potential foreign donors and native Venetians — he was one of those on offer. Come to the zoo and meet the animals that your donations help survive in their native habitat. Come at feeding time. Brunetti was not fond of the part of himself that entertained such thoughts, but he knew too much to stifle them.

Contessa Lando-Continui had been trying for years, he knew, to get her hand into Count Falier's pocket. He had been both gracious and adamant in deflecting her every attempt. 'If so much weren't stolen, Demetriana, the city could pay for restorations, and if politicians' families and friends didn't get public housing, you wouldn't have to ask people to help you restore the apartments,' Brunetti had once heard the Conte tell her.

Unrebuffed by Count Falier's remarks, she continued to invite him to her dinners — she had even invited him to this one in

25

his own home — and each time she did, the Conte remembered a last-minute meeting in Cairo or a dinner in Milano; once he had begged off by mentioning the Prime Minister; tonight, for all Brunetti knew, it had been an appointment with a Russian arms dealer. Brunetti thought the Conte didn't much care how believable his excuses were, so long as he could amuse himself by inventing stories that would agitate the Contessa.

So there they were in his absence, he and Paola and his mother-in-law, offered as a sop to the insistence of the Contessa and, perhaps, as a treat to the visitors: not only Contessa Lando-Continui but Contessa Falier, two real aristocrats for the price of one. And the next generation tossed in as lagniappe.

The dessert came, a *ciambella con zucca e uvetta* that delighted Brunetti, as did the sweet wine served with it. When the maid came around again to offer a second helping, Paola caught her husband's eye. He smiled back and shook his head at the maid's offer as if he had meant to do it, failing to persuade Paola but managing to convince himself.

That done, he felt entirely justified in accepting a small glass of grappa. He pushed his chair back a bit, stretched out his legs, and lifted his glass.

Contessa Falier, as if there had been no interruption, returned to their former subject and asked, 'Are you curious because he works for her?' She moved to one side the glass of grappa the waiter had left in front of her.

'I'm curious about why he thinks it necessary to flatter her so,' was the best answer Brunetti could provide.

The Contessa smiled and asked, 'Is it being a policeman that makes you suspicious of human motives?' She spoke naturally now that the conversation was more general and individual voices were covered by the others.

Before Brunetti could answer, Contessa Lando-Continui set down her spoon and, glancing at her friend at the other end of the table as if for permission, announced, 'I think coffee will be served in the *salone*.' Sandro Vittori-Ricciardi got immediately to his feet and moved around behind her chair to pull it back for her. The Contessa stood and nodded her thanks, allowed him to take her arm, and moved off towards the *salone*. She passed through the door that led from the dining room towards the front of the *palazzo*, the guests falling into a disorderly

27

line behind her.

Palazzo Falier provided a view of what in Venice were considered not particularly distinguished *palazzi* on the other side of the Grand Canal. Some of the guests, unaware of their mediocrity, exclaimed at their beauty.

Brunetti took his mother-in-law's arm as they walked to the other room, where they went to stand next to Paola. Brunetti saw the coffee, sitting on an inlaid onyx table. Sugar, he noted, but no milk, which might explain why only the Italians were drinking it.

Seeing that Vittori-Ricciardi was deep in conversation with the banker and his companion, Brunetti moved slowly over to one of the windows and stood just within hearing distance of them.

'It's another part of our heritage that's being destroyed by time,' the Venetian was saying.

'If it's such a small island, why's it so important?' the banker asked.

'Because it's one of the first places where people lived and built: the earliest ruins are from the seventh century. The church — the one with the mosaics — is older than most of the churches in Venice.' From the energy with which Vittori-Ricciardi spoke, he could have been talking about events that had taken place last year, or last week.

'And that's what you're asking us to restore?' The banker sounded less than fully persuaded that this was a good idea.

'To help restore; yes.' The Venetian reached aside to set down his cup, turned back to the others and told them, 'There's a mosaic of the Last Judgement, and we're afraid there's water coming in somewhere behind it. We need to find the source of the water and stop it.'

'What's so special about it?' the Englishman inquired.

The answer was a long time coming, and Brunetti read the pause as a sign of Vittori-Ricciardi's exasperation with the question. No sign of that was audible, however, when he answered, 'If we don't intervene, it could be destroyed.'

'You aren't sure?'

Brunetti took a step away from them and set his cup and saucer down on a table, then turned back to the window to give his undivided attention to the study of the opposite façades.

'Yes, we're sure. But to prove it, we need to get behind the mosaic, into the structure of the wall, and it takes a long time to get permission for something like that. It has to

29

come from Rome,' Brunetti heard Vittori-Ricciardi say. A note of pained resignation slipped into his voice. 'We've been waiting five years for an answer from Rome.'

'Why does it take so long?' the banker asked, making Brunetti wonder if this were his first visit to Italy.

'There's a commission — the Belle Arti — that has to approve restorations. You need their permission before you can touch anything as precious as this.' Vittori-Ricciardi's explanation made it sound like a sane system, Brunetti had to admit.

'You're not going to damage it: they ought to know that,' the banker insisted. His tone demonstrated that he was struggling to understand.

'Their job is to keep unauthorized people from damaging art objects,' Vittori-Ricciardi told him.

'Or stealing them?' the woman asked, leading Brunetti to suspect she had spent more time in Italy than her companion.

Brunetti glanced aside just in time to see the thin moustache turn up at both ends as Vittori-Ricciardi gave a stiff smile. 'It's rather hard to steal a mosaic.'

'So when will we be able to take a look at it?' This from the banker.

'If you'll tell me when you're free, we

could go out this week.'

'When can work begin?' the Englishman asked, ignoring the previous exchange. Brunetti was curious about the expression with which the law professor's face would greet her partner's question, but he kept his attention directed across the Canal, quite as if these other people were speaking a language he did not understand.

'As soon as we have the permission. We're hoping to have it in a few months,' Vittori-Ricciardi answered. The Englishman, Brunetti reflected, would hear 'few months' and not 'we're hoping' and have no idea how much closer to the truth the second was than the first.

A silence fell. Vittori-Ricciardi linked his arm with the other man's, trying but, Brunetti thought, failing to make it seem a spontaneous gesture and succeeding only in startling the other man, who pulled his arm free. They disappeared, followed slowly by the woman, through a door that led to the *salone* that held the painted beams, one of the architectural details for which the *palazzo* was known.

Paola and her mother surprised him by appearing almost immediately through the same door, Paola bringing with her the promise of escape. As she came towards

31

him, she extended her right hand in a gesture rich in supplication. 'Get us out of here, please, Guido. Tell Demetriana you have to go and arrest someone.'

'I live to serve,' said a modest Brunetti, and led them into the other room to say their farewells to Contessa Lando-Continui, whom they found standing alone in the middle of her friend's *salone* as comfortably as if it had been her own. There followed an exchange of kisses; Paola and her mother left the room, leaving Brunetti alone with Contessa Lando-Continui.

Before he could thank her for the invitation, she placed a hand on his arm. 'Donatella's spoken to you?'

'Yes, she has.'

'I'd like to talk to you as a policeman and as a member of her family,' she said, speaking slowly, as if to convey some special message.

'I'll try to do my best,' Brunetti said. He thought she'd ask him which was more important, but she merely added pressure to his arm and asked, 'Can you come to see me tomorrow?' A contessa did not take the vaporetto and then walk along to the Questura.

'Tomorrow afternoon?' he suggested.

'I'll be at home.'

'About five?'

She nodded, shook his hand, and turned to the lord, who had come to take his leave.

A few minutes later, Brunetti and Paola were at the bottom of the bridge in front of the university. 'It's good to walk after a meal,' Brunetti said, hoping to deflect any discussion of the evening. He said nothing about his last conversation. They paused briefly at the top of the bridge to see what the firemen were up to. Nothing.

Summer had given way to autumn a few days before, and the flocks of tourists had begun their autumn migration. There was no one in Campo San Polo; all the bars were already shuttered; even the pizzeria over at the far end was closed.

'What did the banker have to say?' Brunetti asked.

'Quite a lot,' Paola answered. 'After a time, I stopped listening and tried to nod when I thought it was necessary.'

'Did he notice?'

'Oh, no,' Paola said simply. 'They never do.'

'They?'

'Men who know everything. There's quite a few of them. All a woman who has to listen to them needs to do is look interested and nod now and again. I use the time trying to remember poetry.'

'Am I one of them?' Brunetti asked.

Paola studied his face. 'You know me all these years and you can still ask that question?' When Brunetti did not answer, she said, 'No, you are not one of them. You know a lot, but you never act like you know everything.'

'And if I did?'

'Oh,' she said and started walking again. 'Divorce is so troublesome, I'd probably look interested and nod at you all the time.'

'And try to remember poetry?'

'Exactly.'

They reached the *calle* that led to their home. For some reason, he thought of how Venice had been when they were children, when few people locked their doors: certainly his family never had. But then, he realized, his family had never had anything worth stealing. In front of the door he took out his keys. But before he opened the door, he put an arm around Paola's shoulders and bent to kiss the top of her head.

2

The next morning, when Brunetti and Vianello went down to the bar at Ponte dei Greci for a coffee, Brunetti found himself telling the Inspector about some of the people at the dinner, first among them Contessa Lando-Continui herself. Brunetti recounted her comments about the sad changes to the city and then told Vianello how she had been struck silent by the flattery of one of her guests.

'No one objects to the person who's telling them how wonderful they are,' Vianello observed, a sentiment to which the barman Bambola assented with a deep nod. After a moment's thought, Vianello asked, 'What's between them? Is he a relative? An employee?' The Inspector sipped at his coffee, having finished his brioche some time before, then continued. 'Only someone who wants something would dare that sort of flattery. But he'd have to know her well.'

Brunetti had already considered this. Only someone who knows us well knows how best to flatter us, knows which virtues we'd like to have attributed to us and which not. Paola was deaf to compliments about her appearance but was a sucker for anyone who praised her for being quick-witted. And he knew that he himself was impervious to comments about the quality of his work, while praise of his understanding of history or taste in books was sure to please him.

'He praised her generosity,' Brunetti explained. 'Her *largesse,*' he added, putting the second word in audible quotation marks. He had no idea of the truth of this praise, for he knew little or nothing about the activities of the Contessa other than what had been said the night before. In fact, he knew very little about her at all. *Largesse,* however, was a quality seldom attributed to Venetians, noble or commoner.

'You know anything about her, or the family?' he asked Vianello.

'Lando-Continui,' Vianello repeated, leaning back against the bar to study the people going past towards the bridge that led to the Greek church. 'There's a notary in Mestre: a cousin of mine went to him when he sold his apartment.' People crossed the bridge, either disappearing deeper into Castello or heading the opposite way, towards the *bacino* or San Marco.

'There's something else, but I can't remember it,' Vianello added, disappointed at his failure to recall the past. 'If it's important, you could ask Signorina Elettra.' Her talents would surely surpass his memory. 'It was something unpleasant, years ago, but I can't remember what.'

'I've known her for a long time,' Brunetti said, 'but I've never had more than a superficial conversation with her. Last night was the first time I had any real sense of her. She's not as stiff as I thought she was.' But then he added, 'She does grumble, though.'

'About?'

'The way our fair city has been turned into a kasbah,' Brunetti said in a sing-song voice. 'No longer the city in which I played as a child.' Then, returning to his normal voice, 'Things like that.'

'Doesn't sound much different from what we say ourselves, does it?' Vianello suggested. Bambola turned away, but not before Brunetti saw his smile.

After quelling his initial resentment at the comment, Brunetti said, 'Maybe.' Was it the unconscious recognition of his own lamentations that had made him not like the Contessa's?

37

He reached into his pocket and put two euros on the counter. Bambola's employer, Sergio, the owner of the bar, had raised the price of coffee to one euro, ten, but not for anyone who worked at the Questura. They would continue to pay one euro, 'until', as Sergio was wont to say, 'they do away with the euro and we can go back to lire, when things will cost less'. No one at the Questura had the courage to dispute this with Sergio and all were happy to pay only one euro for coffee.

Back in his office, he found a sealed manila envelope on his desk, the signature of his colleague, Claudia Griffoni, scrawled across the flap.

He opened it and pulled from it six plastic folders containing the latest reports from those officers who were permitted to hire and pay informers. Brunetti knew that other officers had informal, sometimes not very licit, relationships with criminals, and would pay their contacts with favours or cigarettes or, he feared, confiscated drugs, should any be kept back when they fell into the hands of the police. The six officers, five men and one woman, whose reports he read every two months, however, passed to their contacts money from the Ministry of the Interior, receipts for which were clipped to their reports, every euro carefully recorded, though there was no way the sums on them could be verified.

Consider the first, a receipt from a restaurant for 63.40 euro, at the bottom of which was carefully penned in, '6.40 euro: tip'. Seventy euros was what it cost to learn, according to what was written in the report, that Afghan refugees were being carried into the country on trucks coming from Greece, information that could be picked up for free on any street corner in Mestre or, for that matter, read at least once a week in the pages of *Il Gazzettino*. The same officer reported that he had been told by a friend who owned a tobacco kiosk in Mogliano that a client, whose name was given, had offered to sell him some jewellery: the only condition of purchase was that he not reveal the source. This had cost twenty euros.

The other officers had little better to offer, though few of them had spent more than fifty euros. Brunetti was left uncomfortable at the thought that betrayal could be had for so little.

He went downstairs and into Signorina Elettra's tiny office. He found her with both hands raised and motionless over the keyboard of her computer, a pianist about to begin the final movement of a sonata. The

39

pause as she decided the precise attack extended as he watched. She read whatever was written on the screen, then her eyes moved up to study his face with no sign that she recognized him. Finally she lowered her hands, sat back and folded her arms across her chest.

He approached her desk. 'Problems?' he asked when she continued to ignore him.

She looked up but did not smile. Her right hand rose for a moment to place a contemplative forefinger on her lips, then returned to the keys and tapped at a few of them. She waited, tapped in further information, then sat back and studied the screen.

She remained motionless for so long that Brunetti was forced to escalate and asked, 'Is it serious?'

She regarded the computer screen with unwonted wariness, as though it had just given a menacing growl. Then she propped her elbows on the desk and lowered her chin into her hands. Finally, she answered him. 'Perhaps.'

'Which means what?'

'I read the Vice-Questore's email this morning and found one with an attachment. The name of the sender was familiar, but the address was new. So I didn't open the attachment.'

She stopped here. Since Brunetti had no idea what any of this could mean, he limited himself to saying, 'Strange,' which is what he thought she wanted him to say.

'Indeed.'

'What did you do instead?'

'What anyone would,' she said, leaving him wondering. After a pause, she added, 'I marked it and the attachment as read, hoping that would be the end of it.'

She looked at Brunetti, as if to test how much he understood, and his expression must have displayed at least part of the truth, for she added, 'That's how they can hack into your system: if you open an attachment.'

'Where did it come from?' Brunetti asked.

'I've traced it back to an address in the Ministry of the Interior,' she said.

Her answer left Brunetti without words. For heaven's sake, they *worked* for the Ministry of the Interior. Why should the sender need to get into their system, which was the Ministry's own system, where there was an internal record of every email or SMS they sent or received?

Signorina Elettra lapsed again into contemplation of her computer screen, and Brunetti lapsed into the contemplation of possibilities. That there would be official

41

surveillance of their correspondence and phone conversations didn't surprise him in the least: he had come to believe that everybody was listened to by at least one uninvited person. Perhaps the fact that so many people were busy spying rather than working explained why it was so much more difficult, today, to get anything done. Brunetti was conscious of the Unseen Listener when he spoke on the phone and the Unseen Reader when he sent an email. Surely things were slowed by the constant need to consider the uninvited participants who read what they wrote or listened to what they said.

Spying at this level would be given into the hands of experts to do, wouldn't it? A secretary sitting in the office of a Vice-Questore di Polizia in a small city like Venice shouldn't be able so easily to detect the attempt at detection, should she? Adept spies would be less clumsy.

'Do you know which office?'

She glanced out of the window behind him. Finally she shook away the question and said, 'It was a fake address.'

'And the real one?'

'I have no idea,' she confessed. 'I've sent everything along to a friend of mine and asked him to have a look.'

Because he did not want to know the identity of the assuredly non-authorized friend she had asked to investigate the attempted penetration of a Ministry of the Interior email address by a fraudulent Ministry of the Interior email address — Brunetti felt exhausted by the mere process of working this out — he declined to ask which friend she'd sent it to.

He had to think carefully about how to phrase any questions he might ask so as not to reveal his ignorance. 'What would they be after?'

'My first guess is that it's someone who hopes we use our office computers for our private emails. Once they get in, they can look at anything.' Did she shudder?

'I don't have a private email address,' Brunetti said.

'You don't have a private email?' she repeated, quite as if he'd told her he didn't know how to use a knife and fork.

'No,' he answered, with the same pose of innocence with which he used to tell people he didn't have a *telefonino*. 'I use Paola's, but for anything official, I use the one I was given here,' he said, waving his hand to indicate the entire Questura. 'I promised Paola I'd never use one of the computers here to check her account.'

'I see.'

'I prefer to phone people, anyway,' he added.

'Of course,' she answered, involuntarily raising her eyes to heaven at the very idea that a person existed who still believed that phones were safe.

'What will you do?' Brunetti asked.

The question seemed to energize her, as if having to give a response unleashed her to think and to act. 'If my friend can tell me where the mail came from, then I'll have some idea how to treat it. It might just be a case of innocent fishing; some hacker kid who wants to play policeman. I hope it's that.'

Brunetti decided not to ask her what else it might be. Changing the subject, he said, 'I have a favour to ask you.' He took her glance for assent and continued. 'Could you have a look at a Contessa Lando-Continui? Demetriana.' To make his request clear, he nodded in the direction of the computer as he spoke.

Curiosity filled her face. 'If I'm thinking about the one you are, she's eighty if she's a day.'

'Yes,' Brunetti answered. 'She's a close friend of Paola's mother, so I have to be very careful with her. She wants to talk to me.'

Again Signorina Elettra's face lit up with curiosity. 'I have a vague memory that something bad happened in her family.' She paused, waiting for memory, and continued when it arrived. 'To her granddaughter. A long time ago. She drowned or something.'

Surprised, Brunetti said, 'I don't know anything. Vianello remembered that there was something unpleasant, but not what it was.'

'Drowning certainly is.'

'Yes,' Brunetti agreed, thought of his family and did his best to try not to. 'Could you see what you can find?'

'Of course. Is there any hurry?'

'It can wait until your hunt through the offices of the Ministry of the Interior leaves you some time,' he answered.

She nodded and dropped her chin into her hands again. Brunetti, seeing her lapse into a trance, decided to return to his office.

3

Brunetti told no one where he was going and took the Number One to San Stae, then made his way to Palazzo Bonaiuti, where Contessa Lando-Continui lived. A maid opened the door to the street and led him across the herringbone-patterned courtyard, where chrysanthemums still thrived against the east wall.

The outside stairway to the first floor was probably original to the *palazzo,* the lions' heads worn smooth with age and rain and the caresses of centuries of hands. The maid stepped into the enormous entry hall and held the door open for him.

'The Contessa will join you in the small reading room,' she said and turned down the corridor. She stopped at the third door on the left and entered without bothering to knock. Brunetti followed her.

He had been in similar rooms countless times in the last decades. He saw the heavy-footed mahogany tables covered with books and flowers, portraits grown dark with age, tall bookshelves no doubt left untouched since the time of those ancestors, and deep and threateningly uncomfortable chairs.

Light entered from three windows on the far wall, but Brunetti had no idea which way they faced. Beyond them, at some distance, he saw the wall of a tall *palazzo*, its brick surface glowing in the richness of the setting sun. Instantaneous computation, the same skill with which pigeons are said to be graced, let Brunetti calculate that the windows looked over the courtyard of the Fondaco del Megio. He walked to one of them to make sure and noticed that the trees had started to toss away their leaves. Putting his face as close to the glass as possible, he looked to the left, to what he remembered was an enclosed sports field.

Behind him, a woman's voice said, 'Commissario?'

He turned quickly and saw Contessa Lando-Continui in the doorway. She was less imposing than she had been the previous evening, today deprived of the evidence of centuries of good taste that had stood guard around her in the borrowed room. He looked again: he saw a small old woman in a sober blue dress.

'Good afternoon, Contessa,' he said. Then, pointing out of the window, 'I think I used to play soccer in that park down there.' She looked at the window but made no move to approach. 'A long time ago,' he added with a smile. He walked towards her, and she offered him her hand. Though his easily enveloped hers, her grip was firm.

In a face less tense, her expression would have been friendly and welcoming: what Brunetti saw was a pro forma smile. 'Thank you for coming to see me,' she said.

'It's a pleasure,' he answered automatically, then quickly added, perhaps still hearing the echo of the flattery he had listened to the previous evening, 'I'd like to be of help, if I can.'

'Donatella was very kind to let me invite my guests to her home: there are few other people in this city who would do that. She was even kinder to bring you and Paola.' When Brunetti started to protest, she raised a hand to silence him. 'We were both grateful that you came,' she said in understanding of their reluctance. 'I wanted my other guests, the non-Venetians, to get the chance to meet some of the people whose lives might be improved by their generosity.'

Before he could speak, she waved him to one of the two chairs that afforded a view out of the windows. When they were seated, he asked, 'Improved how, Contessa?'

'There will be other Venetian children and grandchildren for yours to go to school with, and perhaps the whole place won't fall down so soon.'

'That's not an expression of optimism, if I might take the liberty of saying.'

There was a discreet knock at the door. When it opened, the same maid came into the room and asked, 'Would your guest like tea, Contessa?'

The Contessa looked at Brunetti. 'I'd prefer coffee.'

The maid nodded and disappeared.

'There's no liberty in your saying that, Commissario,' she said, returning immediately to their conversation. 'Mine is not an optimistic view. I think it's the only view possible.'

'And yet you go to the trouble of providing dinner for wealthy foreigners in hopes that they will contribute to your foundation?' Brunetti asked.

'Donatella told me you were direct,' she said. 'I like that. I don't have time to waste.'

'Was your time wasted last night?' he asked, though it was none of his business.

'No, not at all. The banker is eager to join and has offered to underwrite a restoration project.'

'Of the mosaics?' Brunetti asked.

Her mouth opened. 'How did you learn about that?' she asked.

'Paying attention to what people say.'

'Indeed,' she whispered and closed her eyes for a moment. 'After dinner, when you had coffee, you heard them talking, didn't you?'

'It would have been difficult not to, Contessa,' Brunetti answered, reluctant to have this woman form the idea that he was a snoop.

She laughed out loud. 'She also said you were not a fool.'

'I can't be if I want to survive in my own home.'

'Paola?'

Brunetti nodded.

'She was a very clever child,' the Contessa said. 'And she's become a very clever woman.'

The maid entered, and they stopped talking. She set a loaded tray on a side table and placed a lower table between them, then set the tray on it and left. There was a single cup of coffee, a silver sugar bowl, a spoon, two short glasses of thick cut crystal, and a bottle of whisky whose label made Brunetti stare.

The Contessa leaned forward and pushed his cup, then the sugar bowl, close to Brunetti. Then she took the bottle, broke the paper tax stamp, and opened it. She poured about two centimetres into one of the glasses and silently tilted the bottle towards him.

Brunetti nodded, and she poured the same amount into the second glass.

Brunetti pushed the coffee to one side of the tray and picked up his glass. The liquid was too precious for him to say something as banal as *'cin cin'*, and so he said, *'Alla Sua salute'*, and held his glass up to her.

'And to your health,' she answered and took a sip.

Brunetti did the same and thought he'd sell up everything and move to Scotland. Paola could find a job teaching, and the children would find something to do with themselves. Beg, for example.

'What was it you wanted to talk to me about, Contessa?' he asked, leaning forward to place his glass on the tray.

'You know about my granddaughter?' she asked.

'I know only that she was involved in an accident some years ago, but I heard that from someone in the Questura, not from anyone in my family.' He decided to omit telling her that someone was continuing to look for more information.

She cradled her glass in both hands. 'You don't need to defend your family,' she said, 'but I'm glad you did.' She took a small sip and added, 'I've known Donatella for more than forty years, and I've trusted her for most of them.'

'Only most?' Brunetti asked.

'I think it's rash to give the gift of trust to people we don't know well.'

Brunetti reached for his glass and held it up to the light, admiring the colour. 'The policeman in me says you're probably right, Contessa,' he said and took a small sip. 'This is glorious.' He set the glass back on the table. 'But I assume you are going to trust me. That is, if you want to talk to me.'

'You drink it very sparingly,' she said, putting her glass beside his to show how much larger her sips had been.

'I think whatever you have to say to me deserves more attention than this whisky, however good it is.'

She sat back in her chair and grasped its arms. Her eyes closed. 'My granddaughter was . . . damaged fifteen years ago.' Brunetti heard her breathing grow difficult and wondered if she were going to collapse or faint. What an odd choice of word:

'damaged'.

Some time passed. Her breathing slowed, and she loosened her grip on the arms of the chair. It was then that he realized they had been speaking in Veneziano, not Italian. He had automatically used the formal *'Lei'* with her, but he had addressed her in Veneziano from the beginning and without giving it a thought. It was a greater intimacy than using *'tu'*.

She opened her eyes and said, 'She was fifteen, almost sixteen.'

'How did it happen?'

'She was pulled from a canal not far from her home, but she had been under the water a long time. No one knows how long, but long enough for it to damage her.' By force of will, she kept her voice level and dispassionate. Her pain was evident only in her eyes, which could not meet his.

Fifteen-year-old Venetians were fish, or at least part fish, Brunetti believed. They went into the water as children, spent their summers on the beach and in the sea, diving off the rocks at the Alberoni, racing through the *laguna* in their friends' boats.

'Did she fall?' Brunetti asked.

'That's what the police said, but I'm not sure any more,' she said, then immediately clarified. 'That it was an accident.'

'Why is that?'

'Manuela was terrified of the water.'

Brunetti raised his eyebrows, one Venetian to another. Terrified of the water?

'She almost drowned when she was a little girl,' the Contessa continued. 'My daughter-in-law took her to the beach at the Lido, and she wandered away and into the water. She might have been four, no older. A man on the beach saw her head go under a wave and ran into the water and pulled her out. He gave her artificial respiration and probably saved her life. After that, she was terrified of the water.'

'That's difficult if you live here,' Brunetti said. His voice was rich with concern, no trace of irony.

'I know. She couldn't go on a vaporetto alone: someone had to hold her hand, and they had to stand inside, just beside the door. If there was no one to go with her, she'd walk.'

'Could she manage that?' he asked, wondering how complicated his life would become if he had to avoid taking boats.

'Yes. She could walk to school and to her friends' homes. But she was always careful to avoid walking alongside a canal. So long as she was a few metres from the water, she was all right.'

'What about bridges?' he asked.

'They didn't seem to bother her,' she said and noticed his surprise. 'It sounds strange, I know, but she said she could cross them so long as she kept concentrating on the stairs beneath her feet and didn't have to see the water on either side. That's what she was afraid of: the sight of the water.'

'Did she have to live here?'

'No, she didn't *have* to: she *wanted* to. Her parents were divorced, and my son remarried.' She gave him a level look and added, 'Men usually do.' When Brunetti failed to rise to that, she went on. 'When Manuela fell into the canal, my son had already had two other children, so it would have been difficult for her to live with them.'

'So she lived with her mother?'

'Yes. In Campo Santa Maria Mater Domini. Where they still live.'

'Was that where she was living . . . when this happened?'

'Yes. It's better for her to be with her mother,' she said, sounding not entirely convinced.

Brunetti was at a loss for what to ask her. He found it hard to believe that the girl had so successfully managed to live with her fear. What would it be like, seeing the cause of your terror every day, having it around you whenever you left your house? 'The fear must affect her life all the time,' he said.

'She loves the city,' the Contessa said, as if playing a trump card. 'She's grown up here, all of her friends are here, and . . . I live here.'

'She went to school here?'

'Yes,' the Contessa said and named a school in Santa Croce.

'Do she and her mother get along?'

Her answer was slow in coming. 'I've always assumed so.' As answers went, that wasn't very much, but he left it alone for the moment.

'I'm not sure what it is you'd like me to do, Contessa,' he said.

'I'd like you to see if there was anything that might have happened . . .' she said with a wave of her hand and covered her eyes.

Brunetti allowed a long time to pass before he asked, 'Did you know of any trouble she might have been having? Any person she might have wanted to avoid?'

'No,' she said immediately and fiercely.

Brunetti decided to leave that for the moment. 'Contessa,' he said, using much the same voice he employed when the children were being evasive with him, 'fifteen years have passed. I can't go back and try to look at this unless I have a reason or a place to start looking.' He would also need some sort of legal justification for looking, but he decided to tell her nothing about that.

He picked up his glass, too long ignored, and rolled it between his palms. 'I'm afraid that whatever suspicions you might have aren't enough,' he said — forcing himself to refer to 'suspicions' instead of 'vague suspicions' — 'to justify an investigation.'

'She didn't fall into that water,' the Contessa insisted with the truculence of age and the sense of certainty peculiar to wealth.

He took a sip and then another and kept his glass in his hand, suspecting he might need it. 'Contessa, there are possibilities you haven't considered,' he began, voice tentative, as he prepared to suggest to this woman that neither her love nor her wealth had been sufficient to stop her granddaughter from going into the water drunk or drugged. But how say it? What words to use?

'Manuela didn't try to kill herself, and she didn't drink or use drugs.' Had she read his thoughts?

'You sound very certain.' He was a man with two children who had recently been of that same volatile age. They were happy kids to whom the idea of suicide was from some other planet and drugs, he hoped, were unlikely, but these were beliefs common to most parents. How well did Manuela's grandmother understand a girl two generations younger than she? Youth and age, and their respective problems, lived in different worlds.

'Nothing could have made Manuela jump into the water. No matter what happened to her, if Manuela had got within two metres of the *riva,* she would have been lying on the ground, vomiting with fear. I saw that happen twice. Once we were on a vaporetto and people crowded suddenly to one side, and it tipped a bit. She started to scream and grabbed the woman next to her and vomited all down her back.'

Brunetti tried to speak, but she talked over him, half rising from her chair. 'Another time, when she was about eleven, one of the boys in her class waited for her after school. He knew she was afraid of water — miserable little sadist — and when she was walking across Campo Santa Marina, he and a friend grabbed her and pulled her down towards the canal and told her they were going to throw her in.'

Brunetti waited.

'She had something like an epileptic seizure. Luckily, it's near the hospital, and two men carried her there. She was there for two days.'

Brunetti found himself incapable of speech at the horror of it and at her rage, twenty years on.

'And you know the worst part of it, Signor Brunetti?'

He shook his head and set his glass back on the table, suddenly not interested in its contents.

'How to get her home.' She saw his expression and went on. 'A taxi?' She laughed the idea to scorn. 'Think of the vaporetti and where they go: how do you get to Campo Santa Maria Mater Domini from the hospital? Take the boat around the back of the island to the train station and then walk along the open *riva* to change from one boat to another? Looking at all that water?' She stopped, and he thought she was asking him to suggest a solution to this trick question.

'What did you do?'

'They put her in one of those chairs that Sanitrans uses to carry people up and down stairs, and two of them, well, four of them because they had to take turns, they carried her home from the hospital.'

Brunetti pushed at his glass with one finger and slid it to the side of the tray. He could think of nothing to say.

'Think of that for an eleven-year-old girl

with her eyes shut tight: being carried across the city in an open chair, like a crippled old woman, or some sort of lunatic being taken to Palazzo Boldù, and everyone you pass on the street looking at you and wondering what's wrong with you.' She gave him a few moments to consider what she had said. 'That's why I know Manuela didn't jump into the water, Commissario.'

Brunetti decided not to say that the possibility still remained that she had been drunk or drugged when she fell into the water.

She looked across the table at him. Her face was stripped of expression, allowing Brunetti to see it as a structure of eyes, nose, mouth, jaw, chin. The expanse of years between the time she would have been a beauty and the present surprised him: he would still have been a child, she a woman with children his age or older.

'It's not only her fear — phobia, if you will — that makes it impossible that she fell in,' she said.

'What do you mean?'

'The man who pulled her out . . .' The faint bell of memory sounded in Brunetti's mind. A man diving into the water to rescue a girl. Yes . . . something . . . something, but what?

'The man who saved her said he saw someone push or throw her into the water.'

'Who did he say that to?'

'To you,' she said with barely disguised accusation.

'I think you must be mistaken, Contessa,' Brunetti said. 'With all due respect.'

'No, not to you, not personally. But to the police who came. He got her out of the water, but he was too drunk to do anything except shout for help. A different young man gave her artificial respiration, but by then the damage had been done.' So carried away was she by the telling of this story that she made fists of her hands and banged them into one another. 'It was the other man, the young one, who called the police.

'When they came, the first man was lying on the pavement, asleep. The police knew him. He was the local drunk, and when they woke him up he was so drunk he couldn't remember his own name, and he couldn't find his wallet. He told the police that he'd seen a man with the girl, and it looked as if he'd pushed or thrown her in.'

'What did the police do?'

She uncurled her fingers and put her hands in her lap. 'They took them both — him and Manuela — to the hospital. When he woke up in the morning, he remembered his name.' Brunetti thought the Contessa had stopped, then she added, with great sadness, 'But she didn't remember hers.'

She gave a deep sigh, so profound that Brunetti could see her chest rise and fall. 'But that's all he remembered. When they asked him about the other man, he said there was someone else, but all he knew was that there was another man. The police assumed he meant the young man who had helped Manuela.'

'What else did he say?'

'That he saw something in the water that looked like a person, so he dived in to grab it.'

'That was very brave of him,' Brunetti said but then recalled the spurious bravery of drunks.

'Yes,' the Contessa agreed but hesitantly and sounding even less certain than he was.

'Both he and Manuela were there when I got to the hospital. I went to thank him and told him I was her grandmother.' He watched her recall the scene. 'He asked me for money,' she said.

'Did you give it to him?'

'Of course.'

'How much?'

'I had a few hundred euros in my bag, and I gave it to him.' Before Brunetti could speak, she went on. 'When I asked the police about him — this must have been a few weeks later — it was after the doctors told us that the damage to Manuela was very bad . . .' Her voice trailed off. She wiped at her forehead with the fingers of her right hand, looked at him and asked, 'Excuse me. What was I saying?'

'You were telling me what he did with the money you gave him.'

'The police told me he was drunk for a month. They said he was a drunk and not to believe anything he'd told me because he was just trying to get my money.' She surprised him by shrugging, a gesture that related to nothing she had said. 'But it wasn't until later that I learned about what he'd said about the man.'

'The police told you?'

Her answer was a long time in coming. 'In a way.'

'What do you mean?'

'The Questore had been a good friend of my husband; he told me what was in the original police report and that the man didn't remember anything about it when he woke up. The Questore told me the police were convinced it was drunken invention and wasn't true.'

'Did you believe him?'

'I had no reason not to.'

'And now?'

She stroked the velvet covering of the arms of her chair. 'And now I'd like to be sure.'

There had been so many recent revelations of police brutality and cover-ups that he preferred to spare them both the embarrassment of asking her to explain her change of mind.

'Did the Questore tell you anything else about him?'

'Only that he saved her life, and was a drunk. That's what the police had already told me.'

Brunetti leaned towards her and held up a hand. 'Let me ask you, Contessa, precisely what it is you'd like me to do.'

Her hands had moved to her lap. She laced her fingers together and stared at them.

Brunetti took up his drink. He studied the surface of the liquid, telling himself he would remain like this until she spoke. No matter how long the silence lasted, he would force her to tell him what she wanted.

Footsteps passed the closed door of the room; for a moment, Brunetti thought he could hear his watch ticking, but he dismissed that as fantasy.

He heard her move restlessly in her chair, but he refused to look at her.

'I want my granddaughter back,' she said in a voice that had passed beyond grief into agony.

4

When he looked at her, Brunetti was astonished to find that she appeared to have shrunk: she sat lower in her chair, and her feet could not touch the floor; broad parts of the back of the armchair were visible on both sides of her shoulders. 'I'm afraid there's no way I can arrange that, Contessa. Knowing what happened won't make any difference.'

'Nothing's helped for fifteen years,' the Contessa said, her voice raw. Like an obstinate child, she refused to look at him, as if by ignoring his gaze she could ignore the impossibility of what she was demanding.

'I'm sorry,' Brunetti said, unable to think of anything better to say.

When she finally did look at him, she had aged even more: her eyes were less bright, her mouth smaller, and she slumped forward, as though her back no longer had sufficient strength to keep her upright. She had spoken with the blind insistence of the very old. There were certain things they wanted before they went, and they believed that having them would help them let go of this world more easily. Perhaps it would, Brunetti was willing to admit; but, he added, perhaps it would not.

It did not sound to him as though the Contessa were after vengeance. Perhaps she believed that simply knowing what had happened to her granddaughter would lessen her pain. Brunetti knew how illusory that belief was: as soon as a person knew what had happened, they wanted to know why, and then they wanted to know who.

Almost without being aware of it, Brunetti had passed from curiosity about this young girl and her strange destiny to a desire to learn about its circumstances and, if possible, its cause. There was a disproportion between the importance of the decision he made and the speed with which he made it, but he chose to ignore this. He gave it little serious consideration, nor did he reflect on what it might require of him. An old woman was in need, and he reacted with as little thought as he would give to putting out a hand to prevent her falling down the stairs. His love for his mother had been unthinking, fierce, and protective, as was his love

67

for his wife and his children: he really had no other choice, had he?

He saw her reach for the bottle and felt his resolution pause or skip a beat. He had not agreed to anything, and there was still time to change his mind and say he could not help, but then she picked up the cap and screwed it back on to the bottle and set the bottle at the back of the tray.

She seemed to have regained some strength and now resembled the confident host of last night's dinner party, as though the confession of her futile wish had purged her of weak illusion. 'I'm eighty-six years old,' she said. 'I don't know how many years I have left.' She dismissed this with a shrug and went on. 'Before I die, I want to know what happened. I know it won't help Manuela and won't give her a second chance to become the person she might have become. But I want to die in peace.'

Brunetti didn't move, didn't speak, tried to give no evidence of anything save attention. He both wanted and needed to understand her.

'I told you suicide was impossible.' She took two deep breaths. 'But I'm not sure about that. I never really have been. Manuela had become a troubled girl; joy had fled her life. I don't want to die thinking I have some responsibility for what she is now.' Then she said, not at all melodramatically but with calm certainty, 'I need to know.'

When it became evident to Brunetti that she was finished, he asked, 'Do you know what was troubling her?'

She looked at her hands, and he thought of the way his own children used to hang their heads when he had to reprove them. 'Something had gone wrong in her life, but I don't know what it was.' She took a white handkerchief from the pocket of her dress and wiped at her nose but did not look up at him. 'Her mother had noticed that she was moody and sad, but she thought it was normal for a girl her age.' She glanced away, then back at him. 'I suppose I wanted to believe that.'

'Is that all her mother told you?' Brunetti asked.

'She asked me for money to pay for Manuela to see a psychologist.' The Contessa cleared her throat and then said in a voice made sharp by remembered anger, 'I told her that she could use the money she was paying for Manuela's riding lessons to pay for the psychologist. Or sell the horse.'

As though frightened by what she had said, the Contessa drew a deep breath and closed her eyes, waiting for her emotions to subside.

Brunetti sat and waited for her and with her.

'I gave them the apartment in Campo Santa Maria Mater Domini, years ago, when they were still married. She kept it after the divorce.' She spoke in a low, tight voice. 'I made her a monthly payment. I paid her bills, and Manuela's. I paid for the horse, the lessons, the stable, even the horse's food. When her mother asked for more, something in me snapped and I refused.' She looked at Brunetti, waiting for his response.

'I see,' Brunetti said.

'After it happened, her mother told me that Manuela had got worse because she didn't go to see someone.' She paused, then volunteered, 'Later I learned that my son had given her the money, but she never sent Manuela to see a psychologist.'

Brunetti realized that she was not going to say any more, and so he asked, 'Did you see her soon before the incident?'

'No. Every time I phoned, her mother told me Manuela wasn't there.'

'How long did this go on?'

'Until about a week before it happened, when she finally let me talk to Manuela on the phone.' The Contessa folded her arms across her chest as though the room had suddenly grown very cold. 'I asked her how she was, and she said she was fine; then she asked me how I was, and I gave her the same answer. But she didn't sound fine to me. She didn't sound all right at all.'

'And then?'

'A week later, my son called me in the middle of the night to tell me what had happened.' She looked up at the ceiling and began to nod her head repeatedly, giving assent to something Brunetti didn't understand.

'So you didn't see her again before it happened?'

'No.'

Brunetti pulled out his notebook and opened it. 'I'd like you to give me the telephone number for your daughter-in-law, and your own,' he said. She gave him both numbers from memory, and he wrote them down.

'Do you know the names of any of Manuela's friends, people she knew here or went to school with? Boyfriends, if she had any.'

While he was thinking of what else she might be able to tell him, the Contessa said, 'Those are things you'll have to ask her mother. I think Manuela's lost contact with her friends.' Hearing that, she edited it: 'Or they've lost touch with her.'

He had once believed that people, parents in particular, would notice unusual behaviour in their children, but he had found that this was often not the case. Most people were observant only in retrospect.

'What sort of terms are you on with her?'

'My daughter-in-law?' the Contessa asked, then immediately corrected herself. 'My ex-daughter-in-law?' She thought about this for a moment, then answered, 'It depends on the day.'

Brunetti almost laughed, so at odds was the remark with the tension of their conversation, but the Contessa was in earnest, painful earnest.

'Because of what?'

'That depends on the day, as well,' she said with what sounded like concern gone bad. 'It could be depression or the pills she takes for it, or it could be alcohol. It doesn't matter to me. I call her when I want to see Manuela and go for a walk with her or perhaps have her here for the afternoon.' She paused, and Brunetti suspected she was considering how much she could reveal to him. 'A woman lives with them, Alina, a Ukrainian woman who used to work for me. She takes care of Manuela.' Then she added, 'It's better for Manuela to be there. She lived with her mother after the divorce, and it seemed to calm her to be with her again. And in a home she was familiar with.'

'Does she remember it?'

'It seems so. But there are times when she forgets who people are. Then sometimes she remembers them again because she's very affectionate with them.' An emotion Brunetti could not recognize moved across her face. 'It's as if she remembers the emotion even if she can't remember the person.'

'I'm sorry,' was again the only thing Brunetti could think of to say.

She surprised him by answering, quite normally, 'Thank you.'

He thought it made no sense, at this point, to try to talk to the girl. Probably not until he knew more about her or what she had been like before . . . before she was damaged. But then it crashed down upon him that he didn't know how much the girl would understand of what was said to her.

He turned a page in his notebook. 'What was the name of the man who pulled her out of the water?' he asked.

'Pietro Cavanis,' she answered. 'I'm sure your colleagues can tell you about him.'

Brunetti smiled his thanks. 'I'll talk to them tomorrow. Is he still living in Santa Croce?'

'I don't know. I never spoke to him again.'

He found this strange but said nothing. He had no more questions, at least none he wanted to ask now. 'If I have to speak to you again . . . ?'

'I'm always here,' the Contessa said. 'Unless I go to see Manuela.' She sat quietly but then added, 'Well, it's more often that Manuela visits me.' Her face was transformed by a smile of such surprising warmth that Brunetti was forced to turn away his eyes.

'Can she get here herself?' he asked, somehow ashamed of the question.

'My maid, Gala, goes and gets her. She's worked for me for years, and she's known Manuela since she was a baby.'

He closed his notebook and slipped it into his pocket. 'I have enough to begin, I think,' he said and got to his feet. Usually, after an interview, he thanked the person who had given him information, but that seemed inappropriate here.

He bowed and kissed her hand when she extended it, left the room, and found the maid seated on a chair at the end of the corridor. She let him out of the *palazzo*.

5

Just as Paola was setting a bowl of *paccheri con tonno* on the table that evening, Chiara said to her father, 'Can I ask you a question?' While she waited for him to answer, Chiara took the serving spoon and gave herself a modest portion and then looked at Brunetti.

'You can't ask me an answer, can you?' he replied, a response that had, over the years, become part of family speech ritual, a trap into which the children seemed unable to stop themselves from falling. It was Brunetti's revenge for the persecution he suffered from his ecologically minded children, who pounded violently on the door of the bathroom the moment he entered the second minute of a shower. They could take care of the environment, and he'd see to the logic, thank you very much.

Chiara rolled her eyes in exasperation, and Brunetti asked, 'About what?'

'The law.'

'Large topic, I'd say,' Raffi interjected from across the table.

Ignoring her brother, Chiara lowered her head and concentrated on her pasta. Paola gave Raffi an icy stare.

'What about the law?' Raffi asked; then, when his sister failed to look at him, he added, 'Specifically.' He smiled at Paola to show the purity of his intentions.

Chiara glanced at her mother, who was helping herself to pasta, and then across the table at her brother, as if to test the sincerity of his question. 'I wondered if it's against the law to ask people for money on the street.'

Brunetti set his fork down. 'Depends,' he answered.

'On?' This from Chiara.

'On who sent you to ask,' he answered after some consideration

'Could you give me an example?' Chiara asked.

'If you're working for Médecins Sans Frontières and you have a permit to be there, then you can ask. Or if you're AVAPO and sell oranges and use the money to give help to cancer patients in their homes, and you have an authorized booth in Campo San Bortolo, then you can, too.'

76

'And if you're not one of these?' Chiara asked, dinner forgotten.

He had to think about this for a moment. 'Then I suppose you could be considered a mendicant.'

'And then?' Paola broke in to ask, suddenly interested in the subject.

'Then you're doing something the law — in simple terms — disapproves of. But you're not breaking it.' It was only after he'd spoken that Brunetti realized how absurd this sounded.

'Is it a real law or just a pretend law?' Chiara asked.

Though well he knew what she meant, Brunetti felt the obligation to ask, 'What do you mean by "pretend law"?'

'Oh, *Papà*, don't go all official on me. You know exactly what I mean: a law that's a law but nobody pays any attention to.' Chiara shook her head at Paola's attempt to serve her more pasta.

How children spoke truths, Brunetti reflected, that parents were meant to deny. He and his colleagues had long since adjusted to the fact that some laws were decorative rather than enforced. People arrested for theft or violence: take them down to the Questura and charge them, tell the foreigners among them to leave the country

77

within a certain number of days, and then let them go. Arrest them a week later for the same crime, and start the merry-go-round all over again, the same horses bobbing up and down with each turn.

He saw the moment when Paola gave in to her impulse to cause trouble when she could. 'Like the law about . . .'

'As I was saying to Chiara,' he interrupted her to say, 'it's somewhere between legality and illegality. If you stop someone on the street to ask them for money it's not a crime, though it's an offence. But if you send minors to beg for money, then it's a crime.'

Brunetti had said this with the voice he used for professional explanations, hoping it would suffice.

But Chiara was still preoccupied. 'What happens to you if you ask for money?'

'It's a *contravvenzione*,' he answered, trying to make the word sound important. Not a crime, but a violation, he told himself. Will she understand the distinction? Did he?

'Does that mean nothing happens if you do it?' Chiara asked.

He took time to finish his pasta and looked across at Paola. 'What's next?' he asked, hoping Chiara would be distracted by the thought of more food.

'Does it, *Papà*?' she asked again.

'Well,' he said in his most Solomonic tones, 'the person who does it gets an administrative sanction.'

'That's just a term,' Chiara said quickly. 'It doesn't mean anything.'

'It opens a record with the police about you,' Brunetti said.

'But nothing happens to you,' she insisted.

Through all of this, Raffi's head had turned back and forth between his sister and his father as though he were watching a shuttlecock. Paola pushed her chair back, collected the plates, and carried them to the sink at the end of the room. Brunetti took a sip of wine and finally asked, 'Why are you curious about this, Chiara?'

'Maybe she's looking for a way to pick up some pocket money in the afternoons after school,' Raffi suggested, 'and she wants to know if she'll be arrested.' His sister snatched up her napkin and flicked it in his direction. Paola turned at the sound, but by the time she saw them, the napkin was already back in Chiara's lap and she was taking a sip of water.

Chiara looked at her father and then at her mother, and then down at her plate. Brunetti waited, and Paola, at the counter, returned to spooning vegetables into two ceramic bowls.

'There's one of those new Africans,' Chiara began at last, then paused for a long time before continuing. 'He stops us all and asks for money. Every day: he's always there when we get out of classes.'

'What do you mean by "new" Africans?' Paola raised her voice to ask.

'Not like the *vu cumprà,*' Raffi interrupted to explain. Brunetti expected Chiara to object, but she simply nodded in agreement. Over the years, Brunetti, like most Venetians, had grown accustomed to the presence of the Senegalese immigrants, called *vu cumprà* by everyone in the city, even though political correctness demanded that they be called *venditori ambulanti.* Brunetti had tried to use the polite term but kept forgetting it and so ended up calling them, as did everyone else, by their original name.

'I still don't understand,' Paola said.

Chiara and Raffi exchanged a long glance, as though asking one another if their parents lived in the same city as they did, and then Chiara said, 'They've been around for only the last year or so, the ones I mean. And they're different.'

'In what way?' Paola asked.

'Aggressive,' Raffi said, then looked across

80

at Chiara for confirmation. 'At least the ones I see are.'

Chiara nodded. 'The *vu cumprà* have been here a long time. They all speak Italian. And they know a lot of us, too. So we joke with them, and it doesn't matter if we don't buy anything: they're still friendly,' she said, confirming Brunetti's impression of the Senegalese street vendors.

'And the new ones?' Paola asked, bending to pull a platter from the oven.

Chiara propped her chin in one hand, something she was forbidden to do at table. Brunetti ignored it and Paola didn't see. 'He gives me the creeps,' she finally said, as if confessing to a crime. 'I know I'm not supposed to say that about immigrants, but this guy is different. He's sort of menacing, and sometimes he puts his hand on your arm.' Her voice grew stronger, as if she were defending herself. 'The *vu cumprà* would never do that. Never.'

Brunetti, whose chair faced the stove, exchanged a glance with Paola, who was suddenly motionless and attentive to the conversation. Brunetti didn't like the idea of any man putting his hand uninvited on his daughter's arm. He realized how atavistic his response was and didn't care in the least.

'While asking for money?' he asked in his

calmest of calm voices.

'Yes.'

Brunetti picked up his fork to give himself something to do while he thought about this. Glancing at his place, he was surprised to see that his plate had disappeared. As he looked at the empty place, it was suddenly filled as Paola set a plate of yellow peppers filled with meat and ricotta in front of him.

When everyone was served and Paola had sat down again, he took an exploratory bite. He ate a little more and was about to speak, when Raffi said, sounding both amused and exasperated, 'And we've got the drug people, but they ignore us. It's only the tourists they want.'

'What drug people?' Paola asked, her own voice rough with badly controlled fear.

Raffi turned to her and raised a hand. 'Calm down, *Mamma.* I said it wrong: the anti-drug people.'

Brunetti glanced at Paola and saw her plaster a look of amiable curiosity on to her face, then mirror it in her voice. 'Which is it, Raffi, pro or con?' Surely this calm voice could not be that of the mother of a teen-age child she'd just heard speak so casually of drugs.

'Oh, they say they're against them,' Chiara said. 'But look at them.'

'At their teeth,' Raffi added, reminding Brunetti of what he had seen in the grimaces of some of the addicts who had passed through the Questura on their way to prison, and of what was to be seen in the photos taken when they were booked.

Chiara looked relieved to be free of her criticism of an African. She came, after all, from the generation that had absorbed the gospel of tolerance and believed in the sinful nature of any criticism of a person less fortunate than herself.

Brunetti thought he knew the people his children were talking about, had seen different groupings of them in the city, always at points of maximum tourist traffic. Of both sexes and indeterminate age, they wore some sort of official tag on a lanyard around their necks, which he assumed gave them the right to occupy public space and ask for money — like the AVAPO people or like Medécins Sans Frontières. Hearing himself class them with those other two groups made Brunetti faintly uncomfortable, as though he'd put salt in with sugar and honey. Although they had brushed his curiosity, they had never attracted his attention: he had always walked by, leaving them to the tourists or, more accurately, the tourists to them.

Paola asked if anyone would like another pepper. When they all declined, she asked, 'May I ask what this is all about?' Her voice was level, curious, not a trace of suspicion to be heard.

Chiara and Raffi again exchanged a glance to see who would speak first. Chiara shook her head, and so Raffi said, 'I see them once in a while in front of the Frari. They stop people and ask them if they want to do something to stop drugs, and when they say they do — it's only tourists who stop — they ask them to sign a paper, some sort of petition, and when they do, they keep talking to them.'

'That's all?' Brunetti asked from the habit of precision.

Raffi considered his father's question, then said, 'My friends say they ask for money.'

'And do they?' Brunetti asked.

Raffi's surprise was evident. 'Why else would they bother asking them to sign the petition? There's no use signing anything: no one cares what petitions people sign, so what's the use of asking people to do it?'

How casually different they were from his own generation, Brunetti thought, not for the first time. They had so little to believe in, so little to hope for. He looked back at the political enthusiasms of his youth and

was forced to admit that they had all come to nothing. But at least his generation had tried.

'So it's just a pretext to make money?' Paola asked, using the Venetian expression, *'ciappar schei'*, probably to allow herself to hiss with contempt at the last word.

'If they've got those ID cards, then they must have permits,' Raffi said, reminding both his parents that the times when he could be silenced by the mere tone of their voices were gone, gone, gone, and not coming back.

Brunetti turned to Paola: this was her fight, not his.

'Maybe it's the only way these people can get money. God knows, the state's abandoned them,' she said.

'The state's abandoned us all,' Raffi said with some heat. 'It's abandoned me, too.' He hammered this home, startling Brunetti with the anger in his voice.

'It doesn't matter how much time we spend at university or what degrees we get; my friends and I will never get jobs.' When he saw his mother about to speak, he ignored her, saying, 'I will because of Nonno and all the businesses he has and the people he knows. But my friends won't, unless they know people too, or they'll have to go to

England, or France, to get a decent job.' Then, roughly, after a moment's thought, 'Any job.'

Across from him, his sister held up her hands in the 'T' that umpires use to call 'time out'. Raffi stopped, Paola refrained from saying anything to him, and Brunetti gave his daughter his attention.

'May I remind you that I started this, and I still don't have an answer,' Chiara said impatiently, sounding strangely adult. 'I told you about the African because I want to know what I can do about it. About him.' Brunetti waited to see if she was going to say she didn't want to hurt the man's feelings or frighten him, things he certainly expected her to say.

'I want him to leave me alone,' she said, her voice even. Paola got to her feet and started to clear the table. Raffi began to help his mother, leaving Brunetti to speak to Chiara.

Vianello would be the person to ask to deal with it, Brunetti thought, although he had no idea what to ask his friend to do. What was it that British Chief Inspector used to say, the one he'd met at the conference in Birmingham? 'Put the frighteners on him'? At the time, Brunetti had been amused by the phrase, however unpleasant

he'd found the reality. But that was precisely what he wanted Vianello, his thick-necked, ham-fisted friend, to do for him: frighten off the person who was frightening his daughter. 'I'll see what I can do,' he said, at which point Paola and Raffi returned, each of them bearing two plates with thick slices of fresh chestnut cake.

6

The following morning, Brunetti stopped in the squad room before going to his office. Vianello greeted him with a friendly smile. He wanted to talk with Vianello about the African before telling him about his conversation with Contessa Lando-Continui, so he asked the Inspector if he knew of any complaints from people being asked for money on the streets.

'Who'd bother to come to us?' Vianello asked. There was no sarcasm, only puzzlement at the question: come to the *police* to complain about beggars? The Inspector shifted a pile of papers to the side of his desk, stared proudly at the empty space it left, and asked Brunetti, 'Why are you asking?'

It was only now, having to explain, that Brunetti realized how vague his understanding was. 'There's a man who keeps asking Chiara and some of her friends for money.

Over near her school. She says he's very insistent.'

'Insistent how?' Vianello asked.

'She said he puts his hand on "your arm". And she sounded . . . troubled.'

'Is it one of the new Africans?' Vianello asked.

'Am I the last one to know about them?'

As if to prepare himself for a longer conversation, Vianello got to his feet so as not to have his superior remain standing while he sat behind his desk as they talked. 'Hard not to notice them,' Vianello said, leaning back to half-sit on his desk.

'How are they new?' Brunetti asked.

'They don't come from Senegal, so the *vu cumprà* want no part of them. They don't seem to work, don't speak much Italian, and they have a very insistent way of asking for money. The Mafia's trained the *vu cumprà* because that's who they work for, so they've learned not to insist, and they certainly don't put their hands on people. They don't cause trouble.' Vianello nodded in appreciation of their behaviour and added, 'The new ones look different, too. The Senegalesi are tall and thin, but these guys are shorter and thicker. And rougher looking.' Reflecting on all of this, Vianello added, 'I've never had trouble with the *vu cumprà.*'

89

It bothered Brunetti that he had not noticed these new Africans, or perhaps had noticed them but not paid special attention to them. They'd hardly approach a man in a suit to ask for charity. Women and tourists would be their chief objects, he assumed, the first rendered generous by sympathy, the second perhaps by shame. Or fear?

'Is there anything we can do about him?' Brunetti asked, aware that, in the absence of a legal option, their only choice was to attempt persuasion. Both of them remained silent for a long time, considering possibilities.

'My God,' Brunetti burst out, 'this is how ordinary people feel.'

'Excuse me?' Vianello asked.

'If you have no official power, there's nothing you can do when someone bothers you. Chiara can ask me, but as a father I can't do anything to make him stop if he doesn't want to.'

Vianello picked up the ball and ran with it. 'We can tell him he has to pay a fine.' He gave a snort of grim laughter. 'Or tell him he'll have to leave the country if he does it again.' Vianello stood up and set the file of papers on another desk.

When he came back, Brunetti had his hands in his pockets and was studying his shoes. Vianello sat in his chair.

'There's nothing we can do,' Brunetti continued. 'And we're the police, for God's sake.'

Vianello shrugged, as though to suggest to Brunetti that they were discussing the self-evident. 'You wonder why people vote for the Lega?' he asked. He pulled a smaller pile of files towards him, looked up at Brunetti, and said, 'I'll walk by the school this afternoon and have a word with him.' The Inspector opened the next file.

Brunetti thanked him, then went slowly back to his own office. He had forgotten about the Contessa. By virtue of his authority, he could send a police officer to speak to the man and suggest to him that he stop bothering the girls at the school. If he succeeded, the African would simply go and bother someone else, somewhere else: a different group of schoolgirls, women on their way to do the shopping, people trying to shop for fish at Rialto.

It didn't matter how he had entered the country: the distinction between legal and illegal immigrants had long since been abandoned by the press, as had the term *'clandestina'*. Brunetti assumed that most of these men wanted work, and he similarly assumed that they would not find it. The state had given them places to stay and paid them a minimum daily sum, enough to survive, but it couldn't provide them with something to do.

He marshalled all his *bien pensant* principles about social justice, equality, and human rights, but was left only with anger that any man could touch his daughter against her will. How close we are to the cave, he thought, but still his anger remained.

To rid himself of these thoughts he turned on his computer and, in the absence of any word from Signorina Elettra, put in the name of Contessa Demetriana Lando-Continui, then hit ENTER boldly, sending a wish off to the cybergods.

His prayer was answered with a long list of entries bearing her name, although he soon understood that the major portion of them were offers to provide the Contessa's address and phone number and nothing else. Her photo appeared in a number of articles about dinners and parties given by Salva Serenissima. He studied the photos and thought he saw her in two of them, nestled amidst small groups of women of her age and, he assumed, social stature and wealth.

After three such articles, as well as repeated references to the Contessa on Facebook, he gave up and switched to reading that day's papers. The experience was hardly more informative.

'How about Salva Serenissima?' he asked himself aloud and turned his attention to that organization. He found a long list of articles. There was no Wikipedia entry, but a Facebook page and a Twitter account were given as possible sources of information. Brunetti was not lured into consulting either one. He found a listing of the board of directors and spent some time studying it. There was the usual sprinkling of noble names, their titles dazzling forth from the screen: he particularly enjoyed reading the hyphenated surnames tumbling one after the other, like otters in a shallow pool. In the shadow cast by the noble titles huddled the commoners, some of whose names he recognized. One name towards the end of the list caught Brunetti's eye because he had, more than once, been in the Questura when this man's wife was brought in, accused of shoplifting.

'Lookie, lookie,' another name caused him to exclaim, having picked up the expression from Paola, who used it to proclaim surprise and delight. There was his old friend Leonardo, Marchese di Gamma Fede, who had been at university with Brunetti, then disappeared into the family textile business in Asia, remaining in intermittent touch over the years. Brunetti remembered the letters and cards Lolo had sent him during the years when the kids were interested in collecting stamps: enormous manila envelopes half covered with scores of brightly coloured stamps of very low denomination, but always more than enough to get the envelope, however slowly, to Italy. There had been a herd of elephants from India, near-fluorescent birds from Indonesia, and a mob of kangaroos from Australia. He still remembered them all, as did the kids.

Brunetti hadn't heard from Lolo in more than a year, even though they now communicated by email. No stamps, alas. It delighted him to see Lolo's name on the list, for it meant that he must be spending time in Venice; only after that did it occur to him to be glad of it for professional reasons. Lolo was not a fool, and Brunetti had always thought him to be an honest person. He made a mental note to contact Lolo.

He returned to his consideration of the list. One of the nobles on it had years ago rented an apartment to a friend of Brunetti's, who had discovered only when he moved in that the elevator shaft also served as a conduit of smells from the Chinese restaurant on the ground floor. The smell from the elevator filled the landing in front of their door, but worse came from an exhaust shaft that ran past their bedroom and flooded it with the same odours. Giving in to the landlord's threats of legal action should they break their contract by leaving, they had, in the end, been forced to pay three thousand euros to be quit of the place, and of him. Seeing this noble name on the 'Honorary Board' brought Brunetti a smile and a sense of the rightness of the world.

Alessandro Vittori-Ricciardi was listed among the members of the 'Administrative Board', whatever that was. He was in company with a count and a viscount as well as three lesser mortals.

It was only after Brunetti finished reading through the list a second time that he noticed that fewer than half of the names were Italian. Then he saw that some appeared on the list twice. He marvelled at the various categories into which they were divided, each group with a title. He recalled being at the Metropolitan Opera in New York, at a particularly tedious performance of something by Verdi; so many years had passed that he couldn't now remember what the opera had been. During one of the intermissions, he had opened the programme and found the seemingly endless list of patrons: at least the Americans had the courage of their vulgarity and listed them according to how much they gave.

His father-in-law had once told Brunetti that he joined only the boards of profit-making enterprises. 'They don't fool around and waste your time by inviting you to parties,' he said, 'and they don't expect you to pay to get your name on the list.'

Contessa Lando-Continui was on the International Board, third in a list that was not in alphabetical order, and that left Brunetti curious about the ranking system and what spats and sulkings must have arisen from it.

He recalled a remark that Conte Falier's daughter, his own dear wife, had made, not about boards, but about Brunetti's response to the people who sat on them. 'I'd hoped you'd learn to leave your past behind you, Guido, and forget your class prejudices,' she'd said to him once, years ago, after listening to him criticize the appointment of the new Rector of the University, who bore the surname of two doges. 'If his name were Scarpa, you wouldn't think his appointment worthy of comment.'

Brunetti had burned with embarrassment

for a week, a feeling that returned whenever he caught himself taking pot shots at the rich and nobly born. His was hardly the resentment of the son of toiling workers, protesting because they had not been recognized for their efforts. His father had returned from the war a hopeless layabout who saw no reason to work if he could avoid it.

As though his spirit had been given a thwack on the head with a rolled-up newspaper, Brunetti looked at the list again and told himself that he, and all Venetians, should be grateful that the Contessa gave of her wealth to help the youth and save the monuments in the city.

He thought of Pucetti, the most promising of the younger officers, who had told him some weeks before that he might be moving to Marghera, should his girlfriend be transferred there to teach mathematics. Castello-born, Pucetti seemed to know everyone in the *sestiere.* He had once told Brunetti that his grandfather was the first person in his family to learn Italian and that his father still spoke it as a second language. His great-grandmother had never left Castello, never once in her life.

Why didn't the other foundations emulate the Contessa and do something for Venetians instead of for Venice? The city, for all its promises, was unlikely to do so. The last time a large public building had been divided up into private apartments and offered for sale at affordable prices, a suspicious number of them had been sold to politicians and their wives. Brunetti pulled his mind back: only trouble would come of thinking of these things.

Going downstairs, he thought of Muhammad and the mountain. As he entered her office, he saw Signorina Elettra at her desk and was instantly alerted to danger by the expression on her face. Her narrow smile was lethal, lips denying her adversary the sight of her teeth, perhaps to minimize the idea of them as a weapon.

Brunetti followed her eyes and found Lieutenant Scarpa standing in front of the window nearest the open door and thus hidden by it from anyone passing in the corridor outside. The Lieutenant, his uniform a study in sartorial perfection, leaned back against the windowsill from which Brunetti usually conversed with Signorina Elettra and which, quite understandably, Brunetti thought of as his place.

'The very last thing I'd ever do, Lieutenant, is question your integrity,' Brunetti heard Signorina Elettra say as he entered

98

her office. 'I couldn't live with myself if I had to entertain the thought that you were less than fully loyal to the service to which you are an adornment.' The dead tone — a bad actress reading a bad script, badly translated from some other language — was so at variance with the words themselves as to render the scene hallucinogenic. Her lips moved horizontally in what Brunetti suspected was meant to suggest a smile, but did not.

'That's a great comfort for me to learn, Signorina,' the Lieutenant said with syrupy piety. He cast his eyes in Brunetti's direction but made no other acknowledgement of his presence. Returning his glance to Signorina Elettra, he went on, 'Then I must look elsewhere for the person who attempted to hack into my computer.' After all the soft pleasantries, this last phrase came like the snap of a whip.

Aha! Brunetti thought: that's what she's been up to. He knew she had access to the Vice-Questore's computer; she was probably more familiar with what was in it than Patta himself. She'd known Lieutenant Scarpa's password for ages, but perhaps he'd changed it and she'd been forced to break in again. Had she left the equivalent of a trace of her perfume, a dropped handkerchief, while she was having a look around?

Drawing himself to his full height and taking one step into the small office, Brunetti waved a hand toward his ear, a gesture Lieutenant Scarpa could interpret as a salute and, if so, would have to stand up straight to return. The habit of obedience brought the Lieutenant forward and upright. He raised his right hand to his forehead, and as he did he gave a very knowing smile that showed how well he understood Brunetti's attempt to impose his power and found it quaint, if not useless. 'Commissario,' he said, as if he'd only then noticed Brunetti.

'Is that all you wanted, Lieutenant?' Signorina Elettra asked, this time not wasting any energy in a smile.

'For the moment, yes, Signorina,' the Lieutenant said and took his leave.

When he was sure that Scarpa had started up the stairs, Brunetti asked, 'Did he catch you reading his emails?'

'Good heavens, no,' she said, voice rich with astonishment at the very idea. 'But someone else has been in there, looking around.'

'Who?' Brunetti inquired.

She shook his question away and said, 'It

might be the same person who's been looking at the Vice-Questore's.'

'Someone from the Ministry?' he asked,
wondering what could be going on if the
Ministry were spying on its own internal
correspondence. 'Is he good enough,' Brunetti asked, tilting his head towards the door
Scarpa had just used, 'to detect it?'

'Perhaps,' she said, and Brunetti had to
confess that the admission came to her
grudgingly.

'Do you have any idea what they might be
after?'

She raised her chin, as though to provide
herself with a better view of the ceiling. Or
the stars. The only sign that she had not
lapsed into a profound coma was her
mouth. Her lips drew together as though
about to sip at a mountain pool, pulled back
in a grimace of mild exasperation, then
relaxed completely as she continued her
communion with something Brunetti would
never grasp.

Without warning, her Higher Power released her, and she looked across at Brunetti
to say, 'Giorgio will find out.'

Giorgio, Brunetti thought, the cyber
equivalent of the *deus ex machina*. 'Do you
need his help for this?'

She propped her chin on her left palm and

poked idly at her keyboard: a pianist in search of a better tune, a small bird pecking for something to eat.

'Yes, I do, Commissario,' she said and looked up at him. 'It matters enough to involve him. What happened to the Vice-Questore's mail was not a friendly thing: it was attempted burglary. So if we can find out who did it, we can perhaps get an idea of what they're looking for. It's always good to know what even the enemies of your enemies are after.'

'Do you think the Vice-Questore and the Lieutenant have enemies?' he asked, goading her into a startled look.

When she refused to answer, he asked, 'Is there any reason they'd have enemies?'

She smiled. 'Let me count the ways.'

7

'And Contessa Lando-Continui?' he asked,

Rather than answer, Signorina Elettra turned away from him and hit the keys of her computer, eyes riveted to the screen. 'Have a look,' she said eagerly, waving at Brunetti to come around and stand behind her.

He saw what looked like the first page of *Il Gazzettino.* The page layout was the one they'd long ago abandoned; the date was fifteen years before. 'Young Noblewoman Injured in Accident,' he read. 'Last night, near midnight, Manuela Lando-Continui, daughter of Teodoro Lando-Continui and Barbara Magello-Ronchi and granddaughter of the late Conte Marcello Lando-Continui and Contessa Demetriana Lando-Continui, was rescued from the waters of the Rio San Boldo. A passer-by who saw her struggling dived into the dark waters of the canal and pulled the girl to safety before himself collapsing.

'Another man rushed to the assistance of both and administered artificial respiration to the girl, who was later taken to the Ospedale Civile, where her prognosis is reported as "critical". The police, who arrived at the scene, are treating the incident as an accident.'

Just as Brunetti finished reading it, Signorina Elettra, who had taken his position on the windowsill, said, 'The next two articles continue the story.'

He scrolled the page down and saw the photo of a young girl dressed in a white shirt, perhaps a man's, the bottom almost reaching the knees of her faded jeans. She stood with her left arm hanging loose in front of her, the ends of the reins woven around her fingers, her right arm draped over the shoulder of a dark horse whose head was lowered and pressed into her stomach, showing only one eye and ear. The horse's mouth was open, and it appeared to be nibbling at one of the buttons on her shirt.

The girl's hair, long and dark, was brushed back from a broad forehead. She smiled happily at the camera, fresh-faced, caught just at the point in her life when she would begin the change from a pretty girl to a beautiful woman. Her expression asked the person taking the photo if this weren't perhaps the most wonderful day of their lives? She wore riding boots and stood on tiptoe the better to embrace her horse.

'Pretty girl,' Brunetti comented, only then realizing this was the first time he had seen a photo of her.

'Yes, she was, wasn't she?' Signorina Elettra asked.

'Was?' Brunetti inquired.

'It was a long time ago; maybe she's changed,' Signorina Elettra said, then, 'Read the articles.'

The first, which was dated two days after the previous one, gave the name of Pietro Cavanis, Venetian, as the man who had saved the girl's life, and named her parents, both of whom were at the girl's bedside, waiting for her to emerge from the coma in which she had been since being pulled from the water.

The next had appeared the same day in the other local paper and described the girl as a promising equestrian — which explained the photo with the horse. Manuela was well known at her riding club near Treviso, although for some time she had not participated in competitions.

'That's all?' Brunetti asked as he looked away from the screen.

'Yes,' Signorina Elettra answered. 'What do you make of it?'

He couldn't let this go on any longer. 'I've spoken to her grandmother.'

'What?'

'I was at dinner with her — she's a friend of my mother-in-law — and she said she wanted to talk to me.' He pointed to the screen. 'About her.'

'When did you see her?'

'Yesterday. I came up to tell you about it.' It seemed strange to Brunetti to be sitting at her computer, she at his usual place, but he didn't want to break the mood of their conversation by suggesting they move.

'What did she tell you?'

'About the accident,' he said, waving at the screen, where the barest facts of the story were given. 'The girl's never been the same. She was under the water so long the oxygen to her brain was cut off.' Brunetti let her consider that and then added, 'The word she used was "damaged".'

'Poor girl,' Signorina Elettra whispered.

'Poor everyone,' Brunetti added and then went on with his story. 'The man who dived into the canal and pulled her out was drunk when he did it. Didn't think about it, just went in after her.' He remembered what the Contessa had told him and added, 'It sounds like he was the local drunk.'

'The article didn't say he was drunk,' she said. 'But I suppose they wouldn't.'

'She said the police told her about him. She also said that when the police arrived, he reported that he'd seen a man throw Manuela into the water, but he was so drunk they paid no attention to him. And they were probably right because the next morning, when he woke up, he had no memory of it.'

Signorina Elettra hopped down from the windowsill and came over to her desk. She picked up a notebook and pencil and immediately went back to where she had been sitting and asked, 'What's his name? I saw it in the article, but I don't remember it.'

'Pietro Cavanis.'

She nodded and wrote it down. 'Did she say anything else about him?' she asked.

'Only that she gave him some money, and he stayed drunk for a month on it.'

'I see,' she said, writing in the notebook. 'What do you think we did?'

'We?'

'The police.'

It could have been anything, Brunetti realized, but it was more likely nothing. The uncorroborated story of a man known to be the local drunk, given at a time of great stress, a story he retracted the day after: no one would have paid attention to it. Brunetti shrugged.

She jabbed at her computer with the eraser on the pencil. 'The date's there. I'll see if I can find a record of the incident.' She wrote a bit more and stopped to look across at him. 'What do you make of it?' she asked.

Brunetti had been considering this since the Contessa spoke to him. A drunken witness who didn't remember his own story? 'I don't know. If he didn't remember anything the next morning, there was nothing for them to do.' She waited, forcing him to admit he had not answered her question. 'The most likely thing is that the girl fell into the water,' he continued. 'Or it would be if it weren't for her phobia.' Her glance was a question; he went on. 'Her grandmother told me the girl almost drowned when she was a child: after that, she was terrified of the water and never went anywhere near it, which means she wouldn't be walking along a *riva,* especially alone and especially in the dark.' Before she could ask, he continued, 'Her grandmother said she managed to live in the city by knowing which *calli* didn't run along a canal. And she looked at the pavement when she had to go over bridges.' Her expression showed that she, as any Venetian would, found this improbable if not impossible.

'More importantly, she told me the girl had grown reserved and unhappy in the months before the incident, so there's the possibility of drugs or drink,' Brunetti added. 'If she were using them, then she might have walked along the *riva,*' he added.

'Ummm,' was Signorina Elettra's response as she continued to write. 'What about the fact that she hadn't ridden in competitions for some time?' Was that an inquisitorial note in her voice?

'She still had the horse,' he answered. 'Her grandmother was paying for it.' He was conscious of how inadequate this sounded, even to himself.

Signorina Elettra raised a hand in a gesture that could mean anything. 'I don't know,' she said, looking down at her feet. She swung them away from the wall one by one, then looked over at Brunetti. 'The story's caught you, hasn't it?'

Brunetti accepted that it had, but he had no idea what might have caught Signorina Elettra's attention in this sorry tale: lost youth, lost possibility, bad luck? It might be no more than an interest in the unfortunate destinies of the noble names of her native city, or just as easily it could be her heightened sensibility to the fate of women. He switched the screen back to the photo of the girl and studied it for a while. 'She could have been away from riding because of a fall,' he suggested. 'Or it could be — we don't know how old she was when this photo was taken — that, like many girls, she forgot about horses when she discovered boys.' He glanced over to see her response, but she seemed occupied with seeing just how high she could raise her feet.

'Her horse could have been injured,' Brunetti added. Paola having long ago declared their family an Animal Free Zone, he had no first-hand information about the relationships between young girls and their horses. He had read, however, that they could be very strong.

She pushed herself off the windowsill and landed silently. Brunetti got to his feet as she moved towards the desk, leaving the chair and computer to her. He thought he knew her well enough to ask, and so said, 'Has it caught you, too?'

She turned to look at him. 'Of course.' She brushed a strand of hair behind her ear, then sat and tapped at the keyboard with one finger. 'There's something wrong about it all. Let me see if I can find the original reports and witness statements, for example.'

'She'd be how old now — more than thirty?'

'Yes, just a bit,' Signorina Elettra said. 'But if what her grandmother said is true, then she hasn't had the last fifteen years in any real sense.'

'The grandmother wasn't precise,' he explained, 'but she spoke of Manuela as though she were a child.'

He watched her hit a few more keys, but she didn't bother to look at the screen: it must be a nervous habit, the way a smoker rolls a pencil in his hand, just to keep his fingers nimble.

He stood there for a long time, but she said nothing. Finally he asked, 'What are you going to do?' as if she were another commissario, and they were planning strategy together.

'I'll start with the stables and see if anyone there remembers her. Same with her school.'

'And when you've done that?' he asked.

'Then I tell you what I've learned.'

'And then?'

'And then we'll see.'

■ ■ ■

That afternoon, Brunetti spent some hours writing 'performance assessments' for six members of the uniformed branch. When he was finished, he allowed himself to leave the Questura, took the Number One to the Lido, and went for a long walk on the beach. Autumn was in the air and visible on the whitecaps, and by the time he got home, he was tired and chilled and very hungry.

After dinner, he and Paola moved into the living room, and he told her about his conversation with Contessa Landi-Continui and her request — entreaty, really — that he find out what had happened to her granddaughter.

'Even though this happened fifteen years ago?' Paola asked.

'The Contessa said she needs to know. Before she dies.'

Paola stopped to consider that. 'Yes, I suppose she does. A person would, wouldn't they?'

'Would what?'

'Need to know they weren't responsible, if nothing else.'

She had chosen to sit in one of the armchairs that faced the sofa, leaving him to stretch out on it. It was late and they were drinking verbena tisane, Brunetti having opted not to have a grappa and Paola fighting a sore throat.

'But why would she be responsible?' he asked, moving around until his head and shoulder were at the perfect angle on the arm of the sofa. 'The girl was living with her mother, and the Contessa didn't see much of her in the last months before it happened.'

'She probably thinks that she should have.'

'She's her grandmother, not her guardian angel.'

'Guido,' she said, putting hard emphasis on the first syllable, the way she did when she was calling the children to account.

'What?'

'You're being heartless. The girl was her granddaughter.' That said, Paola sipped at her tisane.

Brunetti realized her voice sounded rougher than it had at dinner. Apparently the verbena had not succeeded in helping her throat, which meant the centuries-old Falier remedy had been bested by the germ theory.

He took the empty cup from her hand, carried it into the kitchen and put it into the sink. When he came back, Paola sat with her head resting against the back of the chair, eyes closed, no book in her hands.

'I think it's time we went to bed,' Brunetti said.

She made no response. He studied her face and noticed that her long nose was red at the end. With that and the two euro-coin-sized red circles on her cheekbones, Paola had the look of a clown, a very tired one. He leaned down and touched her shoulder. 'That's it for tonight,' he said and helped her to her feet.

8

Brunetti passed a restless night. Paola, as was her wont, well or ill, slept the sleep of the heavily sedated beside him. At three, some urge to fear woke him and lifted him to his feet beside the bed. Fully awake, shaking, he tried to remember the dream that had shocked him, but it was gone: he remembered only fear and concern for Chiara's safety.

He went down the corridor to the kitchen and drank a glass of water, then another, trying to remember any detail, however small, that might have chilled his soul to this degree. Leaving the light on in the corridor and telling himself he was not behaving like a superstitious fool, he went to Chiara's room and pushed open the door. Having done this countless times when she was a child, Brunetti knew exactly how far he could open it without having the light shine on her pillow. He stuck his head

115

around the edge of the door. When his eyes had adjusted to the darkness, he saw her ruffled head, lying where it was supposed to lie, her jeans lying where they were not meant to lie, the rest of her clothes in a joy-inducing heap on the chair at the end of her bed.

He pulled his head back and closed the door silently, rejoicing in the glimpse of her and of her desk, dripping papers and laden with abandoned books. Oh, thank heaven for the mess my children make. Give praise that they do not clean up after themselves but give proof of youth and energy by leaving a trail of objects, clothing, books, shoes, videos, everything and anything, all shouting out that they are alive.

Brunetti went back to the kitchen and leaned forward over the sink, his hands braced on the edge. He stood like that for some time, until the euphoria passed. When it did, he remained where and how he was, thinking about children and the terrifying cost of having them. When he had grown calm, he pushed himself back from the counter, turned off the light, and went back to the bedroom. He slipped noiselessly under the covers, though well he knew he could bring drummers and a band and Paola would sleep on. He turned to her and wrapped his left arm around her and saw again the photo of the girl with her arm draped over the shoulder of her horse. But then sleep had him, and the girl and the horse rode away into the night.

By the time he got to the Questura the next morning, the effect of the dream and his response to it had worn off, and he arrived in good spirits aided by having given in to weakness and stopped for coffee and a brioche at both Ballarin and Rosa Salva. He stopped to see Vianello in his office, intending to ask if he had managed to go over to Chiara's school to have a look at what was going on.

The Inspector was at his desk, reading that morning's *Gazzettino*. 'You know, there should be a warning wrapper on that,' Brunetti said, nodding towards the newspaper.

'Saying what?' Vianello asked.

'That it could be harmful to your health,' Brunetti answered, touching his head, then waving his fingers in front of his face to signal madness.

'I've been reading it for thirty years,' Vianello answered. 'So I'm either crazy or immune.'

Brunetti refused to pay for a paper copy

and seldom found time to read it online, and so he was leading a relatively *Gazzettino*-less life. Had he been asked, he would have said he regretted it. Certainly it, along with the other local paper, *La Nuova di Venezia,* was essential for a well-informed life, even if the information pertained to which pharmacies were open on Sunday or at night, what weather was predicted, the forecast of the level of *acqua alta,* and the deaths of local residents. There was also passing reference to the rest of the world.

'My friend Bobo Ferruzzi always warned me: *"Per diventar cretin', leggi il Gazzetin' ",*' Brunetti said by way of comment.

He paused, remembering his late friend, 'But it must not work because Bobo read it every day, and he never became a cretin.'

Vianello, apparently having exhausted his interest in the newspaper, said casually, 'I went over to Chiara's school yesterday. I stopped in a bar for a coffee and waited for the kids to get out of class.' He smiled and added, 'It was like a visit to my own schooldays: hanging around and waiting for the girls to walk by.'

Brunetti smiled but said nothing.

'After I'd been there about ten minutes, an African appeared from the *calle* to the left of the school. About five minutes after he got there, the kids started coming out, and he started asking them — but only the girls — for money. At least that's what it looked like to me.'

'How'd they react?'

'Most of them ignored him and continued walking as if he weren't there. But some of them couldn't avoid him.'

'What did he do?'

'He got very close to them, stood in their way. Once he touched a girl's arm, but she pulled it away from him,' Vianello said. 'It looked to me as if he was only trying to get her attention.'

'Did any of them give him money?'

'No, not one.'

'How long did this go on?'

'About ten minutes. I stayed at the bar, watching. I wanted to see what he'd do. A couple of the boys said things to him, and he answered them, but there wasn't any aggression or trouble. Finally, when there were no more kids coming out of the school, he turned back into the *calle* and walked away, heading towards Accademia.'

'What did you do?'

'I followed him.'

'And?'

'When we got out into the *campo,* I walked up beside him and showed him my warrant card and asked to see his identification,' Vianello began. 'I could see him thinking about running, but then he said he'd left it in his room and it was all in order. He had only a few words in Italian, but he made that much clear.'

'And then?'

'I asked where he was from, and he said the Central African Republic. Then he tried to charm me with his big smile and calling me *"amico".*'

Vianello sounded un-charmed, and Brunetti said nothing.

'I told him I wasn't his *amico* but *la Polizia;* then I told him to stay away from the school.'

'Did he understand?'

'I think I made it sufficiently clear,' Vianello said.

'You don't sound very sympathetic,' Brunetti observed.

'Why should I be? He's here, he has no job, so I'm paying his way with my taxes. The state's given him a place to live and fifty euros a day . . .'

Before Vianello could continue, Brunetti asked, 'How do you know it's fifty euros?'

'Everybody knows it,' Vianello said.

'Everybody might say it,' Brunetti admitted, 'but I'm not sure that anybody knows it. You ever multiply fifty by thirty?' he asked.

'What?' Vianello asked defensively.

'You ever multiply fifty by thirty?'

Before Vianello could say anything else, Brunetti said, 'That's how many days there are in a month. Times fifty.'

He watched Vianello work out the numbers. 'It's one thousand, five hundred euros,' Vianello said, making no attempt to hide his surprise.

'Do you think the government has that much to give to each one of them?' Brunetti asked. 'Plus a place to live?'

Vianello ran his hands through his hair. 'But . . .' he began. 'But it's what everyone says.'

After a while, he added, 'They also say that they don't have to pay tax on it.' He looked at Brunetti. 'If that's the case, then it's what a person who makes about three thousand euros a month would take home.' He folded the newspaper in half and slid it slowly to the edge of his desk.

Looking at Brunetti he asked, 'It can't be true, can it? That they'd be given so much?'

'I doubt it,' Brunetti answered. 'I've heard lots of variants on the same story: that they have entire apartments, not just rooms in an apartment. That their names always go to the top of the lists for housing, so Italians have no place to live.' One of the circulars he'd been sent from the Ministry of the Interior estimated a cost of fifty euros, but that was the cost to the government for each day it kept an immigrant at one of its shelters or housing facilities: very little went directly into their hands. 'The government might spend fifty euros a day on them, but it doesn't go to them,' he concluded.

'*Mamma mia,*' Vianello exploded. 'Next thing you know, I'll be voting for the Lega Nord.'

As if to justify his critical stance, Brunetti said, 'Logic was my favourite class in school. I liked it because it's a way to see *how* what someone says is nonsense.'

'For example?' Vianello asked.

'As with these immigrants and the argument that they impoverish us as a country, take all of the money that should be ours. And our jobs and our women.'

He paused, but Vianello did not prompt him with another question, so he went on. 'In logic, that's the appeal to fear. Make people afraid of something and you can make them do what you want.'

Vianello, who had just joked about joining the Lega, added, 'Once you multiply the fifty euros a day by a couple of months, you do see it's impossible.'

Brunetti shrugged. 'Exactly. Appeal to fear,' he said.

'Lot of that around, isn't there?' Vianello asked.

This time a silent Brunetti nodded. He was about to ask Vianello if Signorina Elettra had told him about the attempt to hack into the Vice-Questore's email, when the Inspector said, 'But still, regardless of whether it goes directly to the immigrants or not, fifty euros a day is still being spent, isn't it?' He gave Brunetti a quick glance and asked, 'Eighteen thousand euros a year?'

This time, it was Vianello's turn to wait. When he had figured it out, Brunetti nodded.

'That's still more than I take home in a year.' Vianello did some calculations and was forced to clarify. 'After taxes, that is.' Was that a grin he saw on Vianello's face?

Brunetti decided it was time to go up to his office.

9

Brunetti met no one on the steps. He went into his office and, rejecting the temptation to close the door behind him, walked over to the window and looked across towards the façade of San Lorenzo. The restoration team had long since disappeared, leaving no trace that they had been there. Worse, the cat condominium that had stood there for years had vanished, as had, unfortunately, the cats.

Over the years, most of the street cats had disappeared from the area, and now their last home, that multi-storey extravaganza, was gone. Brunetti realized he minded more for the humans than for the cats. They were wily and would find new safe places to hide in and go on living, but the people from the nursing home who took such pleasure in the cats' presence and their survival in the face of terrible odds, what of them? And what of Vianello, to whom he had been so condescending with his talk of logic and all its wonders?

He heard a noise at the door, called *'Avanti,'* and turned to greet his guest.

It was Signorina Elettra, today dressed in something that might have been mistaken for battle fatigues. The cloth of her jacket was mottled green and grey, with twin breast pockets buttoned closed. Things got a bit confused with her trousers, which were charcoal grey and very narrow — hardly the sort of thing to wear into battle. Her boots, however, slipped back into role: heavy-soled, thick black leather brushed to a mirror-like shine, tied halfway up her shins with elaborately choreographed white laces. In her hand she held a folder, not a weapon.

'Are you planning to repel an invasion?' he asked.

'I've got some information about Contessa Lando-Continui's granddaughter,' she said by way of response. Perhaps he had only imagined speaking?

'Please tell me,' he said, waving a hand towards the chairs on the other side.

She sat and crossed her legs. She opened the folder.

'Manuela,' she began, 'has been declared 80 per cent mentally handicapped, and her mother receives a monthly payment of six hundred and twelve euros to help care for her.'

Signorina Elettra glanced at Brunetti, who nodded, urging her to continue. 'Her oxygen supply was cut off for a certain time. The official report gives this as the reason for her handicap and the resulting payment and further states that the damage manifests itself in permanent child-like behaviour. They estimate her mental age at seven, though for some things it is estimated that she has greater capacity.' She looked at Brunetti, but he shook his head: that was more than enough to know.

'I found the school she was attending and spoke to the *preside*, who's been there only four years. Manuela's file is online and states that she was absent from classes for a good portion of her last three months there. Only one of her teachers is still there: he taught Italian but doesn't remember much about her save that she was beautiful.'

Brunetti realized that, although the facts kept rising around him like a tide, he had discovered little to suggest a crime of any sort. If he wanted to make any real progress, he could no longer continue without an official request.

Signorina Elettra saw his attention move away from her and asked, 'What is it?'

'The Vice-Questore doesn't know anything about this. I've not had time to mention it to him.' Hearing himself, Brunetti recognized how lame the excuse was.

'Ah,' she said, eyes moving away from his face, as though a solution were written on the far wall and she had only to study it to discover what it was. 'It would be best,' she began and paused to consult the wall again to read the rest of the message. '. . . if he believed that this was an investigation that would somehow help his career.'

Brunetti turned his attention to the wall she had studied with such success. Their eye-beams threaded on one double string, the same their postures were, staring at the wall in hope of some revelation.

'Have you met Dottor Patta's wife?' he broke the silence by asking.

'Once. At a reception for the Praetore. She wanted his attention, not mine.'

Brunetti was struck by her last sentence and by the idea of a person who wanted attention. Finally he said, 'That's how to do it.'

'How?'

'By using the Contessa's attention as bait to offer his wife.'

He watched as Signorina Elettra worked

this out. Her eventual smile was sufficient reward.

In his desk drawer, Brunetti kept a ten-year-old Nokia that he had bought for Raffi on sale for nineteen euros. The *telefonino* had served his son for four years, then passed to Chiara until her embarrassment at owning a phone so out of fashion — but that refused to die — grew so great that she used her allowance to buy herself a newer one. The phone, now battered and cracked, had ended up in Brunetti's briefcase and then in his desk. In it was a chip that had been bought for him, with cash, by one of his contacts, purchased with a false *carta d'identità* and thus untraceable. Brunetti left it in the drawer, sure that no one would bother to steal it.

He used it only when he wanted no trace of a call to lead back to him.

The Contessa had given him her number, told him to call if he had to, and had also told him she would do anything she could to help him. She answered the phone with a simple '*Si*', no doubt because she did not recognize the number.

'It's me, Contessa. You said I could contact you.'

'Ah,' she whispered.

'Would you be willing to invite two people

128

to dinner and, if necessary, ask the wife to be on the board of Salva Serenissima?'

'If you asked me to, I would,' she answered immediately.

'Thank you,' he said and hung up.

He glanced across the desk at Signorina Elettra and, in keeping with her outfit, held his fingers up in a triumphant 'V'.

Twenty minutes later, Brunetti was sitting in front of his superior's desk, doing his best to look awkward, almost embarrassed, no doubt the result of his having been chosen, a mere mortal, to help arrange a conjunction of the stars.

'No, Vice-Questore, I have to admit I didn't bring it up. It was the Contessa who did.' He carefully avoided meeting Patta's glance and kept his eyes on the top of the desk. 'As I told you, we were there for dinner a few nights ago, and she was talking about her foundation, Salva Serenissima, and said that there was an opening for a board member, but she wanted to appoint a woman — definitely a woman — and one who would have objectivity in relation to the other members. She said she was tired of social climbers and wanted a serious person who was deeply committed to the best interests of the city.'

Brunetti looked up and into Patta's eyes. 'It was then that Paola thought to mention your wife.'

Patta had leaned ever more forward with each sentence and had insisted that Brunetti tell him again exactly what had happened, almost as if he wanted to be sure to give an accurate account of it, should it happen that he repeated it to some other person. 'Go on,' he said in a pleasant voice. 'Please.'

'Of course, Dottore. As I said, Paola has heard so many good things about your wife that she suggested the Contessa might want to speak to her about the possibility of her joining the board.'

'Did the Contessa ask your opinion?' Patta said, trying to sound affable but managing only to sound menacing.

'She did. And I said I thought Paola was right.'

'Good,' Patta affirmed in a more pleasant voice. 'And so?'

'I took the liberty of giving her your phone number, sir. I hope you don't mind, but I didn't have your wife's to give her.'

'And?' Patta asked.

'She said she'd call you this week and see if . . .' he was about to say, 'if your wife would be willing to speak to her', but he realized in time that this was too obsequious, even for Patta, and so, instead, said, 'your wife might be interested in a position such as this.' Brunetti recrossed his legs, and awaited his superior's words.

'I'll discuss it with her this evening,' Patta said, doing his best to sound nonchalant, as if this were the sort of offer he and his wife had to deal with every day. Then, 'Can you tell me a bit more about the Lando-Continui family?'

'It's one of the oldest families in the city,' Brunetti lied. 'And the Contessa's foundation is renowned.' He'd let Patta think about that. 'The *palazzo* is impressive.' His father-in-law had said it was second-rate, but that was surely not an opinion Brunetti was meant to publicize.

'There is one thing, however . . .' Brunetti began.

'What?' Patta asked.

'The granddaughter.'

'I don't know what you're talking about.'

'Well, sir, few people remember, but the Contessa — I know this only because my mother-in-law told me about it — is very troubled by something she thinks we're responsible for.'

'You and your wife?'

'No, sir,' Brunetti said with a smile he made sure looked nervous. 'The police.'

'How can a woman of that stature have anything to do with the police?' Patta demanded.

Now that Patta had bit at the hook, Brunetti decided to give it a hard tug by using Paola's mother's title.

'Contessa Falier told us about it at dinner the other night. Years ago, Contessa Lando-Continui, who is her best friend, told her how dissatisfied she was with the way the police investigated what she thinks was an attack on her granddaughter.'

'I know nothing about this,' Patta said, as Brunetti knew he would. Brunetti was surprised he didn't ring a bell and have Lieutenant Scarpa bring in a basin of warm water so that he could wash his hands of all responsibility.

'It was before you were here, Dottore. Of course you can't know about it. But she's apparently convinced there was some error.' Brunetti held up his hands and shrugged, as if to suggest that his superior's wife would have other opportunities to break into Venetian society.

'Have you studied the case?' Patta demanded.

'I remember it from the past, sir,' Brunetti said, lying more easily this time. He moved his head from side to side, either to give his imitation of an Indian actor he'd seen in a Bollywood film some weeks before or to express uncertainty.

'What?' Patta asked, voice grown crisper.

'I think it's possible that some details might have been overlooked during the original investigation,' Brunetti answered vaguely.

'Could it be reopened?' Patta asked.

'If you asked a magistrate to order it, I'm sure it could be, Dottore.' Brunetti could not have been more helpful and accommodating.

'Right,' Patta said in his voice of command. 'Send me an email with all of the information: case number, dates, people involved, and I'll see about finding someone who will authorize it.' He paused for a moment and then added, 'Gottardi would be the right one. He's new, and he won't give any trouble.'

Brunetti knew when to disappear. He got to his feet. 'That's very good of you, sir. I'm sure Contessa Lando-Continui will be pleased.'

The very idea that a member of the aristocracy would be pleased with him brought a smile to Patta's lips. Brunetti took his leave.

Outside Patta's office, uncertain as to

whether Patta would call his wife immediately or wait to surprise her at dinner with the news, he was reluctant to linger and talk to Signorina Elettra. She, however, waved him nearer to her desk and said, 'I've spoken to Giorgio. He's just been promoted and is very busy, but he said he'd look into that matter as soon as he can.'

So enchanted had Brunetti been by his exchange with Patta that it took him a moment to realize she was talking about the attempt to break into the emails of both the Vice-Questore and the Lieutenant.

'What is it that he's doing now?' Brunetti asked. Her look assessed Brunetti's right to know as well as his ability to be trusted with information. He must have passed both tests, for she said, lowering her voice, 'He's working on a way to erase all record of the numbers that have been called from a person's phone as well as to erase any recordings that might have been made of actual conversations.'

'Am I to understand that this can all be done with his computer?'

'Well,' she said with feigned hesitation, 'not from *his* computer, but from *a* computer.'

'From one of Telecom's own computers?' Brunetti asked, astonished to learn that

Giorgio had turned on his employer and even more surprised that he would risk using one of their own computers to work against them.

'I thought I'd told you, Dottore. He doesn't work for Telecom any more. He hasn't for some time.' She might as well have pasted a DO NOT TRESPASS sign across her forehead and switched it on.

'Ah,' Brunetti said in sudden understanding. 'I hope he's still willing to . . . ?' he began but proved unable to complete the sentence or, in fact, to find the proper term for whatever it was Giorgio had been doing for Signorina Elettra for years. Most of the terms that occurred to him would ordinarily lead to criminal prosecution.

'Yes, he's willing.' It was evident that this was the last thing she had to say for now. He nodded and went back to his own office.

Half an hour later, Brunetti still sat in his office, uncertain about what he wanted to do. He had read his way through most of the papers accumulated on his desk and would have been able to recall them, so strongly had he forced himself to concentrate. But none of the cases required his attention. The one regarding the Bangladeshi porter who had stabbed another porter to death during a furious argument over territory at the train station had been solved within a few hours of the victim's death; the body found floating in the *laguna* four days ago was quickly identified as a retired electrician who had had a heart attack and fallen out of his boat while fishing; the postman on the Lido who had set fire to the camper van of the new boyfriend of his ex-wife had been found and arrested.

Brunetti knew that he would use the speedy resolution of those cases to justify his investigation of a fifteen-year-old accident that might well not even be a criminal case.

Is this what retirement would be for him? he wondered. Sticking his nose into other people's business whenever he had the feeling that something wasn't consistent in a story? Must every death come in a tidy package before ex-Commissario Brunetti would leave it alone and let people get on with their lives?

He dialled Rizzardi's number in the office at the morgue. The pathologist answered with his name.

'It's me, Ettore,' Brunetti said. 'I have a favour to ask you.'

'Fine, thank you,' Rizzardi said in a pleasant voice. 'And you?'

'It's about patient records at the hospital. I thought you might know something.' Rizzardi remained silent, so Brunetti plunged on. 'From about fifteen years ago. I'm going to have a magistrate's order that will let me have a look, but not for a few days, I'd guess, so as of the moment, I'm not authorized to ask questions or see files. Is there anyone in the Records Office who might be able to help?'

'Are you talking about one of my patients, if I might call them that?' the pathologist began. 'Or one of the patients in the wards?' If possible, Rizzardi's voice had grown even more friendly, as if he were enjoying the exchange.

'Someone who was taken to the hospital,' Brunetti answered. 'And who left.'

'Why don't you simply ask the Vice-Questore's secretary to break into the system?' Rizzardi asked affably. 'Unless by now you're able to do it yourself.'

'Ettore,' Brunetti said, 'I think you're not supposed to know about that. Or at least talk about it.'

'Ah,' Rizzardi answered. 'Sorry. Secret best kept, I realize.' The pathologist said nothing for so long that Brunetti thought he might have replaced the phone, but then Rizzardi said, 'I have to disappoint you,

Guido. The one person I knew in the Records Office — that is, knew well enough to ask this sort of favour — retired last year. There's no one there now who'd be willing to circumvent the rules.'

'Thanks anyway, Ettore,' Brunetti said, then added, 'Soon it'll be like working in Sweden.'

'I know,' replied Rizzardi. 'Shocking.'

10

Brunetti thought of looking online for the phone number but, instead, reverted to his Luddite ways and pulled the phone book from his bottom drawer. The only Cavanis, Pietro, was listed as living in Santa Croce.

The phone was answered by a machine that gave a message in gruff-voiced Veneziano, telling the caller to leave his name and number and what he wanted, and perhaps he'd return the call.

Brunetti gave his name and the number of his *telefonino* and said he'd like to speak to Signor Cavanis about an incident near Campo San Boldo some years before.

Restlessness attacked him. He remembered one of the phrases Paola had picked up from an American friend and had used to admonish the kids, ever since they were little more than babies: 'You've got ants in your pants', an expression that had delighted them for years. Brunetti stood and went to the window, telling himself it was to check the weather. What he saw surprised him: the morning's clement sky had been replaced by a mass of dark grey clouds that tumbled and rolled over one another and promised nothing pleasant. He looked at his watch and told himself that, if he left now and walked quickly, he could get home before the rain threatened by those clouds could begin.

It started just as he reached the top of the Rialto bridge, so he cut left at the bottom of the steps and into the underpass. Through the arches on his right, he saw the rain intensify.

Within minutes, he could barely see the shops on the other side. It shouldn't rain like this, not even at this time of the year. This was monsoon; this was the end of the world. He continued on to the turning, where he had a longer view across the small *campo*. He could barely make out the storekeepers on the other side, hurrying to carry inside the racks of scarves and trays of wallets standing in front of their shops.

He opened his umbrella and, persuading himself that the rain was less heavy, stepped into the by now almost empty *calle* and started walking quickly towards home. Before he got to the bridge, his shoes were soaked through, and the arms of his jacket proved incapable of keeping him dry beyond the radius of the umbrella.

He told himself he could have waited, that he was wet because he was impatient. But he kept walking. The narrowness of the next *calle* protected him from the rain. He came out into San Aponal, then left at the corner, other hand in his pocket to get his keys, up to the door, zap the key into the lock, push the door and into the enormous entrance hall.

Soaked. His shoes leaked water at every step and were probably ruined, water flowed from his hair and down the collars of his shirt and jacket. Don't stop. Up. He climbed, one hand holding the dripping umbrella, the other his keys. Up. At the final landing, he looked back down the steps and saw that he was still leaving wet footprints. He stopped in front of the apartment, set the umbrella upright in a corner, and opened the door.

He stuck his arms out sideways, and as he did, he could hear the cloth of his shirt pull away from his body. Paola called from the kitchen, and then she was standing in the doorway to his right.

'Oh, good,' she exclaimed when she saw him.

Brunetti sought sarcasm in her tone but heard none.

'Come into the kitchen,' she said.

He paused only long enough to push off his shoes and then squished after her.

He was relieved by the warmth of the kitchen; until then, he hadn't been aware of how cold it had become. He glanced around, grabbed a kitchen towel and wiped the water off his face and hair.

'Look,' she said, pointing at the window that gave a view of the mountains to the north.

The mountains were hidden behind the falling rain; no, behind a cascade of water that fell at a distance of ten centimetres from the window.

'What's that?' he asked, waving the towel in the direction of the window.

'I think the drainpipe must be blocked.' Paola stood beside him and took his arm, not seeming to mind how wet it was, nor that he was dripping on the tiles. She pulled him back a step and pointed to the wall above the window through which they could see the curtain of water still pouring down. Just at the top, the white paint was beginning to turn a light grey as the damp began to permeate the brick.

'The water in the drainpipe's backed up

and going down the wall outside,' she said.

It looked that way to Brunetti, too. He stood and studied it. He took off his jacket and hung it over the back of one of the kitchen chairs. Eyes still on the water beyond the window, he told Paola, 'Go and get me an umbrella with a hooked handle.'

She disappeared. Brunetti swept everything on the counter to one side. He pulled over a chair and used it to step up on the counter. He was now too high for the window, so knelt in front of it.

Paola came back with the umbrella. Brunetti opened the window and moved aside as a vagrant burst of wind swept the rain into the room and over him. Ignoring it, Brunetti reached for the umbrella. He stuck the hooked end out of the window and anchored himself to the frame with his other hand. He leaned out, sticking his arm through the sheet of water, and fished around in the gutter above his head. He moved the umbrella handle back and forth. When he met resistance, he shoved harder, careful to tighten his grip on the window frame, conscious that he was four storeys above a stone pavement.

Back and forth, back and forth, pushing ever more strongly in the direction of the drainpipe at the corner of the building. He leaned out even farther and felt something give way above him. Suddenly Paola was behind him on the counter, her arms wrapped around his chest.

In an instant, all resistance ceased and the umbrella slid freely through the gutter towards the corner of the building. Just as quickly, the curtain of water turned itself off as the trapped water poured towards the drainpipe. He lifted the umbrella and pulled it back through the window, then leaned aside and pushed the window closed.

Paola scrambled off the counter and stood facing him. She put both hands to her head. 'We're both crazy. What would have happened if you'd lost your balance?'

'The window's too small, I think,' he said, turning back to assess its size. 'Especially with you as an anchor, I could never have fitted through it.'

When he turned back to her, he saw that he had not managed to calm her residual fear. 'Look,' he said, patting his stomach, made more evident by the wet shirt that clung to it. 'Your cooking probably saved my life.'

11

As he walked back to the Questura, restored by a long, very hot, shower, and lunch, Brunetti found himself thinking about Patta and about how easy it had been to outwit him: all he'd done was hold out the possibility of his wife's social advancement, and his superior had fallen like a ripe pear. What was it the woman wanted: to be president of the Lions Club? A Dame of Honour and Devotion of the Order of the Knights of Malta? She had been in Venice for years, and to the best of Brunetti's knowledge had not managed to enter into any of the religious or social orders that bestowed prestige upon those allowed to join them. Yet he, by the magic of his family connections, was about to make her dreams come true. He felt no triumph in the deed.

It was well after four when he reached the Questura. On the second landing he met Signorina Elettra coming down. When she stopped above him, he asked, 'Has he told you?'

'No. Nothing,' she said, her curiosity evident.

'He's going to request an order to open an investigation,' Brunetti told her.

She leaned back against the railing. Brunetti, only just recovering from his own experience leaning out the window of his apartment building, involuntarily put a hand on her arm.

'What is it?' she asked, unable to hide her surprise. She didn't exactly pull her arm away but she did free herself from his grasp.

'Sorry. It makes me nervous when anyone leans against a railing like that.' He braced both hands on the railing and extended his head over the void. He estimated the metres: eleven? twelve? Surely enough.

Signorina Elettra stepped away from the railing and moved up one step. She shifted to the other side and turned to lean against the wall. 'Is that better?' she asked.

'Yes. Much. Thank you.'

'Not a pleasant feeling to have if you work on the third floor,' she said.

Brunetti shrugged. 'I always walk close to the wall; then it doesn't bother me so much.'

She nodded, acknowledging the good sense of this. 'You were saying?' she asked

146

in an ordinary voice.

'The Vice-Questore thinks we should take a closer look at what happened,' he said.

'And he's going to have you do the looking?'

It made him uncomfortable to hear Signorina Elettra hold so close to the truth. 'There are certain social advantages that are to be had from this.'

'How lucky that Contessa Lando-Continui is so well known. Would you like me to be involved in this investigation?' she asked, conveniently ignoring the fact that she already was.

'Of course.' Whatever would prompt such a question, he wondered. From her? 'You know how to deal with the Vice-Questore should his enthusiasm begin to waver or should he begin to offer . . . ?'

'Resistance?' she suggested.

'Once again, you follow my thoughts exactly, Signorina.'

'The duty of every woman, Dottore,' she answered.

He smiled, relieved that they had so easily slipped back into easy banter. He continued up the steps, suddenly aware that what he had said was true: he did stay close to the wall.

Nothing on his desk needed his attention,

so he took his phone and called the number he had listed for Leonardo Gamma Fede.

'How'd you know I was back home?' Lolo said when he answered.

'Remember, I'm a commissario di polizia,' Brunetti said and added what he hoped sounded like a wicked laugh. 'You're never safe from us.'

'Don't say it, even as a joke,' Lolo said, not as a joke.

'Trouble?'

'Nothing I'm not used to,' Lolo answered ambiguously, then asked, 'You free for a drink before dinner?'

'That's why I called.'

'Good.' Then, 'You at work?'

'Yes.'

Silently, they shared geographic calculation as both tried to think of a conveniently located bar somewhere between them where they could sit and have a drink and be left in peace.

'There's a place in Campo San Filippo e Giacomo,' Brunetti said.

'The one on the corner?'

'Yes. I'll see you there in half an hour.'

'Good,' Lolo agreed and hung up.

Left with time to kill, Brunetti read reports until the tedium drove him to the window to study the traffic in the canal below his window. A heavy-bodied transport boat went slowly past, forcing a *caorlina* to hug the side of the narrow canal until they passed one another; a taxi cruised by, passengers invisible in the cabin; two men in white rowed a *sàndolo* towards the entrance to the *bacino.*

There had been a time in his life when Brunetti's hands were calloused over by the months he'd spent rowing in the *laguna.* It was the only thing his father had ever taught him, taking him out in his *puparìn* from the time his son was seven years old. Brunetti still remembered the joy of feeling his father's body bent over his, his rough hands on top of his as he showed him just where to put them on the oar.

His father was an irascible and impulsive man, unable to keep a job, or a friend, for any length of time. He always had to be right, could not bear opposition. Worse, he had no patience with incompetence, would criticize a plumber for using the wrong tool, the butcher for a badly trimmed cutlet, the postman for a delayed letter, though he never minded if the bills arrived late. Walking on the street with him was both joy and horror for the young Brunetti, for he never knew when his father would begin to rage at the person who walked too slowly in front of him or too close to his side.

But once on the water, he could have been Patience on a monument, so easily did he slough off all concern with time or efficiency of movement. He spent hours with Brunetti, placing his son's hands back in the right places, then, after a few minutes, stopping the boat and moving forward to where his son stood to slide them gently back. 'Just there, Guido,' he remembered him saying, patting his son on the shoulder or head when he managed to keep his hands in the right place long enough to row five metres.

He remembered, too, the time when — he must have been fourteen — his father had suggested, oh so casually, that he try rowing from the back of the boat that day. His heart could still thump at the memory; first at the fear of not being able to establish command of the boat and then with unfettered joy when his father called back to him, 'Well done, Capitano.'

He returned from his reverie and looked at his watch; he had only ten minutes to get to his meeting with Lolo. He arrived late, but so did his friend: they entered the *campo* from opposite sides at the same time.

Seeing him after so long a time, more than a year, Brunetti was struck by how happy he was to see Lolo and how deep were his feelings for his old friend. 'Lolo,' he called, and the Marchese, who had been walking towards the bar on the corner, turned in his direction. He quickened his pace towards Brunetti, and they embraced warmly, holding one another like two bears and then letting go, only to hug one another again, even more strongly.

As they did each time they met, for it was always after lengthy intervals, first one and then the other said, 'You look just the same,' after which they pounded each other on the shoulder and embraced again.

'Where have you been?' Brunetti asked, taking a closer look at his friend. Only then did he see how pale Lolo looked, no trace of the deep tan he often brought back from his international adventures. He was thinner, too, his cheekbones prominent under his dark eyes.

'Argentina,' he answered, taking another whack at Brunetti's shoulder, as if words could not sufficiently express his delight at seeing him again. Then he added, his smile fading a bit, 'For my sins.' And then, more brightly, 'And trying to keep an eye on my investment.'

Curious as he was, Brunetti thought it would be better if they could continue over two glasses of wine, so he put his hand on

151

Lolo's shoulder and guided him towards the bar.

The place had been renovated since Brunetti had last stopped there for a drink. The wooden counter with the worn pink linoleum surface was gone, replaced by a slab of white marble that could have been looted from an Etruscan tomb. Customers no longer stood in front of it to drink a quick coffee or glass of wine but were encouraged to sit on high, seemingly precarious, steel stools with neon-orange plastic seats. The bottles lined up on the shelves in front of the very clean mirror carried graphically sophisticated labels that made no attempt to suggest their contents.

The six old wooden tables, scarred, scratched, and burned by generations of clients, had followed the counter into retirement. Brunetti and Lolo hesitated momentarily at the door, and then by unspoken agreement went to the back of the room and took their places at one of the three-legged tables that stood against the wall. Because they were both tall men, they found themselves sitting high above the mirrored surface of the table.

Brunetti saw a thin-faced man in his fifties, tall and muscular, his eyes surrounded by the tiny lines that come from too many years of too much sun, looking now out of place in his strangely pale face.

A waiter approached, and Brunetti asked for a glass of white wine. *'Due,'* Lolo said, apparently as uninterested as Brunetti in the long list of possibilities the waiter had begun to suggest. So long as it was white and cold.

'Argentina?' Brunetti prodded when the waiter left them.

Lolo lowered his head and rubbed at his hair with both hands. His hair, Brunetti had noticed, was still thick and dark; indeed, it rustled audibly as Lolo rubbed his hands through it. That finished, he looked at Brunetti and said, 'One of my brothers has a cattle ranch there. He asked me to go down and help him out of a mess.'

'How long were you there?'

'Three months.'

'On the ranch?'

'In the office of the ranch, mainly,' Lolo said and looked up at the arrival of the waiter, who set the glasses on the table and went back behind the bar. 'Doing what I could to save things.'

That, Brunetti surmised, as he picked up his glass and tapped it against his friend's, explained his lack of colour. But what could have taken three months? 'What about your family?' he asked.

Confused, Lolo said, 'My brother *is* family. They're all there now.' He took a long taste of the wine, set the glass down and said, 'Argentina's is better.'

'Wine?'

'Yes. And beef. And that's all.' Lolo took another sip, swirled the glass around, and then said, 'I will never again in my life criticize the bureaucracy in this fair land.'

'Here?' Brunetti asked, unable to disguise his astonishment.

The waiter drifted over to their table, set a bowl of salted peanuts between them and then left.

'Guido,' Lolo said, digging up a handful of peanuts and leaning his head back to drop them into his mouth one by one, 'compared to Argentina, we are living in Switzerland.' He chewed, swallowed, dropped in more peanuts. 'Sweden. Norway.' More peanuts. 'Finland.' He grabbed another handful and tossed them after the others. 'You have no idea.'

'It's hard to believe,' Brunetti said in what he tried to make sound like a calm voice.

'I know it is. But trust me.' He set his glass down and pushed his chair back far enough to allow him to cross his legs without doing himself or the table an injury. 'What do you

154

want to know?' he asked, reminding Brunetti that he was a man who hated to waste time.

'I'd like information about Salva Serenissima: I saw your name on the board of directors. But mainly I wanted to see you again and see how you are,' Brunetti said, knowing it was the truth.

Laughing, Lolo said, 'Don't tell me Demetriana's got her hand in your pocket, too.' He shook his head in mixed appreciation and exasperation. 'She's a wily thing, but I can't help liking her.'

'Do you know her well?'

'I sort of inherited her from my parents,' Lolo said, sipping his wine. 'I can't remember a time when my parents didn't know them, her and her late husband; she's almost an aunt by adoption to me.'

'And Salva Serenissima?' Brunetti asked.

Lolo leaned back in his chair, raising its front legs from the floor. He crossed his arms and gazed into the far distance as he considered Brunetti's question. 'I think it's her baby.'

'I beg your pardon.'

Lolo let his chair fall to the ground. 'Maybe better to say it's what gives her most satisfaction.'

'She's got a son, hasn't she?' Brunetti asked.

'Yes. Clever fellow, Teo. He's taken over half of the family businesses and is making his own fortune. Most of it's out of the country now, and he's away most of the time. Thailand, Indonesia, India.' Before Brunetti could ask, he said, 'He and Demetriana have never understood one another.'

'Did you know his first wife?' Brunetti asked.

'Ah, yes,' Lolo said, then picked up his glass and emptied it. 'Barbara.' He looked around for the waiter and, catching his attention, held up his glass, then glanced at Brunetti, who nodded. *'Due,'* Lolo called to the waiter.

Lolo rested his elbows on the table and clapped his palms softly together a few times. 'You know about their daughter?' he asked.

'Yes. That's what I want to talk to you about,' Brunetti answered.

Lolo's expression changed, and he looked at Brunetti in long appraisal. 'Aha, and I thought it was the charm of my personality that led you to call.'

'That, above all,' Brunetti answered in the same joking tone. Then, more seriously, 'I've asked the Vice-Questore to open an investigation into what happened to her.'

'Is that necessary?'

They were interrupted by the waiter, who set down two glasses of white wine and replaced the half-eaten peanuts with a fresh bowl.

Brunetti ignored his glass while telling his friend the few facts he knew, ending with the story of Manuela's drunken saviour.

Lolo picked up his glass by the stem and turned it around repeatedly before setting it down untasted. 'Well, he did and he didn't,' Lolo said at last, then added immediately, 'Save her, that is.' His eyes were on his glass, but Brunetti saw the bleakness that had taken over his face.

'Have you seen her since then?' he asked.

'Yes.'

'What's she like?'

Lolo drained half his glass. He set it down clumsily, making a loud clack, and said, 'She's a lovely woman with a vacant face and is often confused by things. She's very sweet, but after a while you see that something's wrong with her.'

With the seriousness that had entered his voice with this description of the woman, Lolo asked, 'Why are you bothering with this? What's done is done.'

'Her grandmother asked me to. She

doesn't want to die without knowing what happened.'

'What good will that do?'

Brunetti shrugged in answer.

'But it won't change anything,' Lolo said fiercely.

'It will change what she knows,' was all that Brunetti could think of saying.

Lolo crossed his arms again and sat for some time, eyes on the far wall, until he finally said, 'Then it's not Salva Serenissima you want to know about.'

'I do. I met some people who are involved with it — or who will be — and I'm curious about their motives, I suppose.' Brunetti shook his head at the vagueness of this, even to himself. 'She — the Contessa — wants to leave the city better than she found it. I don't think there's any doubt about that.'

'But?' Lolo asked.

'But some of the people around her . . . I don't understand what they want.'

'Who are they?'

'An English banker and his companion. I think he's a fool and she's not. He seems to want to help, so long as it gets done quickly.' Brunetti suddenly remembered his wine and took a sip.

'And he gets the credit for it?' Lolo asked.

'Do you know the people I'm talking about?'

'He's short and insignificant looking, and she's got very large brown eyes and doesn't say much?' Lolo asked.

Brunetti nodded.

'You're right about both of them,' Lolo agreed, then as quickly asked, 'But what of it, so long as they give the money and something gets done?'

Brunetti laughed and answered, 'I see what three months in Argentina have done to you.'

Lolo at first looked surprised, then he tried to look offended, and then he smiled. 'A lifetime in Venice has done more.' Brunetti laughed at this, making it unnecessary for Lolo to explain. Instead, he asked Brunetti, 'Anyone else?'

'Not among the foreigners.'

'Who, then?' Lolo asked and picked up his glass.

'There was a Venetian at the dinner; he flattered the Contessa terribly. A bit younger than us, beard like the last Tsar.' Then, reluctantly, because part of him did like the Contessa, Brunetti added, disappointment in his voice, 'She seemed to like hearing it.'

'Ah, Vittori,' was all that Lolo said.

'Doesn't he have one of those double-barrelled names?' Brunetti asked.

Lolo snorted into his glass. When he had recovered, he surprised Brunetti by asking, 'Tell me the name of someone your father worked for.'

'Excuse me?'

'The last name of someone who employed your father, for any job at all. Tell me his name.'

Brunetti thought of the fruit and vegetable vendor who had, when his father was in a period of relative calm, given him a job delivering produce to restaurants. 'Camuffo.'

'Then you could call yourself Guido Brunetti-Camuffo with as much right.'

'You mean he invented it?'

Lolo crossed his arms and leaned back. Lapsing into contemplative mode, he stared at the ceiling and then said, 'I always wonder, if people like him are capable of adding a name to their names, what are they capable of adding to their bills?' He let his chair slam back to the floor and went on. 'It's really closer to the truth to say he borrowed the name,' Lolo said with barely disguised contempt. 'His father worked for the Ricciardis: gardener or something. Everybody knows that.'

Brunetti, who hadn't known, asked, still

pondering the thought of having gone through life as Guido Brunetti-Camuffo, 'But why would he do that?'

Lolo reached across the table and gently ruffled Brunetti's hair. 'You're wonderful, Guido, really wonderful. Your wife has the bluest blood in the city, and still you just don't get it.'

'That this stuff is important to people?' Brunetti asked indignantly.

This time, Lolo actually pushed his chair back until it banged against a chair at the next table. He looked across at his friend and finally said, 'It's one of the reasons I love you, Guido, and why you're such a friend.'

'Because I don't understand?'

'No, because it doesn't matter to you. What people are called.' Then, after a pause, 'What I'm called.'

Brunetti looked at the peanuts and, needing something to do, stuck his finger into the bowl and moved the nuts around, shifting them from one side to the other and then back again. When he had them arranged to his satisfaction, he looked at Lolo and asked, 'What else can you tell me about him?'

'Only that Demetriana's not the only elderly woman he flatters.'

'To get what from them?' Brunetti asked, familiar with the race of man.

'Work. Dinner. Invitations. Trips. Whatever happens to fall from the table, or whatever he can nudge just a little bit until it falls from the table and lands near his feet.'

'I see,' Brunetti said. 'What do you think he wants from the Contessa?'

'Work, probably,' Lolo answered, making it clear that the subject did not interest him much.

'Can you tell me anything else about the granddaughter?'

Lolo closed his eyes and pulled his lips together, then opened his eyes and said, 'You know I hate waste, Guido. Doesn't matter what it is; I just hate to see anything lost or spoiled.' Brunetti nodded to tell him to go on.

'That's what happened with Manuela. She was a sweet, lovely kid. I didn't see her often, maybe five, six times when she was growing up, when she was at Demetriana's place. And then suddenly, when she was about fourteen, fifteen, all I knew about her was what Demetriana told me, that she had "problems", the kind that are never defined.' He waved a hand in the air. 'You know how it is when people use that word when they talk about the people close to them: it can be anything: drugs, anorexia, bad friends.'

Brunetti kept his face impassive as he heard his friend read off a list of his own deepest fears.

'And then it happened, and she was in the hospital, and when she came out, she wasn't the same.'

The waiter appeared, and Lolo paid him, waving away Brunetti's offer to contribute. 'We don't talk about her, Demetriana and I. Nothing's going to change. Ever. That's the waste; her life was tossed away, and nothing's ever going to change. So there's nothing to say.'

'And if anything happens to her mother?' Brunetti asked.

Lolo thought for a long time, perhaps trying to assess how much he should tell Brunetti. Then he said, 'She'll have to stay with her grandmother or her father. Demetriana's more than eighty, and Teo has a new wife and kids. So I imagine she'll have to go somewhere. To a place.' He got to his feet, as did Brunetti.

Outside, in the *campo,* they exchanged another bearish hug, then Lolo turned back towards San Marco, and Brunetti went out to San Zaccaria to get the vaporetto.

12

Dinner passed quietly. Raffi had gone out for a pizza with Sara Paganuzzi, who was back after a year studying in Paris. It seemed to both Brunetti and Paola that Raffi spoke of her with less enthusiasm than previously. Perhaps it was only Raffi's nervousness with the beginning of a new academic year, with three new professors and the necessary adjustment to their habits. It could just as easily be the fading of first love's intoxication: he and Paola could do no more than stand and wait.

Chiara filled the gap created by her brother's absence by asking her parents if they would let her go to London the following summer with a friend from school to work as a waitress in the restaurant of her friend's uncle. 'What do you know about being a waitress?' Paola, who had been taking part in the conversation from the stove, asked.

'I know that you're supposed to serve

from the left,' Chiara said right back, then added, 'though you always serve me from the right.'

Paola had just turned towards her husband and daughter to bring them their farfalle with *radicchio* and gorgonzola. She stopped and set the two plates down on the counter beside her and raised her head to address the Spirits of Offended Motherhood. 'I serve her from the right,' she said in an entirely conversational voice. 'From the right, did you hear? While waitresses are supposed to serve from the left.' She folded her arms and leaned back against the counter. 'I hope that means she's recognized that I am not a waitress, but her mother, who gave a three-hour lecture on *The Rape of the Lock* this morning, after which she sat in a committee meeting for two hours to discuss changes in the pension system for professors at the university.'

Knowing that she had their interest, she looked at them and then returned her attention to whatever Spirits might be circling in the air above them. 'The universities I've attended have failed miserably to prepare me to be a waitress, and thus I've gone through life serving from the right. Perhaps I do this because it saves my having to walk around my daughter — who is sitting at the table and waiting to be served — and then return to serve my husband. Who, I might add, is similarly engaged.' Then, to remove any doubts either one of them — or the Spirits — might have about what Brunetti was doing while sitting there, she explained, 'Waiting to be served.'

That said, Paola turned and picked up the two dishes and approached the table. From Chiara's right, she set down the dish, then Brunetti's, after which she walked back to the stove to prepare her own plate of pasta.

Chiara looked at her father, who held a finger to his lips, enjoining silence. He pointed at his face to tell Chiara to leave it to him to take care of things.

Paola, plate in hand, returned to the table and took her place. She looked across at her daughter and inquired brightly, 'Did you have a nice day at school today, dear?'

The rest of the meal had been strained, though Chiara did her best to help clear the table, even dried and put away the dishes before going silently to her room to do her homework. Brunetti had left them to work things out between them and gone into the living room to continue reading the *Argonautica* of Apollonius of Rhodes, a book he'd let sit ever since he'd struggled through parts of it in Greek in his last year in *liceo*. He had found an Italian translation in a second-hand bookshop a few weeks before, and he looked forward to being able to read it with less difficulty than it had presented decades ago.

Lolo had been the star pupil in Greek, could read it with the ease with which he read Italian. No one, least of all Lolo, could understand why that was, what place in his brain held the secret of language, for Lolo had the gift in a way Brunetti had seen in no other person. He needed a month to become comfortable in a language and to be able to read it; by the time they left school, he was fluent in English and French, and could read both Latin and Greek with no trouble. Since then, he'd picked up — that was his phrase — German, Spanish, and Catalan. He had once told Brunetti that, after a certain point, he no longer felt that he was translating a language into Italian but was simply reading it as though it were his own language.

When Paola came in, carrying two cups of coffee with spoons upright in them, he said, 'I saw Lolo this afternoon.'

Her delight was evident and served to banish the scene she had made at dinner. 'I didn't know he was here. Where did you see him?'

'We met for a drink. He's been in Argentina sorting out some sort of mess his brother found himself in.'

'Is he the one with the cows?'

'Yes. Do you know him?'

'I knew him in school. We used to do our chemistry homework together.' She gave the spoon a stir and removed it, then sipped at her coffee. 'Hopeless. We were both hopeless idiots. God knows how we got through the exam. I'm sure he charmed the teacher into giving him a passing grade: he understood less than I did.'

'Is that how you got through it? With charm?' Brunetti asked. It was hard for him to imagine Paola passing an exam in chemistry by any other means.

'No, I simply memorized the textbook, even though I didn't have any idea of what it all meant.' She sipped again.

It had taken Brunetti years to become familiar with her extraordinary memory, and he still found it difficult to believe that she could memorize anything simply by reading it with special attention and telling herself to remember what she read.

'That's all any of us had to do. I've been suspicious of scientists ever since then.'

'I know,' Brunetti said and drank his coffee.

'Tell me about Lolo,' she said, coming to sit beside him.

'He said Argentina makes Italy look like Switzerland.'

'Oh, my,' she said. 'How long is he back for?'

'I don't know.'

She turned to stare at him. 'You don't see him for more than a year, and you don't ask him how long he's staying here?'

'We talked about other things.'

'What?'

'Manuela Lando-Continui,' he said, although he had not intended to use her full name. Brunetti realized he did it to make her — even if only for the time it took for him to say her name — a person, her own self.

'Ah, that's right,' Paola said, sitting back and resting her head against the cushions. 'He's known them all for ever. I think he and Barbara, her mother . . .'

'He and Barbara what?' Brunetti asked.

'There might have been something between them, years ago, when he was at university.'

'And she?'

'Oh, she was at the beginning of throwing

169

her life away.'

'I never met her,' Brunetti said. 'You know her well?'

'No. There's about six years' difference in age between us, so we didn't have friends in common and weren't ever at school together. So I know her only by reputation, though I did see her occasionally, back then.'

'What's she like?' Brunetti asked. Before Paola could begin to answer, he stood and went into the kitchen and was quickly back with two glasses and a nearly empty bottle of the home-made plum schnapps a friend gave him every Christmas. He poured two small glasses and returned to his seat.

She thanked him and took a small sip, as if barely willing to try it, which was the way she always drank this schnapps, a sort of transferred manifestation of the suspicions she entertained about the man who had given it to her husband.

'She was very pretty: tall, with long, straight blonde hair and pale blue eyes. She could have been a Scandinavian exchange student, so little did she look like one of us.' Coming from a light-eyed blonde, this seemed strange to Brunetti.

Paola seemed to drift off. She gave her attention to the night sky, the still-lit *campanile* of San Marco just visible from this corner of the living room. 'We couldn't live anywhere else, could we?'

'Probably not.'

'It makes me understand why Demetriana wants to save it. Or at least try to.'

'Good luck to her, then,' Brunetti said and went back to work. 'How did Barbara throw her life away?'

'The usual way for rich young girls who aren't very bright: men, some drugs, some more men, lots of parties and lots of trips, and then some more drugs, and then she was twenty-five, and she was lucky enough to meet Teo, who's really a very nice man, and she married him and had a baby and sort of settled down.'

'Sort of?'

'Sort of,' Paola repeated. 'Teo finally ran out of patience. Unfortunately for Barbara, he met someone else at the same time, so things were over for her.'

'You make it sound easy.'

'I think, for men, it is, especially when there's enough money and another woman waiting.'

'And his child?' Brunetti asked, trying to sound neutral.

'What judge would give a child to the father, Guido? In *Mamma*-worshipping Italy?'

'So he left them?'

'He left them, but Barbara had someone waiting, too.' He watched her consider whether to say something and then decide she would. 'But he didn't stay around very long.'

'And Manuela?'

'According to Demetriana, she was in love with her horse, and that seems to have made life with her mother easier for her.' Brunetti detected none of the irony or sarcasm he had expected in Paola's voice. 'Manuela lived with her, spent a lot of time with her horse, and then she fell into the water, and that was that.'

'Has your mother ever spoken about Manuela?' Brunetti asked.

Paola spent a long time looking at the *campanile* before she answered. 'Only after she sees her at Demetriana's. She's a very sweet girl. Woman.' She paused, busying herself with her glass, then said, 'None of us talks about her much.'

'Don't you find that strange?' he asked.

'Guido,' she said in a very soft voice, 'sometimes I don't understand you.'

Brunetti thought this was because she forgot that he was a policeman but chose not to say anything.

'We talk about her, of course, because we

172

see her. But we've never talked about what happened to her.' Then, setting her glass down, she said, 'There's no other decent way, is there?'

'No, there isn't,' Brunetti said and got to his feet to take the bottle back to the kitchen.

13

As he walked towards the Questura the next morning, Brunetti considered the ways this case differed from the others he'd dealt with during his career: there was an injured person but no evidence that she had been the victim of a crime, and there was no need to hurry the investigation, for, in the absence of both victim and suspect, what need of haste to seek a guilty person?

The whole thing had taken on the feeling of an academic exercise, carried out to allow the wife of the Vice-Questore to rise a few steps up the ladder of Venetian society, and to help an old woman die in peace. Yet Brunetti was incapable of ridding himself of his concern for the girl's fate.

Ahead of him as he entered the Questura, his colleague Claudia Griffoni was just starting up the steps. She turned at the sound of her name and paused on the third step to wait for him.

'Are you working on anything important?' Brunetti asked as he approached.

'A tourist was mugged and robbed last night,' she answered. 'In Calle degli Avvocati.'

Brunetti was surprised: the street was home to a small hotel and a number of people of ample means. He closed his eyes and called up the memory: a narrow cul-de-sac leading off from Campo Sant'Angelo, it ended against the door of a building and was a place where the unwary could be trapped.

'What happened?'

She pulled a notebook from the pocket of her jacket and opened it. 'The victim's Irish; twenty-three years old. I was at the hospital this morning at eight to see him. He was in a bar last night, chatting up a girl. Bought her a few drinks, had a few himself, and then she suggested they go to her home together. When they got to the end of the *calle,* two men jumped him from behind. He doesn't remember any more than that.'

'What time was this?'

She looked at the notebook. 'About one-thirty. The call came at 1.37.'

'Who called?'

'A man who lives in the *calle:* the noise woke his dog up, and the dog's barking woke him up. When he saw a man lying in the *calle,* he called the Carabinieri. But by the time they got there, he was gone; the Carabinieri found him in the *campo,* propped up against a building. They called an ambulance that took him to the hospital.'

Common as this might be in any other city, the attack astonished Brunetti. This sort of crime did not happen here. Had seldom happened here: he corrected himself.

'You talked to him?' At her nod, Brunetti added, 'What did he say?'

'That he was too drunk to defend himself, especially against two of them.'

'Was he badly hurt?'

'His head needed a couple of stitches, and he's bruised, but nothing's broken.' After a moment, she added, 'It could have been much worse, I suppose.'

'The girl?'

'No sign of her. He didn't remember anything about her except that she spoke a little English and seemed to know the way they were going. He doesn't know what happened to her.'

'So she could have led him there,' Brunetti suggested.

'Or she could have reacted with good sense and run like hell when the punching

176

started,' Griffoni shot back.

'Of course,' Brunetti temporized. 'Did you get a description?' he asked.

'He was still fuddled when I talked to him,' Griffoni said. 'I don't know if it was the drink or the shock or maybe what they gave him when they put the stitches in his head. He wouldn't know them if he saw them, although he'd remember the girl.'

'You think it's worth pursuing?' he asked her.

She waved the notebook in a vague circle and said, 'I doubt it. There's no video camera near there. He doesn't remember what bar he was in or how they got to where it happened: everything looked the same to him. He thought they went over three or four bridges.'

'So it could have been anywhere,' Brunetti observed.

'Exactly.' They began to climb the steps. At the second landing, she stopped and asked, 'May I say something that will sound strange?'

'Of course.'

'Where I last worked, this sort of thing happened ten times a night, twenty. Every night; more on the weekends. We kept up a steady stream in and out of the hospitals.'

'Naples,' he stated. He knew it was her

home as well as her last posting.

'*Casa mia,*' she said with a laugh.

'And so?' Brunetti asked.

'One mugging — and it's only the third since I've been here — and I'm shocked by it. When I realize that, I begin to suspect I've been reassigned to a different planet.' She shook her head in wonder.

Brunetti turned to the last flight of steps that would take him up to his office but stopped and turned back to her. 'We're spoiled, aren't we?' he asked.

She pulled her lips together, the way a student would when confronted with a difficult question from a teacher, perhaps a trick question. Brunetti watched her formulate her answer. 'Perhaps it would be better to say that you're lucky,' she finally said.

'What are you going to do about it?' he asked, gesturing towards the notebook that was still in her hand.

She tilted her head and raised one shoulder in a resigned gesture. 'Unless the girl suddenly shows up and gives us a description of the two men, there's nothing we can do.'

'Other than sit and wait for them to come in and confess?' Brunetti suggested.

'I hadn't thought of that,' she agreed drily.

'Then if there's nothing for you to do,

come up to my office and let me tell you about another case where it seems there is little to be done.'

It took Brunetti some time to tell her about Contessa Lando-Continui and her grand-daughter, as Griffoni frequently interrupted to ask for explanations and write the answers in her notebook.

When he was finished, though the events made no more sense to him than they had before he tried to explain them, Brunetti was aware of how strong were the opinions he had formed of people he had never met. He felt nothing but pity for Manuela, whom he continued to think of as a girl, although she was at least thirty. He disliked her mother, whom he defined in Paola's terms as someone who had 'thrown her life away'. Unfortunately, she might somehow have created the circumstances in which her daughter's could be thrown away, as well. The father was little more than a shadow with a double name. An emotional Schettino, he had stayed on board his own *Costa Concordia* until the marital seas got rough and then jumped ship and found a new crew with whom to sail away from the wreck. Brunetti realized he also pitied Contessa Lando-Continui for her aching need

179

to know what had happened to her grand-daughter before she ceased knowing anything at all.

'You really convinced Patta to ask a magistrate to open a case?' Griffoni asked with open admiration.

'I told you what he's getting in return,' Brunetti answered.

'You make it sound so easy,' she said.

Brunetti laughed. 'I've known him so long, I've begun to feel something close to affection for him,' he confessed. Seeing her surprise, he added, 'Though only at times.'

Griffoni closed her notebook and sat back in her chair. 'If you will allow me to say this, I can never trust a Sicilian.'

Brunetti's first response was amusement, thinking she was joking. But when he realized she was not, he managed to disguise his startled reaction by raising his hand to his mouth and then moving his fingers to rub against his jaw in a manner he sought to make seem contemplative. Is this, he wondered, what it sounds like when I say how little I can trust Neapolitans? Why are other people's prejudices so strange, while our own are so thought-out and reasonable?

To get away from this subject as quickly as possible, Brunetti asked, 'Do you have time to help with this?'

'Yes, of course,' she said. 'Otherwise, I might be tempted to take another look at the baggage handlers.'

'Claudia, my dear,' he said in his most patient and philosophical voice, 'you and I will become grandparents many times over and the baggage handlers will still be opening suitcases and helping themselves to whatever it is they please, and the videos of their doing so will by then fill a warehouse. But it's our grandchildren who will be handling the investigation, not us, and the investigation will continue into the fourth generation.'

Griffoni steered away from the topic, saying as quickly as she could, 'What is it you'd like me to do?'

By way of an answer, Brunetti asked, 'Do you know anything about horses?'

'Who told you?' she asked, raising her eyebrows.

'Told me what?'

'About the horses,' she answered.

Raising his hands in feigned surrender, Brunetti said, 'No one told me anything about horses, or about you and horses. It was a simple question.' She remained silent, and so he asked, 'Why did it surprise you?'

'I haven't mentioned it to anyone here.'

He shook his head, more confused with

181

every remark.

'I ride,' Griffoni said. 'Dressage.'

'Is that the one where the horses sort of dance?' Brunetti asked, as ignorant of horse riding as he was of pigeon racing. 'I see it on television sometimes. The riders wear tall hats, don't they?'

'Yes.'

'Do you ride here?'

'No,' she said, her disappointment audible.

'Why not?'

'Guido,' she said, voice tight, 'could you tell me what you want to know and let this other stuff go?'

'Of course,' he said apologetically, seeing how troubled this conversation — he realized it was really more like an inquisition — had made her.

'Her granddaughter had a horse and kept it near Treviso. I want to talk to them, and I'd like to take someone with me who knows about riding.' Then, as if he thought she might not follow his explanation, he added, 'That's why I asked you.'

'You just told me all this happened fifteen years ago,' Griffoni said. 'And you think the same people will still be there?'

'Perhaps. Perhaps not. Whoever's there, I want to understand whatever answers I get.'

'You make it sound like they're going to

make you take a test ride on a horse and not answer your questions unless you do.'

'It's not the questions I'm concerned with,' Brunetti said. 'It's the answers. If they talk about her and riding or her and horses, I need to understand what it is they're telling me.'

She appeared utterly confused. 'It sounds as if you think they're foreigners.'

Brunetti smiled at this and said, 'No, I'm the foreigner. I don't know enough about what goes on between the rider and the horse, especially if it's a young girl.' When she said nothing, Brunetti was forced to add, sounding defensive, 'Please don't tell me I'm crazy. Or that it's all pop psychology.'

Before he could continue, she interrupted. 'If anything was troubling her, the horse would have known about it, that's for sure.' Then, grinning, she added, 'Unfortunately, they're hard to interview.'

The idea made Brunetti smile. 'What I'm hoping,' he said, 'is that someone there will remember her. At the time, it was reported as an accident, so I'm sure no one bothered to question these people.'

'Have you seen the report?'

'Signorina Elettra should have found it by now.'

'Shall we go and find out?' Griffoni asked and got to her feet.

Signorina Elettra appeared to have given herself a promotion, for today she wore a double-breasted blue jacket with epaulettes and gold braid at the cuffs. Griffoni's glance was a mixture of envy and appreciation, which she did nothing to disguise.

Brunetti stepped forward since he had made the request. 'Did you find the report of her accident?' he asked.

'Are you sure of the date, Commissario?' Signorina Elettra asked, but she said it as a statement and not a question.

Signorina Elettra had found the newspaper accounts of the incident, as had he, so there was no doubt as to the date. She knew this and he knew this, so her remark was a coded announcement that . . . Brunetti's mind flashed to but immediately excluded: 'she had failed to find it but was still searching', 'it did not appear in the files', and settled on 'she suspected it had been lost'.

'Those files were all computerized, weren't they?' Brunetti asked.

'At the time, yes.' Signorina Elettra answered. 'Everything from the paper reports was transcribed and entered into the system.'

'And the paper copy?' Griffoni, who had moved over to prop herself against Brunetti's place at the windowsill, asked.

'Destroyed, of course,' Signorina Elettra said and, as though she had been waiting for them to catch up with her, relaxed back in her chair.

Both heads swivelled towards her at the same moment, both faces registering comprehension. Brunetti left it to the other commissario to state the obvious. 'So if the computer doesn't have the report, then it's gone.' Never had the simple word sounded so final to Brunetti.

Signorina Elettra nodded but went on to say, 'Before you start suspecting conspiracy, you should know that about a third of the reports that were put into the system are missing, at least for that year. There was a bug in the program, and before they found it, they continued to enter material and destroy the originals.'

'How long did it take to discover what was happening?' Griffoni asked.

'They'd entered almost everything before they noticed.'

Brunetti and Griffoni exchanged a glance. In her shrug, he read her irritation with

185

incompetence and error. She asked, 'What about the hospital? If they took her there, then a medical report must exist.'

Ah, Brunetti thought, is this how southerners imagine us to be? Creatures of order, routine, method? The last time he had been to the hospital, it was to visit his sister-in-law the night before she was to be operated on for varicose veins. He'd walked in on his brother taping a plastic folder to her leg; inside the clear plastic was a sheet of paper on which could be read, 'Operate on THIS leg.' He had chosen not to comment.

'Let me see what I can find out,' Brunetti said and picked up Signorina Elettra's phone.

14

Because he was Venetian and had the rank of commissario, Brunetti was quickly put through to the Records Office. He explained his request to a man with a voice that sounded machine-generated, who proceeded to explain the process for requesting a copy of a patient report. So long as a magistrate submitted a formal request, the hospital would provide a copy of the services administered on a given day to the person named in the request.

Before he could pass this information to the others so that they could engage in universal rejoicing, the man added that those files, from fifteen years ago, existed only in paper form and would have to be searched for and found by someone familiar with the filing system.

'Have you any idea of how long this might take?' Brunetti asked.

In the long pause, he heard the real

answer. The man, however, gave the official one: 'It shouldn't take more than a few days.' Well, thought Brunetti, it shouldn't take more than thirty years to build the dykes meant to protect the city against *acqua alta,* either. But he said, 'If I were to have my friend, Dottor Rizzardi, call you and ask how long it will take, what answer would you give him?' He put as much amiability as he could muster into his voice.

'Is he a good friend?' the man asked.

'For more than thirty years.' It was an exaggeration, but it was made in a worthy cause.

'I'd tell him not to bother waiting,' the man answered in a voice that was now recognizably human. Brunetti liked the fact that he made no attempt to excuse or justify what he said. He thanked him, and hung up.

He looked at the two women and shook his head. 'Hopeless,' he managed to say.

Griffoni, who was now sitting on the windowsill, having pushed herself up on to it while Brunetti was on the phone, jumped down and started towards the door. 'I'll be in my office. I have to write the report on the mugging,' she said and left. Brunetti, telling Signorina Elettra he had calls to make, went upstairs to his office.

Signorina Elettra had found the name of the riding school near Preganziol, not far from Treviso. Using the internet as though he were an adept, he found the phone number, and, horses on his mind, typed in 'dressage' and read a general description of the sport, though he found it difficult to think of it as such. The grace and elegance of the horses and their riders reminded him of ballet. But art belonged to humans, didn't it, not to animals?

He read quickly, growing more and more interested as he learned more. There were the top hats, white saddle blankets, boots, jackets, braided manes and flash nosebands: endless paraphernalia for man and beast. He studied a chart of the various tests imposed upon horse and rider, saw how they could move at an angle while appearing to move straight forward, looked at photos and prints of *capriole* and *levade*. When he read that one of his favourite writers, Xenophon, had written about the systematic training of the horse, he knew he had been right to find it interesting.

He went back to Google and added 'Claudia Griffoni' to 'dressage', curious to see what he would find. A silver medal, as it turned out. Griffoni had won it for the Italian Olympic Team eighteen years before. In all of the time they had worked together, she had never mentioned much about her past, had definitely never spoken about horses, yet here she was, a silver medallist. His first thought was how important it was that this be kept from Patta, who was sure to tell Scarpa about it, a possibility that rendered Brunetti nervous.

Like many men on the force, Scarpa didn't like women, although in his case it would be closer to the truth to say he disliked them. He went out of his way to show his disrespect for Signorina Elettra; she countered by ignoring him unless he addressed her directly, when the sweetness of some of the responses Brunetti had heard her give the Lieutenant had caused his insulin level to rise.

The Lieutenant especially didn't like women with authority. He made a point of being slow to acknowledge any orders he received from Griffoni, but eventually he had no choice but to obey them, and her. Signorina Elettra, on the other hand, was, in the end, only a secretary, and he was a Lieutenant of police, and so it set his universe on end to have to do what she told him to do. Even now, he refused to believe that his patron, Vice-Questore Giuseppe Patta, was completely in thrall to her powers and abilities and would, if asked to choose, happily chop up his Lieutenant for bait, should that be necessary to maintain his rapport with his secretary.

Better that a man with opinions such as these floating around in his head not learn that Commissario Griffoni not only knew how to ride a horse, but rode it in something as frivolous as dressage and, worse, had won an Olympic medal doing so. Brunetti feared that learning this might well unhinge the Lieutenant.

Brunetti dialled the number of the school and introduced himself, explaining that he was calling about someone who had kept a horse there fifteen years before and would like to speak to anyone who might have worked there at that time.

The woman who answered the phone said, 'It's Signora Enrichetta you need to talk to.'

'And she is?' Brunetti asked.

'The owner. Now, that is. She took over when her husband died. She's the only person who might know.'

'Is she there?'

'She might be out in the ring. Could you call back in ten minutes?' she asked.

'I'll wait, if you don't mind,' Brunetti said, life having given him long experience of those ten minutes, after which too often no one was there to answer the phone when he called again.

'All right,' she said and set the phone down. Brunetti put his own phone face up on the desk and grabbed a stack of papers. Most of them concerned new regulations from the Ministry. One specified how officers were to secure their weapons at home: the gun in one locked box and the ammunition in another, the gun to be left unloaded at all times when it was in the house.

He had been reading similar regulations, it seemed, for decades. Yet often he read newspaper accounts of the children of officers who managed to get their hands on their parents' guns and shoot some other member of the family, or themselves. Nothing more terrible, nothing more true.

The next contained new regulations for parking a service car when the officer driving it was not in service. Curious, Brunetti leafed through it, not to read the text but to see how many pages it was. Four. He set it aside.

He heard a voice speaking from the receiver on his desk. *'Sì?'* he answered.

'Are you the policeman?' a woman asked.

'Yes. Are you Signora Enrichetta?'

'Yes. My helper wasn't too clear about the message. Could you tell me who you are and what it is you'd like?'

'My name is Brunetti: I'm a commissario in Venice. I'm calling to get information about a girl who kept a horse at your stable about fifteen years ago.'

'And you expect me to remember?' she asked, but with amused surprise and not with the certainty that she would not remember.

'I hope so,' Brunetti said in his friendliest manner. 'The girl's name is Manuela Lando-Continui. Though she's a woman now.'

'Ah,' she said, and then, 'Manuela. Poor thing. I know about her. My husband liked her a great deal.'

'Would it be possible for me to come out and talk to you?' Brunetti asked.

'Yes, of course,' she answered. 'But not until Monday. I'm sorry. We have a competition in Desenzano this weekend. It's lucky you got me because we're leaving in an hour: we're taking two horses there.'

'Then I'd like to come out on Monday,' Brunetti said.

'Good. We should be back on Sunday evening, so any time in the afternoon would be all right.' Brunetti was just about to continue when the woman asked, 'How is she?'

'I haven't spoken to her yet, but her grandmother says she's peaceful.' It was the best Brunetti could think of to say.

'Well, at least that's something,' the woman said, sounding not fully convinced. 'I'll see you Monday afternoon, then.' She replaced the phone.

Remembering that Pietro Cavanis had failed to return his call, Brunetti took out his *telefonino* and found the number again.

The voice that answered on the seventh ring, a man's, sounded fuzzy with sleep.

'Signor Cavanis?' Brunetti asked.

'I think so,' the man answered. 'Tell me what you want, and that will give me time to remember who I am.'

'I'd like to speak to you about Manuela Lando-Continui.'

'You police?' the man asked. 'You sound it.'

'Yes, I'm Commissario Guido Brunetti. I've been asked to look into the incident near Campo San Boldo.'

'Yes, the incident,' Cavanis said, still sounding dull with sleep. 'What do you want to know?'

'I'd like to talk to you about what happened.'

'And if I say I don't remember?' Before Brunetti could answer, the man said, 'Wait

194

a minute.' Brunetti heard the phone being set down, a rustle of paper, the scratching sound of a match and then a long sigh of satisfaction. There was a fumbling as the phone was picked up. 'You were saying?' the man asked.

'I'd like to speak to you about what happened.'

'Isn't fifteen years a long time to take to get around to this?' the man asked with counterfeit amiability, as if it were a serious question and not a reproach. Brunetti heard a clinking sound, followed by a rushing noise it took him a moment to identify. Ah, the day's first drink. He wasn't sure if he'd heard the swallowing noise or only imagined it.

'Yes, it is a long time, but this is a new investigation. Would it be possible to talk to you?' Brunetti asked, deciding to ignore the other man's provocation.

'Of course. But it will be to no purpose. I told you: I don't remember anything, and the farther I get from it in time, the less I remember.' He spoke with great insistence, Brunetti thought.

'I'd still like to talk to you,' Brunetti said, using his friendliest voice.

'I'm not available this weekend. How about Monday?'

'I've got a meeting in the afternoon,' Brunetti said.

'Tuesday?' Cavanis suggested with the ease of a person who did not have to go to work and the rigour of one who did not think of the morning as a suitable time for a meeting.

'Fine,' Brunetti said. 'Tell me where to meet you.'

Cavanis named a bar Brunetti was unfamiliar with, explaining that it was on Rio Marin, a few doors down from the gas office, heading away from the station. He suggested the late afternoon, but Brunetti said it would be more convenient to meet around noon; perhaps he could invite Signor Cavanis to join him for lunch? That seemed to convince the other man, who said he'd be there at twelve, and Brunetti, having heard a glass click against the phone a number of times, repeated that it was on Tuesday that they would meet.

'If I'm not there, ask the owner of the bar to give you the keys and come across the canal — I'm just opposite the bar — and wake me up, all right? Green door. Second floor. Just come in and give me a few shakes.' Brunetti, thinking that the invitation to lunch had struck some vein of humour, perhaps even amiability, in Cavanis, said he would. Cavanis replaced the phone without speaking, and that was that.

Because it was Friday afternoon and because he was bored and restless and felt himself growing thick with the anticipation of winter, Brunetti called Lolo and asked if he still had his *sàndolo* and if it was still in the water. When his friend said he did and it was, Brunetti suggested that they run away from home the next day and go out into the *laguna* and spend the day rowing.

'And if we like that, then Sunday, too,' Lolo said without hesitation.

Late on Saturday afternoon, Brunetti returned home to show Paola the four bandages on his hands and the blister on his left heel where his tennis shoe had rubbed repeatedly against the skin as he concentrated on relearning the shift and balance, thrust and dig that the single oar forced upon each of them. After dinner, he collapsed in front of the television and slept intermittently during the local news: fire in an apartment in Santa Croce, wildcat strike of the ticket sellers for the vaporetti, and a brief interview on the local channel with Sandro Vittori-Ricciardi, the man he'd seen at the Contessa Lando-Continui's dinner, talking about his new project. Brunetti, however, was so exhausted by the late-autumn sun, cold wind off the water, and the hours spent rowing that the only thing he registered from these three segments was that the man had shaved off his beard and looked years younger as a result.

When Paola switched to a rerun of the first series of *Downton Abbey,* Brunetti pushed himself to his feet and made it as far as their bed before collapsing in a heap of exhausted muscle. He barely moved until he got up at eight to creak off and meet Lolo and climb back into the *sàndolo.*

There had been a freak *acqua alta* the night before, but the only remaining sign was the damp pavement next to the *canale* where Lolo tied up his boat. They spoke little as they headed out into the *laguna,* aware that words were an intrusion. Occasionally Brunetti called a warning about a log floating in the water, and they adjusted course. Brunetti saw two long-beaked birds sunning themselves, wings extended, on a tuft of grassy mud. He no longer remembered their name. 'Isn't it time they headed south?' he called to Lolo, rowing at the back of the boat. They slipped past the birds, which ignored them.

'They winter here now,' Lolo said.

Stroke, cutting deep, then tilt and lift the

oar from the water and slide it to the front, then dig it in again. Time after time, silently, with very little conscious effort; the endless flat expanse all around them, the sky gun-metal grey, the wind much too cold to justify being so playful with their sweating bodies.

At two, they decided to rest for a while and rowed to a stop at the side of the small canal that cut through a series of grass-covered semi-islands. From where he stood at the front, Brunetti turned in a half-circle to one side, then to the other. Spread out around them was the emptiness of the *laguna:* grass, water, tufts of reeds; no sound save their breathing, still heavy, and the far-off cawing of a bird. The day had lightened, but still the sun hid itself from them, though it managed to warm them now, out of the wind.

'Guido,' Lolo called from behind him. When he turned, Lolo tossed him a paper-wrapped sandwich. Brunetti was suddenly so hungry that he didn't bother to look to see what was in the sandwich. He ate it in six bites, still standing, looked back at Lolo and said, 'I've never eaten anything so good in my life. And I have no idea what it was.'

15

Monday morning brought paralysis, or something very near to it. Brunetti had gone to bed a happy man, one who had proved his stamina by six hours of rowing, come home bursting with pride in his prowess, eaten two plates of *polpette* with potatoes and *porcini,* four pieces of *merluzzo* with spinach, and then found room for a large slice of *torta della provvidenza* before retreating to his bed with the *Argonautica* and falling asleep before he'd finished two pages.

He woke a different person, a crippled old man who could barely push himself to the edge of his bed and whose body, as he walked towards the shower, made strong protests from a different place with every step. He was unable to step out of his pyjama bottoms, so he let them fall to the floor and left them there, gingerly removed the top, and reached into the shower to turn on the hot water. It finally arrived from five floors below, and he stepped into its healing warmth. He turned the nozzle to the right and moved to stand with his forehead pressed against the tiles, letting the water pound, splash, course, and flow across and down his back.

After five minutes, he felt some of the knots in his spine loosen, as the burning in the muscles of his shoulders was replaced by the burning of the water and the steam that was slowly enveloping the entire bathroom. A few minutes more and he was able to contemplate the possibility that he would be able to reach his office that morning, though it would be wonderful to be able to phone Sanitrans and have himself picked up by two strong young men, propped in a chair, and carried down four flights of steps by them and not by these stumps that had once been his legs.

As if one of those young men had been summoned, someone called his first name from the door of the bathroom, but it was a high voice and sounded agitated. He hadn't had enough of standing there, but he decided he was ready to make the effort of getting dressed and so turned off the water and stood in the growing silence.

'Guido?' a familiar voice said. 'Are you all right?'

Through the dripping glass, he saw what he thought was Paola, standing in the doorway. 'Of course I'm all right,' he answered, wondering if he would have to put up with a comment about his use of hot water.

'Oh, good,' she said and was gone.

He stepped slowly out of the shower and took a towel, dried most of himself and left his lower legs and feet to take care of themselves. Wearing the towel, he went down to their room, where Paola was in bed, reading.

'You came all that way to check?' he asked.

She peered over her glasses at him. 'It was a long time. I was concerned.' That said, she returned to her book.

'Concerned about what?'

Over the glasses again. 'That you might have fallen.'

'Ah,' he said and reached for the drawer in which his underwear was kept. His back and right shoulder screamed at him, but he ignored them and, however slowly, began dressing, then pulled out a pair of socks and went over and sat on the bed. The tops of his feet were still wet, but he ignored that and pulled on the socks.

Trousers — not easy, that — a shirt — child's play — the heavy shoes Griffoni had advised him to wear — difficult — a tie, and his jacket. When he was dressed, he went over to the bed, bent and kissed the top of Paola's head, and said, 'I'll go somewhere for lunch. I have to go out to the mainland to talk to people.'

Paola mumbled something. He moved closer, the better to see the title at the top of the page of her book. He read the last words, 'the Dove', and realized there was no sense in trying to talk to her. The stairs were painful at first but became easier the more of them he descended, until he got to the ground floor and felt in control of his limbs. As he opened the door and stepped out into the sunny day, it occurred to him that she had left Henry James to go and check on him in the bathroom. He was immeasurably cheered by the thought.

By the afternoon, he had learned how to use his body and could walk, bend to pick up objects — as long as they were on desks and not on the ground — and both sit down and get to his feet with reasonable ease. None of these actions was painless, but all were bearable. At two, having had only sandwiches for lunch so as to save time, Brunetti and Griffoni got into a squad car at Piazzale Roma, and the driver set off to the highway that would take them to Pre-ganziol, on the outskirts of which was to be found the riding school.

Griffoni wore a short woollen jacket, jeans, and a pair of boots, attire that, at first, made Brunetti suspect she had dressed for what the English called 'mucking out', which he thought was pretty much what Hercules had done with the Augean Stables. But a closer look suggested that the jeans would hardly lend themselves to work, and the tan boots, however worn they might be, had the thin double belt and metal toggle at the top that Paola had once pointed out to him on a similar pair in a shop.

Her blonde hair was pulled back in a ponytail tied with a black ribbon: he won-dered whether she perhaps had a black rid-ing helmet in her bag.

It was always a strange experience for Brunetti to travel by car. He'd become ac-customed to them during the periods he'd been assigned to work in different cities on the mainland, but he hadn't grown up with them, and so cars were ever alien to him and seemed unnecessarily fast and danger-ous.

Griffoni, perhaps sensing his nervousness, did most of the talking, finally drawing on her former career as a rider. 'It's true what people say, about a horse being able to read our feelings, although I think most animals manage to do that.' She looked out of the window as she spoke, at the far-off fields, barren and dry, and, between them and the road, the endless low clusters of shops, restaurants, and factories that lined the road on both sides.

'I suppose all of this was once farmland,' she said by way of general observation.

The driver, who might have been ten years older than she, answered from his seat in front of her, 'It was, Commissario. I grew up around here: my parents were farmers.'

They passed an enormous agglomeration of buildings on the right: supermarket, garage, one shipping warehouse then another, a furniture store, enormous trucks backed up to the metal doors at the back of a single-storey building.

'Why do we need so much stuff?' Brunetti asked, turning to look at the buildings on the other side, equal in kind, variety, and size.

No one answered him. Perhaps because so many of us had second houses, he reflected, we had more space to fill with stuff, or perhaps people now had what was called 'disposable income', while his parents had barely had an income.

'It's only another couple of kilometres,' the driver said.

'You know the place?'

The driver laughed at the thought. 'I know about it, but I've never been there.' He concentrated on passing another car and then said, 'The only horse I ever touched was my father's, and all that horse did was pull a wagon and eat a lot of grass.'

'And you saw that?' Brunetti asked, unable to stifle his reaction. 'A wagon?'

'Well, only for us kids. My parents never really used it, but every once in a while they'd hitch him up to it and take us all for a ride. We were mad for it. I was just a little kid, but I still remember.'

'What happened to the horse?' Griffoni asked.

'Oh, he died.'

'What did your parents do?' Brunetti asked, curious to know how a dead horse could have been disposed of.

The driver waited a long time before he asked, 'Can I tell the truth?'

'Of course,' they both answered.

'My father dug a hole in the field with his backhoe, and then he picked him up with the front end of it and lowered him into the grave, and we kids all threw flowers on him, and then he covered him over and told us not to tell anyone what he'd done.' The driver had slowed down while he told them this, and first one car, then another, passed them without his seeming to notice.

No one spoke until a wooden fence appeared and ran beside them on the right. 'That's it,' the driver said, leaning forward to tap his finger on the screen of the GPS.

Not far ahead of them, they saw a gate set back about ten metres from the road. The driver pulled up to it and stopped. There was a hand-printed sign saying to close the gate after entering, so he got out, drove through, and then went back to close it. Brunetti noticed a speakerphone system in place on the left side of the gate, but the handset was cracked and hung from a wire.

When he was behind the wheel again, the driver started up the narrow road running between twin wooden-fenced paddocks on either side. 'Just like Texas,' he said.

Neither of them answered. They drove forward on an asphalt road that had seen better times. Leaves from the plane trees on both sides lay thick but failed to buffer them from the holes into which the car drove, bouncing them about on the seat. They followed a curve in the road and drew to a stop in front of a low stone building with arched windows and a tiled roof.

An old brown dog of indeterminate ancestry ambled around the corner of the building and approached the car. He ignored them and didn't bother to bark, moved to the driver's door and flopped down on the ground. The driver opened the door very slowly and climbed over the dog. He looked up at the driver, put his head down and appeared to go to sleep.

Brunetti and Griffoni got out and all three of them closed their doors very quietly. A woman with short wispy grey hair came out of the front door of the house, looking worried. 'Hector didn't frighten you, did he?' she asked with real concern. Her eyes were hazel and seemed lighter in contrast to her tan, the permanent sort common to people who spend most of their time outdoors. She smiled as she approached them. Small, well into her sixties by the look of her, she was wiry and quick-moving, and wore jeans, riding boots, and a thick man's sweater a few sizes too large for her.

'You must be the police,' she said, sounding delighted, as though the name cards on the dinner table said 'Police' and, now that they were there, dinner could finally begin. She smiled again, smoothing out for a moment the barcode wrinkles above her lips.

'Yes,' Brunetti said, taking her extended

hand. 'I'm Commissario Brunetti.' Her grip burst two of the blisters on his right palm and, had he been of weaker stuff, would have brought him to his knees.

As it was, he sucked in some air and turned to his colleague, saying, 'And this is Commissario Griffoni.' The woman released his hand and took Griffoni's, saying, 'I'm Enrichetta degli Specchi. Thank you for coming.'

Griffoni showed delight at her greeting and asked, 'Are you Giovanni's cousin?'

The woman stepped back and took another look at Griffoni. 'Yes, I am. Do you know him?'

Griffoni's face radiated her own pleasure. 'We rode together, years ago,' she said, then, after she'd spent a few seconds counting them, added, 'almost twenty.' And immediately, 'He often spoke of you.'

'Tell me your name again, please,' the woman asked, tilting her head and staring at Griffoni with great interest.

'Griffoni. Claudia.'

The woman's face changed, her smile tossing away years and giving a flash of what a beauty she must have been before the sun had its way with her. 'Claudia,' she said, her voice filled with delight: Marcellina discovering her lost child. Unable to restrain her emotion, she put her arms around Claudia's shoulders, though she had to stand on her toes to do it, and said, 'Oh, thank you, thank you. You saved Giovanni's life.' Brunetti noted that she had unconsciously begun to address Claudia in the familiar 'tu'.

As the woman removed her arms, Griffoni said, 'I think that's a bit of an exaggeration.'

'But if you hadn't spoken to him, he wouldn't have ridden, and then he would have died,' the woman insisted, stressing the final verb.

'No, no, no,' Griffoni insisted. 'He just needed someone to tell him he was the best on the team.' Then, with the force of truth, she added, 'And he was.'

'But still . . .' the woman said, not convinced. She turned to Brunetti and explained, 'My cousin has always suffered terrible panic attacks before competitions.' Brunetti nodded, as if familiar with the emotional vagaries of athletes. 'So you can imagine what the Olympics did to him. Jumping. He froze. Friends who were there told me he could barely walk.' She glanced at Griffoni for confirmation. Griffoni nodded.

'He couldn't ride,' the older woman went on, speaking to Brunetti. 'The horse was saddled. But Giovanni was paralysed. And then she,' she said and gave a dramatic pause to point to Griffoni, 'took him aside and talked to him, and then he went back and got on his horse as if nothing in the world was bothering him.'

Griffoni bent down and worked at removing a small stone embedded in the heel of her left boot.

'Gold! He won the gold medal,' the woman said, clapping her hands in delight. 'And it was all due to you.' She grabbed Griffoni's right arm with both hands and gave her a little shake of thanks, then turned to Brunetti and said, 'It's true. He wouldn't have done it if she hadn't talked to him.'

'How is he?' Griffoni asked, completely ignoring everything the woman had said.

'Fine. Fine. Three kids. Growing olives in Tuscany: God knows why, when . . .' She let this go and gave herself a little shake. 'But you're here about that girl, aren't you?'

'Manuela Lando-Continui,' Brunetti said. 'Did you know her well?'

'No. It was my late husband who ran the place then. I came here only twelve years ago, when we married.'

'So your husband would have known her?' Brunetti asked.

'Yes, he did. He told me what happened to her.' She held up her hands in a gesture

211

that signified helplessness in the face of life.

'Did he tell you anything else?'

'No, only that she had the gift with horses.' She looked at Griffoni, who nodded in understanding.

Griffoni asked, 'Is there anyone working here who might have been here then?'

'Let me think,' the woman said, and Brunetti watched as she started counting. She got to seven, extending a finger for each, then closed them all back into her palm until everyone had been eliminated.

She looked at Brunetti. 'No. They're all gone.' Her eyes drifted off to a field behind the house, where he saw a few horses grazing on the remaining grass. 'Most of the horses are gone, too, I'm afraid.' It sounded to Brunetti as though that were the part she regretted.

'Are you still in contact with any of them?'

She didn't bother to use her fingers to count the possibilities. 'No, I'm not.' Then, with mixed explanation and apology she added, 'People don't stay a long time at this sort of job.'

Brunetti saw that the driver was standing at the wooden fence, rubbing the head of one of the horses. As he watched, the driver bent down and ripped up a few tufts of grass on his side of the fence and held them out to the horse, who took them from his hand and munched on them. When she'd eaten them, the horse bumped her head against the man's hand, and he obeyed by bending down for more grass.

'They're very smart,' Griffoni said and walked towards the railing. Brunetti followed her, and the woman followed Brunetti. When the humans were all standing in a line, the horses in the field started to drift in their direction, and within five minutes the four humans were all busy pulling up grass to feed them.

Griffoni stood on the bottom rung of the fence and leaned over towards the horses, two of whom responded and nuzzled at her hands and then her neck and then her face. She embraced them, arms spread, a hand on each of their necks, and then began slowly to scratch at the place just under their ears. The three of them seemed to enter into a trance, and only when a third horse approached and nipped at the flank of one of the others did they jerk away from Griffoni and, losing interest, turn and trot away.

Griffoni turned to Brunetti and smiled, and he saw a new person hiding behind her face.

From behind them, Signora degli Specchi

said, 'Come in and at least have something to drink.' Griffoni started towards the building, and Brunetti followed. The driver bent down to tear up more grass.

She led them through the house to the back, passing through rooms where the furniture all seemed to have served as resting places for Hector and whatever dogs had preceded him. Saddles occupied two chairs in the kitchen, where a large fire burned to challenge the cold that seeped up from the stone floor. It blazed and succeeded in making it warmer than outside, but not by much.

They both said coffee would be fine, and she surprised them by going to a small Gaggia machine. With the ease of familiarity, she made three coffees quickly and brought them back to the table, where she'd told them to take seats.

As they stirred sugar into their coffee, Brunetti asked, 'If you knew nothing about Manuela, why did you tell us to come out here?'

Keeping her eyes on her hands as she stirred her coffee, the owner said, 'I had the idea that you were going to bring her.'

'Her?' Brunetti asked.

'Manuela,' she said, still not looking at him.

'But what sense would that make if you never knew her, and no one who knew her is still working here?' Brunetti asked. Half-way through his sentence, he realized how irritated he sounded and so moderated his tone until, by the end of it, he was merely asking a simple question.

Clink and clink and clink, until she set the spoon down on the saucer. She took a sip, set the cup back and used the spoon to make a few more clinks. Finally, she tired of the attempt to delay and said, 'Her horse is still here.'

Brunetti set his own cup down, and Griffoni asked, 'How old is she?'

'She's twenty-one.'

'And you thought . . .' Griffoni started to ask but then ran out of ideas.

'I thought she'd remember her.'

The pronouns refused to make sense to Brunetti. 'That the horse would remember her?' he asked.

'No. My husband told me about what happened to her. In the water.'

Brunetti still didn't understand. He waited.

'I hoped she'd remember the horse.'

16

'My husband told me, before he died, that she'd suffered brain damage — people in the city told him — but he didn't know how bad it was. Because he was so fond of her, I thought that, hoped that . . . well, that she'd be well enough to remember her horse or recognize her, and it might . . . it might help her. Somehow.' As she spoke, she picked at a tiny flap of skin near one of her fingernails, reminding Brunetti of a much younger Chiara when she had to confess having done something stupid or wrong.

Entirely at a loss, he looked at Griffoni, who held up her palm to silence him. 'Did your husband say anything else about her?' she asked.

The silence expanded so much that Brunetti thought the woman was not going to answer. He leaned back in his chair and looked around the room. It was much cleaner than the other rooms, the counters uncluttered, plates and glasses neatly stored in open cabinets on either side of the sink. The stone floor was spotless. The walls were filled with group photographs of horses and humans. He was close enough to see that some of them showed people with the haircuts and clothing of decades before. He saw young people wearing glasses with thick, rectangular plastic frames, a style so old it was on its way back. Other photos showed fashions closer to those of today. The horses always looked the same.

The woman got to her feet and left the room without saying anything to them. Brunetti stood and walked over to the photos, some in colour and some older ones in black and white, wondering if Manuela was in any of them and forced to accept the fact that, even if she were, he might not recognize her. The likelihood would depend on his ability to carbon-date clothing and hairstyles. What had young people — for most of the people in the photos were young — worn fifteen years ago? How had their hair been cut? In the photo he'd seen, she'd worn jeans and had long hair: that description would fit most of the people in these photos.

He recognized, in a photo that must be recent, the young journalist who read the

8.30 news on local television. Usually he appeared wearing suit and tie, but here he was, looking not much younger, in sweat-shirt and jeans, with tousled hair and his arms around the shoulders of the boy and girl on either side of him. Brunetti looked more closely at the photos. He saw a very faded photo of a light-haired girl who looked a bit like Paola, but with a smaller nose. She stood beside a long-haired young man who was not much taller, as smiling and fresh-faced as she. He looked familiar, but Brunetti couldn't place him. Perhaps this one had grown up to become the weatherman.

He heard footsteps behind him; when he turned, the woman was back with papers in her hand. She went over to the table and laid them, only two of them, on the table: they were photos.

'This is Manuela,' she said. 'The only thing my husband ever said was that she was as good as she was beautiful and what happened to her was horrible.' After a long pause, she added, 'He cried about it once.' Then, pointing to the photos, she said, 'You can see why.'

Brunetti and Griffoni joined her beside the table and looked at the photos, one in black and white and one in colour. It was the same girl he'd seen in the photo in the newspaper, looking just as young — or old. But here she sat on the fence where they had stood a half-hour before, her face raised to the sun, eyes closed, apparently unaware of the camera.

In the second, she was mounted, high boots and helmet, tight jeans, sweater and scarf. She was as radiant and as beautiful as in the other, her face a collection of perfections.

The horse was a dark chestnut, quite as beautiful — at least to Brunetti's ignorant eye — as the girl. The hair on its left flank gleamed, the light creating shadows among the muscles and tendons of the leg. From under the saddle peeped the edge of a red saddle blanket. The girl looked serious, and the horse looked happy.

'Is that her horse?' Brunetti asked.

'She's beautiful,' Griffoni said. Brunetti somehow knew she was talking about the horse.

'Yes. My husband always liked her because she was so sweet-tempered, so when Manuela didn't come back and the family said they didn't want her any more, he kept her, and she became the beginners' horse.' Then, reflectively, she added, 'She was here when I came, and she's the only one left — horse or human — who was. Nobody much rides her now.' In answer to their evident curiosity, she went on. 'There's not a lot of work for me today. I board a couple of horses, but the days are gone when people could afford lessons for their children. Or to keep a horse.'

'But you still keep her?' Griffoni asked.

The woman smiled. 'She knew my husband.'

Griffoni nodded and said, 'Of course.' Then, 'Could I ride her?'

'Now?' the woman asked, surprised.

'No, some other time. If I came out.'

'Of course. She'd love the company, I'm sure.' Then, after a moment's reflection, she added, 'She's a bit slow, I'm afraid, but it's a joy to ride her. She's not what she was.'

'None of us is,' Griffoni said, then laughed out loud. She got to her feet. 'We have the number, so I'll call, all right?'

'Yes. Oh, she'll be so happy.'

'Me, too,' Griffoni said and turned away to go back to the car.

When they emerged into the sunlight they saw the driver standing on the first railing and scratching the space between the eyes of a dark brown horse.

'Let's go,' Brunetti called over to him.

The officer jumped down and came towards the car. Hector was still asleep and did not wake when the officer stepped over him. Brunetti and Griffoni gave their thanks to the woman and made their farewells. As they started to get into the car, Signora degli Specchi said, speaking to Griffoni, 'You'll really come back, won't you?'

'Is that her?' Griffoni asked, pointing to the horse the driver had been scratching. Brunetti looked over at the horse, who was looking back at them. She was thinner than in her photo, her coat less glossy: he supposed this made horses look older, but he wasn't sure.

'Yes. Petunia.' As if to prove it, she called over to the horse, 'Petunia, who's a pretty girl?'

The horse gave an answering whinny.

'I'll be back,' Griffoni said and got into the car.

The return journey to Venice was subdued, but there was an atmosphere of satisfaction and complicity that made speech unnecessary. As they started across the bridge leading to Piazzale Roma, the driver said, 'Petunia,' and laughed at the memory. Neither of the people in the back said anything; the car pulled up in front of the landing, where the driver had ordered a boat to pick them up.

Away from the freedom provided by a day in the country, back into routine, the driver came around to open Griffoni's door. As she got out, he raised a hand in what might have been a salute but might have been the friendly wave of one colleague to another.

She followed Brunetti down the steps and on to the police launch. When they were seated in the cabin, Brunetti said, 'Do we bother to look for the people who were working there fifteen years ago?'

Her answer was immediate. 'The fact that you didn't ask her for a list of names means you don't think it's worth it, I'd say,' but she said it with a smile, then asked, 'What's left for us to do?'

'Talk to the mother,' he said, already dialling the number the Contessa had given him.

'*Pronto,*' a woman's voice answered on the seventh ring, sounding anything but pronto.

'Signora Magello-Ronchi?'

'*Sì,*' she answered, as if she found this an interesting question and might like to discuss it further.

'This is Commissario Guido Brunetti,' he said. 'I realize this must come as a surprise to you, but I've been asked by the Public Magistrate to examine the circumstances of your daughter's accident in case something was overlooked in the original handling of the event.' Brunetti decided that was sufficiently confusing to sound convincing. 'And I wondered if you'd be kind enough to speak to me about it.'

He thought of the way, as a child, he'd dropped stones down the still-uncovered wells in the city and waited to hear the answering splash, often long delayed. Finally it came. 'Ah, yes, the accident.' A pause extended out from that last word, until she was back to ask, 'What did you say your name was?'

'Brunetti.'

'The Public Magistrate, you say?'

'Yes, Signora.'

'Then I suppose I should talk to you?'

'It would be a great kindness.'

She spent some time considering this before saying, 'Then I suppose I must.'

'Would it be convenient for us to come to see you now, by any chance?' he asked. 'My colleague, Commissario Claudia Griffoni, is with me.'

'A woman?' she asked.

'Yes.'

'In the police?'

'Yes.'

'How very interesting,' she said, then

asked, 'Where did you say you were?'

He looked out of the window of the launch and saw the familiar façade. 'At Ca' d'Oro.'

'Can you get to Campo Santa Maria Mater Domini from there?' she asked.

Entirely at a loss for words, Brunetti decided on a simple 'Yes.'

'Then why don't you come here? I never get to see anyone.'

'We can be there in about fifteen minutes,' Brunetti said, knowing they could be there sooner, but not wanting to frighten her by appearing too eager.

'Oh, fine. I'll expect you, then. It's just to the left of the church. Top floor.'

When the call was over, he turned to Griffoni and said, 'She asked me if I could get to Campo Santa Maria Mater Domini from here.'

'She's Venetian?'

'Yes.'

Brunetti told himself, but did not say aloud, that Manuela might not be the only one who was brain damaged.

The pilot of the launch slowed down when Brunetti explained that they had fifteen minutes to get there, allowing them a slow passage up the Grand Canal: taxis passed them, a boat loaded with washing machines left them in its wake, until finally the pilot made a U-turn and went back to Rio delle Due Torri and proceeded slowly towards the Campo. While they moved, Brunetti used Google Earth to locate the house: he recognized it to the left of the church. How did tourists find things, with only street addresses to guide them? He didn't like this new age, much preferred having someone tell him the address he was looking for was the house with the new shutters to the right of the greengrocer opposite the flower shop that had the cacti in the window. Any Venetian would understand that.

The *campo* threw windows at them, as it always did: a Byzantine and a Gothic *quadrifora* competed with one another, and straight ahead two *pentafore,* one on top of the other, battled it out for public admiration. The lower, Gothic one always won Brunetti's vote, even if two of the windows were bricked up.

Just beyond the house was the church: poor little church, Brunetti always thought, to have such a lovely façade wasted in such a narrow *calle.* No one could stand back far enough to see it all from the proper perspective, but past builders knew nothing of zoning laws, and so it could be seen only from close up.

He found 'BMR' on the top bell on the right and rang. After a full minute, he rang again, and this time the door snapped open.

The staircase was surprisingly grand for a house with such a modest exterior: low marble steps rubbed smooth by centuries of climbing and descending feet. The marble balustrade had been worn down by the hands that had sought its help. The walls were unplastered brick, completely free of adornment or decoration. What he was seeing was the ancient, barefaced Venice of working merchants who had no desire that their wealth be seen beyond their homes.

They continued to the top, where they saw an open door. Brunetti stopped in front of it and knocked a few times, calling out, 'Signora? Signora?'

A tall young woman emerged from a room on the left side of the corridor, turned and came towards them. She had shoulder-length dark hair, pulled back by pink barrettes on both sides. She wore a grey sweater, dark blue jeans, and red tennis shoes above which peeped pink socks.

Brunetti studied her face as she approached them and found the same perfections he'd seen in her photo, frozen into place as if carved on the face of a statue.

Manuela — for this must be Manuela — approached them, her entire bearing showing confusion, though Brunetti wasn't sure what made him think that.

'Are you the policemen?' she asked in a tentative voice. She managed to move her lips and tried to smile.

'Yes, we are,' Brunetti said in as pleasant a voice as he could muster.

'But you don't have uniforms. And she's not a man,' she said, pointing an agitated finger at Griffoni.

'But I do work for the police,' Griffoni said calmly. 'We're called policewomen, and we don't have to wear a uniform.' She produced a smile, warm and large enough for a person to plunge into.

Manuela nodded, but Brunetti wondered if her mental capacities had a category for policewomen.

She turned to Brunetti and pointed at him, but spoke to Griffoni. 'He isn't wearing a uniform, either.'

'He doesn't have to wear one,' Griffoni said smoothly. 'We're bosses, and bosses don't have to wear them.'

'But you can if you want?'

'Of course.' Then, with real interest, Griffoni asked, 'Do you think it would be better if we wore them?'

Manuela stopped to consider this. Brunetti watched her face as she tried to decide. First her lips tightened, and then her eyes. She brought her right hand to her forehead, the way a bad actor would, to show indecision. Then her face flushed, and her breathing quickened. A low humming noise came from her mouth.

Griffoni intervened when she heard this. 'Oh, who cares, anyway, Manuela, so long as we're here and can talk to your mother. She said you'd answer the door and take us to her. Do you think you can do that now?'

Manuela took a step towards Griffoni and latched her arm in hers. Her face cleared and her breathing returned to normal. 'Oh, yes. She's in the sitting room and told me to bring you there.' She smiled and then lost her smile when she said, 'But I forgot.'

'Oh, I forget everything, too,' Griffoni said. Then, to her new best friend, placing her hand on hers the better to anchor their arms together, she said, 'Let's go and see your mother.'

'Yes, please,' Manuela said.

Brunetti had watched all of this, marvelling at the woman's beauty. No makeup, hair pulled back and hanging straight, but she'd cause heads to turn on the street. As she walked away, arm in arm with Griffoni,

228

Brunetti noticed that her left foot did not rise as high as the right. She did not drag it, but it was evident that it did not make a matched pair with the other.

He followed them down a corridor that led towards the back of the house. Manuela stopped abruptly outside a door, as though she had walked into something solid. Then she turned to the left and said, 'In there,' leaving it to Griffoni to open the door. They walked in, still arm in arm, and Brunetti followed fast upon them.

A woman a bit taller than her daughter stood looking out of a window, her pose so studied and artificial that Brunetti had to stop himself from laughing at the sight of her. 'Signora Magello-Ronchi?' he asked formally, as if uncertain who this woman might be.

She turned slowly to face them but said nothing. Brunetti used her consciously dramatic pause to study her face. In it, he saw the eyes she had passed to her daughter: clear blue and almond-shaped. Human intervention had thinned Barbara's nose: either nature or her father's genes had thinned that of her daughter. Her hair was artfully streaked with blonde, and she was careful to stand straight, shoulders back, as if she had been told she'd be punished if her hair touched her shoulders.

Her mouth, a colour somewhere between strong pink and delicate red, was poised in a half-smile as she formulated the proper greeting. *'Buon giorno,'* she said, having found it.

She looked at Brunetti and graced him with a smile, then nodded in Griffoni's direction, leaving it to her to decipher if the nod were meant for her or for her daughter. Griffoni nodded in return, and Manuela said, '*Mamma*, these are the policemen, but they don't have to wear uniforms to be policemen and they don't have to be men, either.' She turned to Griffoni for confirmation, and Griffoni smiled, patting Manuela's arm as she did so, as if to praise her for having learned so much, so fast.

Manuela laughed, a bright tinkle that filled the room with delight and caused Brunetti's hands to curl into tight fists. He looked at his shoes until the moment passed and then returned his eyes to the mother.

'That's very interesting, Manuela,' she said with enough interest to make it sound as though she believed it herself. 'But aren't you helping Alina in the kitchen?' Before Manuela could answer, her mother went on. 'Why don't you go and ask her to make coffee for our guests?'

Then, to Brunetti, 'You'd both like some coffee, wouldn't you?'

'That would be very nice,' he said.

Griffoni slipped her arm from Manuela's and echoed, 'Oh, yes, I'd love a coffee.' She looked at her watch and added, 'I always have one about this time of day.' Then, after a silent exchange with Brunetti, she said, 'Manuela, why don't we both go and help Alina?' When Manuela was slow to answer, Griffoni said, 'You'll have to show me where the cups and saucers are, you know. You'll have to help me.'

Manuela's face glowed with delight. She took Griffoni's arm and gave it a gentle pull, saying, 'All right. Let's go to the kitchen and I'll show you. I'll help.'

Seeing that Manuela's mother was at a loss for how to behave, Brunetti decided to take the initiative and said, 'Shall we sit down, Signora? I have a number of things I'd like to ask you.'

She walked to a chair that stood in front of the window. The light fell on the chair facing her, so Brunetti pulled it to one side and sat out of the direct light. 'Thank you for agreeing to see us, Signora.'

Sitting closer to her now, Brunetti saw that she had applied a layer of flesh-coloured makeup to her face but had not succeeded

231

in applying it smoothly under her chin, so the colour simply ended, creating a colour change as evident as that on the fur of a Jack Russell. 'I don't understand what's going on,' she said.

'A magistrate has initiated a re-examination of the circumstances surrounding Manuela's accident,' he said, intentionally avoiding any reference to his own interest in the subject. Let her think he was merely a cop sent to do some unimportant job.

'Ah,' she said, prolonging the sound. When Brunetti made no comment, she said, 'I didn't know there had been an examination to begin with.' Her tone caused Brunetti to do a sudden reassessment. Perhaps she was not drugged at all, merely leading them on.

Brunetti gave an easy smile. 'Perhaps it's more correct to say that there was the usual police report of the incident. That's what the magistrate wants us to look at again.'

'After fifteen years?' she asked, deadpan.

'Yes,' Brunetti answered but supplied no explanation.

'Has my mother-in-law got anything to do with this?' she asked.

Brunetti narrowed his eyes in confusion, as if hearing for the first time that this woman had a mother-in-law. 'I'm afraid only the Public Magistrate would know that, Signora. I was asked to speak to you.' Then, with interest obviously aroused by her question, he asked, 'Is there something your mother-in-law knows that we should hear about?'

Her answer was immediate. 'Not that I know of.'

Brunetti indicated his acceptance of her remark. In a more serious voice, he began, 'Signora, you must excuse me if I ask this, but can you tell me how much . . .' Brunetti broke off, seeking a word less savage than 'damage' to use. '. . . harm was done to Manuela?'

'You've seen her,' she said, suddenly fierce with the anger of someone who has nothing to lose. 'What do you think?'

'I think she has a very sweet character,' Brunetti said in the girl's defence.

'Children usually do,' the mother said bitterly, then clapped her hand over her mouth, as if surprised to hear herself say such a thing. She put her palms on her knees and leaned forward to take a few deep breaths. As Brunetti watched, she rocked back and forth a few times, eyes closed. Finally she said, voice calmer but not calm, 'The doctors say she has a mental age of six or seven, and that's what she's going to be for ever.'

Brunetti thought back to what Chiara had been at that age: sweet, affectionate, able to sound out and read aloud any text given to her and to understand some of what she read, trusting of all adults, in love with the neighbour's dog. What a lovely age; how horrible to have it be prolonged year after year.

He looked at Manuela's mother with new eyes, and she looked back at him with a flash of the intelligence he had chosen not to notice before. 'I can't tell you how sorry I am, Signora,' he said.

She nodded. 'Thank you. It doesn't help in the least, but I thank you for your sympathy,' she said sounding like an actress who had stepped out of role.

The moment passed, and he laid all father aside and returned to being only a policeman. 'Did you learn this from the hospital report, Signora?

She considered that then said, 'I don't think I ever read it.'

'I beg your pardon.'

'I said I think I never read it,' she repeated. 'By the time Manuela came home from the hospital, it was obvious to me what was wrong with her. So what did I have to learn from the report? That I'd spend the rest of my life taking care of her? I could under-stand that myself: I didn't need their medi-cal jargon to tell me.' Saying that had ap-parently provided her with momentum, and she continued. 'You've seen her. Do you think there will be a time when I'm not go-ing to have to take care of her?'

Then, seeing his surprise, she added, 'Her father took her to doctors all over Italy, to specialists, and for tests, and they all said what anyone could see — what I saw when they brought her home.'

Brunetti remained silent. She asked him, 'Do you have children?'

He nodded, unable to find words. For the first time since entering it, Brunetti took a look around the room. Normal, everything was normal: sofas, chairs, a table, a book-case, carpets, windows. Nothing out of place, nothing upset or broken, everything normal except for the lives of the people who entered and left this room.

'I'm concerned about the original report, the one from the hospital here, Signora,' he said. 'Do you remember if they gave you a copy of the file?' he asked, hoping to keep to the past and avoid the present and, please God, the future.

'I suppose they must have.'

His voice calm, as though this were the

most normal thing in the world, he asked, 'Would you still have it, do you think?'

'Why do you ask that?'

'I'd like to see it,' Brunetti said.

'There were so many doctors, so many reports,' she said.

'Could you try to find it, do you think?' he insisted.

She rose to her feet and said, suddenly eager, 'I'll have a look,' then left the room.

Brunetti walked over to the window, which was at the back of the house and thus provided a long view of Marghera and Mestre, a view he'd rather be spared. The *laguna* wasn't visible from the top floor, but he could see the chimneys of the Marghera factories, busy with their life's work: killing him. Over the last years, Brunetti had come to this conclusion about most industries: their desire was not to produce chemicals, refine petroleum, or make plasterboard, or jewellery, or indeed — in the factories of the hinterland — make anything. On the contrary, Big Business wanted nothing more than to take the life of Guido Brunetti and everyone in his family. His children's concern for the environment had nudged him into reading and that had nudged him into paying attention and reading more widely, and that had led him down the slippery slope of information to arrive at this conclusion, one he had so far spared his children. Off there in the distance sat the daily reminder: a vast petrochemical complex that had spent decades pouring anything it wanted into the waters of the *laguna,* into the fish he ate, the clams his children loved, the *radicchio* grown on the farm someone in his wife's family owned on the island of Sant'Erasmo, not to mention what had also been tossed up, ever so carelessly, within those enormous clouds that had billowed out of their smokestacks all these years.

The sound of the opening door pulled Brunetti from his reflections. He turned to see Manuela entering the room, pushing in front of her a wheeled trolley draped in a white linen cloth, on which sat three cups of coffee, a chocolate cake the size of a pizza, plates and forks, and a large bowl of whipped cream. Manuela's excited pleasure radiated from her, seeming to bounce around the room, calling out that there was cake and cream for everyone. Behind her came Griffoni and, carrying a manila envelope, Manuela's mother.

Manuela parked the trolley in front of the sofa and called to her mother, 'Alina made a chocolate cake, *Mamma.* Alina made a cake.'

'Oh, wonderful, *Tesoro,* and it's your favourite, too.'

'And my favourite,' Griffoni chimed in.

Brunetti did nothing more than smile, but Manuela, who had turned to see what he had to say, seemed pleased that he liked it, too. She waved to them all to take their places, and they responded to the lure of the cake and cream and took seats around the trolley, Brunetti holding chairs for both her mother and Griffoni.

Manuela picked up the cake knife and looked tentatively at her mother, who nodded. Carefully, guiding her right hand with her left, Manuela set the point of the knife in the centre of the cake and cut down through it, then went back and cut an enormous piece, certainly twice as large as a normal piece would be.

'Oh, good. May I have that one?' Brunetti asked Manuela, knowing that Griffoni disliked sweet things.

She started to turn to her mother for approval but couldn't wait and said, 'Oh, yes, please.' Manuela tried to lift the slice of cake but had to use the fingers of her left hand to guide it to a plate, which she passed to Brunetti. He thanked her effusively and leaned forward to slather a mound of cream on it. Taking it upon himself to help, he placed cups of coffee in front of Griffoni and Manuela's mother and, assuming that it must be hers, a glass of what looked like Coca-Cola in front of Manuela's empty chair.

There were three moments of shared anxiety as Manuela cut the remaining three pieces of cake, but she managed to do it without creating much mess, giving her mother a small piece and cutting one as big as Brunetti's for Griffoni and setting down the knife long enough to pass it to her, smiling.

Last, she cut herself a normal-sized piece and sat down.

Her mother put a drop of cream on her cake and passed the bowl to Griffoni, who heaped three large spoonfuls on hers. Brunetti knew that she'd prefer not to, but also knew that she would eat it all, perhaps even ask for a second slice. In the past, he had watched her eat pies and cakes in order to placate possible witnesses or to win trust from people who should not have trusted her. Here, however, it had nothing to do with her profession: food is love, he believed, and Manuela needed to love.

Griffoni asked her if she'd like cream and at her nod put a large spoonful on top of Manuela's cake.

'*Buon appetito,*' her mother said, and they picked up their forks.

Ah, Brunetti thought as he piled cream on his second bite of cake, who says that good actions are not rewarded?

Automatically, the level of conversation became appropriate for Manuela: how good the cake was, how good Alina's apple cake was, too, and Manuela always helped by peeling the apples; why is cream so good with chocolate cake, and where does cream come from; and would it be possible to ride a cow?

When Manuela asked this question, her mother quickly ate her last bite of cake and asked her daughter if she could have another, although Brunetti suspected she was enjoying the cake as little as Griffoni.

'Would you like another piece of cake, Signora?' Manuela asked Griffoni, who put both hands over her stomach and said, 'If I ate any more, I'd go "pop" and they'd hear it all over the city.'

This set Manuela off into giggles, and the idea of riding a cow — of riding — was abandoned.

When cake and more coffee had been refused, and then refused again, Brunetti and Griffoni got to their feet and said they had to go back to work. Manuela found this thrilling and asked, 'Do you get to chase bad guys?'

'No, Signorina Manuela,' Brunetti said, 'usually we sit at our desks and read papers all day long. It's really very boring. Much more fun to come here and have cake.'

She laughed at this as though it were the funniest thing she'd ever heard, and again the bright sound of her laughter cut Brunetti to the heart.

She went with them towards the door, leaning close to Griffoni as they walked. Just as they got there, Brunetti heard Signora Magello-Ronchi call after him. 'Commissario,' she said, coming towards them. 'You forgot this.' She held up the manila envelope she had brought back from some other room.

He took it and thanked her. Manuela's name was on the cover. He turned the envelope over and looked at the flap. 'Didn't you open it?'

'I told you. There was no need to,' she answered, voice moving away from pleasantness.

Griffoni, perhaps in response to the tension that had suddenly entered the room, asked Manuela a question and moved off from the others to hear the answer.

Manuela's mother closed her eyes for a

moment and concentrated on taking a breath. When she opened her eyes, she said, 'You can read it if you want. It doesn't interest me.' She looked towards the door, where Griffoni and Manuela stood close together, talking happily. 'Only she does,' she said in a tired voice. 'Only my baby.'

Brunetti reached out and took her hand and held it. 'Thank you for talking to us, Signora,' he said.

'I hope you liked the cake,' she chirped back in best hostess fashion, then smiled easily, looking remarkably like Manuela when she did.

Griffoni and Brunetti took their leave, but not before having promised to come back and see Manuela another time.

17

The fastest way to get to the Questura was to take the Number One from San Silvestro. As they waited on the *imbarcadero* for the vaporetto, Brunetti said, 'She's a sweet girl, isn't she?' realizing only too late that he had referred to Manuela as a girl.

Griffoni nodded but said nothing.

'You got on with her very well, it seemed.'

'All I had to do was think of my nieces.'

'How old are they?'

'One's six and one's eight. I said to her what I say to them.' She walked back outside and leaned against the railing with folded arms, looking towards Rialto for a sign of the boat.

Brunetti, without glancing at his watch, said, 'Four minutes.'

'Are you joking?' Griffoni asked in surprise. 'Do you all have computer chips in your ears with the boat times?'

'It's my stop,' he said. 'So I don't need a chip.'

She turned and glanced across the canal and said, 'It's strange: there are times when I begin to find all of this normal. It's where I live and I move around on boats, and addresses mean nothing, and it's faster to walk to work, and I'm even beginning to get used to the sound of Veneziano.' She let her voice trail off and stop.

'And other times?'

'Other times I see how strange it all is. Everyone in my building is very friendly if we meet on the stairs, but no one's invited me into their home, not even for a coffee, and I've been there for several years. The young people call me *tu,* but the old ones never will. I find the food insipid. I've almost died from every one of the pizzas I've tried to eat here. And I know the sun is going to disappear in about two months and we won't see it again until March, except for a one-week break in January, usually about the end of the first week.'

Brunetti laughed out loud, as he suspected she wanted him to. 'And at home, you'd be walking around in a sweater and eating pizza at every meal?'

'No, not really. I'd probably be trying to figure out a way to get around the magis-

244

trates who are working for the Mafia; the same with my colleagues. And I'd be in the habit of carrying my pistol. Here,' she began and pulled open her jacket to show that she was not wearing one, 'I forget to carry it most of the time.'

Brunetti, who did the same, said nothing.

'What's in the envelope?' she asked, pointing to the one he was carrying.

'It's what the hospital gave her mother when she took Manuela home.' He turned it over and showed her the sealed flap.

'And she couldn't open it,' she said, sounding as if she understood such reluctance. 'How awful it must be for her.' She turned away from Brunetti and looked at the buildings on the other side of the canal, but they offered little solace.

'Why?' Brunetti asked, curious about Griffoni's concern for the mother when she had spent most of her time with the daughter.

'Because she understands. And the daughter doesn't.'

He turned and walked into the *imbarcadero,* and she followed him. 'You heard it coming, didn't you?' she asked as she noticed the boat approaching. When it tied up, they moved on board and towards the back of the cabin, where some seats were empty.

'I suppose I did. I've been listening to them all my life, so maybe my body feels their vibrations before I hear them. Never thought about it before.'

He stood back and let her pass in front of him to take the seat by the window. When he turned to speak to her, he saw only the back of her head: she was glued to the window as if she were a tourist seeing these *palazzi* for the first time.

He stuck his finger under the flap and prised it up. It opened easily, noiselessly. He reached in and pulled out a dark blue manila folder. Having heard the sound, Griffoni turned and watched him read.

She gave him plenty of time. When he turned to the second page, she said, 'Well?'

'It gives a general description of her condition when she was brought to the Emergency Room: she was unconscious, but breathing; an X-ray showed there was still water in her lungs; there was a wound on the side of her head.' Brunetti had gradually been moving the papers farther away from him as he read but finally reached into the inner pocket of his jacket for his reading glasses.

He read quickly down the second page then told Griffoni: 'Aside from the wound on her head — there is no speculation here

about what the cause might have been —
there were bruises on her arms and neck.'
He flipped back to the first page. 'These
were written when she was admitted. It
seems their chief concern was the water in
her lungs.'

He turned back to where he had been and
again read quickly, skimming the text,
searching for the point when the doctors
began to understand the extent of her injuries.

He took his eyes from the paper and
stared ahead, blind to the people sitting in
front of them, blind to the glory on both
sides of the boat.

'What is it?' Griffoni asked.

He pointed to the third paragraph and
passed the papers to her, saying, 'The
second day. Look.'

Griffoni read it and, just as Brunetti had,
looked away from the page blankly in front
of her.

'Bloodstains seen on patient's sheets
necessitated a pelvic exam, performed in
place on the still-unconscious patient.
Evidence of recent sexual activity of a
violent nature, very likely rape.'

Griffoni continued reading the report to
the end. 'She was unconscious for a week,'
she said. 'And then she woke up naturally

but could remember nothing — nothing — of the events before her fall — fall — into the water.' She handed him the papers, saying, 'Read the rest.'

He did and had barely finished when the boat pulled up to the San Zaccaria stop. He followed Griffoni from the boat. They walked along the *riva,* both on autopilot, towards the Questura. At one point, uncertain of his memory of what they had both read, Brunetti stopped and took another look at the report. 'When she finally did wake up, it took them only a day to see that something was wrong,' he said, then read aloud: ' "Patient has no memory of incident and great difficulty in explaining the events preceding it. Her language is childlike, and she seems not to understand her condition." ' He continued reading the doctors' day-by-day evidence that far more was wrong with this girl than they had at first assumed, until that evidence became incontrovertible: an adolescent had fallen into the water, and a child had been pulled out.

'They didn't bother with a full examination when they brought her in,' he said and closed his eyes. 'A wound on her head, bruising on her body, pulled from the water, and they didn't give her a full examination!'

'And then, I suppose,' Griffoni said in a

voice she struggled to contain, 'they thought they'd wait until she woke up before they told the mother or told the police.'

Brunetti thought Griffoni's anger might blossom into something else, but it did not. He started towards the Questura again. He wondered if the mother even knew; surely, they would have to have told her; the girl was a minor. Or maybe they thought that by giving her the medical files they were fulfilling their obligations.

Griffoni followed him up to his office and sat opposite him; the sun streaming in from the windows turned her hair into a golden crown. 'What now?' she asked.

'I still have to talk to the man who pulled her out of the water,' Brunetti said. 'I'm supposed to see him tomorrow at noon. I had to invite him to lunch to get him to talk to me.'

'Do you think he knows anything?'

Brunetti waved a hand in the air to show his uncertainty. 'He's a drunk. Everyone who's spoken of him says he is. When I called to ask to speak to him, I could hear a glass clicking against the phone.'

'They're unreliable, drunks,' Griffoni said.

'And if his brain's been soaking in alcohol for the last fifteen years, it's even less likely he'll remember anything.'

'Then why bother?'

'There's nothing else,' Brunetti admitted.

They sat in silence until Brunetti said, 'The medical report changes everything, doesn't it?'

'Yes,' she agreed.

Griffoni stared out the window while together they listened to a boat passing from left to right under the windows. 'Maybe. So are you suggesting that her fall was more likely . . . involuntary?'

'Maybe,' Brunetti answered. 'Her grandmother told me that Manuela had become very withdrawn in the months before it happened.

'How did she know that?'

'Manuela's mother told her.'

She nodded. 'She'd know, I suppose.' Griffoni crossed her legs and slumped down in her chair. She folded her arms and looked out of the window. 'You know,' she said, 'if I think about this, I want to cry.' She pressed both hands to the sides of her mouth and smoothed the skin back.

'She could be my younger sister.' She shook her head and went on, 'That hardly matters. She's a young woman who's lost her future. She could be like this for another half a century. My God, think of it.' Her voice had grown unsteady and trailed away on the final words.

'I think it's time we went home,' was all Brunetti could think of saying.

That is what they did.

18

The next morning he woke with an ache, but this time it was in his mind, not in his joints. He'd spent the better part of the last week getting nowhere, involving not only himself but another commissario, a magistrate, his superior, Vice-Questore Patta, and Patta's secretary, Signorina Elettra. Five people's attention had resulted in no discoveries save unprovable information about a rape committed fifteen years before, of which there existed no possibility that the victim would remember.

He lay in bed and stared at the ceiling, then turned his head and looked out at the roofs of the city, which glistened with autumnal rain.

He looked at the clock and saw that it was almost nine: Paola had let him sleep. He turned on his side, telling himself that he would plan his day, and went back to sleep.

Half an hour later, Paola woke him by saying his name and setting a cup and saucer down next to him. The sound, and then the smell, bored down into wherever he was and pulled him free. He flopped on to his back, pushed himself up against the back of the bed, and rubbed at his eyes.

'Here,' Paola said, handing him the cup and saucer. 'There's already sugar in it.'

She sat on his side of the bed and watched as he took his first sip of coffee, closed his eyes, and rested his head back against the pillow. 'The patient will live,' he said and finished his coffee. He set the cup and saucer on the bedside table. 'Aren't you supposed to be teaching?' he asked her.

'Not until ten.'

'I'm not doing anything until twelve today,' he boasted.

'Why is that?'

'Because I don't feel like it.'

'That's certainly a compelling reason,' she agreed.

'When's the last time I missed even a half-day of work?' he demanded. 'How many days have I taken sick leave in all these years?'

'You were in the hospital for almost a week.'

'That was years ago.'

'Yes,' she admitted.

'I can't bear it today,' he said: he had told her about the medical report the night before. 'I don't know why that is, but it's true. Just for one morning, I don't want to think about it, go there, do it.'

'Is this a life-altering change?'

He had to consider this. 'Probably not.'

She bent over him and pressed his shoulder, then got to her feet.

'Why'd you stay?' Brunetti asked.

'To bring you coffee.'

'Don't let your feminist friends find out you did that,' Brunetti said.

'Love trumps principle,' she said and left.

Brunetti spent another hour reading Apollonius. How often it was true in these stories: love trumped principle. Paola tossed out these things so easily. Did she sit on the vaporetto and make them up or did they come to her in flashes?

He set the book aside, took a shower and got ready to leave the house. While he had been lolling in swinish sleep and reading, the sun had come out and got immediately to work: the streets were dry, and it was warm enough to wear only a sweater and jacket.

In the street, he decided to walk: it was faster than taking a vaporetto and making the long S towards Riva di Biasio. Besides, the air was an inducement to walk. Brunetti set out in what would be, in a normal city, a straight line, heading north-west. Venice, however, took him left and right, over bridges, around corners he wasn't aware of turning or planning to turn. Within fifteen minutes, he was walking along the embankment of Rio Marin, heading towards the gas office. A few doors before it, he saw the windows and door of a bar, stopped and glanced inside, searching for a man he wouldn't recognize.

There were two women at a table, each with a coffee cup in front of them. Three young tourists, two girls and a boy, sat at another table, a map spread out in front of them, each holding a glass of beer as they bent over it.

Brunetti entered and went to the bar. The barman looked at him and nodded. Brunetti had eaten nothing that morning and so did not want wine or a spritz. Nor did he want a coffee so close to lunch. He asked for a glass of mineral water and said, 'I'm supposed to meet Pietro Cavanis, but he doesn't seem to be here.'

'No,' the man said as he set a glass in front of Brunetti. 'He hasn't been in for a couple of days. At least, I haven't seen him. He might have been here in the morning, when

255

my son works, but he's not much of a one for the morning, Pietro.'

'I know,' Brunetti said with a friendly smile. 'He told me.' He took a few sips of his water and set the glass down. 'He told me to ask you for the keys if he wasn't here.'

The barman smiled and stepped over to the cash register and pulled a much-handled envelope from where it was stuffed between the machine and the wall. He took out a set of keys and handed them to Brunetti. 'It's the green door on the other side of the canal. Top floor.'

'I know that, too,' Brunetti said, thanked the man, and took the keys. Without asking what he owed, Brunetti left two euros on the counter and started for the door. Holding up the keys, he turned at the door and said, 'I'll bring them back.'

The barman, who had already removed Brunetti's glass and was wiping at the place where it had been, waved the cloth in his direction.

The bridge on the left was closer, so he crossed that and went along the *riva* to the green door. He stepped back and looked at the façade of the building: the shutters on the first floor were all closed and sun-bleached, as were the four on the left side of the second floor. Two of the shutters on the right side were open, the inside bleached to a dull grey-green, suggesting that they were never pulled closed. The building looked sick, as if withering away to death. There were two empty rectangles on the left side of the bells; only Cavanis' name was there: top row, right side.

He put the larger key into the green door. It opened easily, and Brunetti crossed the small entrance space and started up the stairs. He paused on the second landing, something he had begun doing on the steps to his own home.

Outside the door on the right, he saw Cavanis' name, printed in a fine copperplate hand, on a piece of cardboard pinned to the left of the door. Politeness or territoriality made him ring the bell, wait, and then ring it again, longer. Familiar with the sleep of alcoholics, he then used the key to open the door, which was not double-locked.

'Signor Cavanis,' he called from the doorway. 'Signor Cavanis.' He waited, and his nose told him what he was going to find. He could have retreated into the corridor and called the crime squad, but instead he left the keys in the door, stuffed both hands into his pockets, and stepped into the room.

It smelled of cigarettes, of decades, eternities of the presence of a heavy smoker. It was a small room. Sofa, low table, facing them a television, all part of a shrine to the flat-faced god. This one was as enormous as it was old. As deep as it was wide, it was turned low but was still audible and was currently giving a blonde young woman in a pink angora sweater the chance to look adoringly at an elderly man in an expensive suit who sat opposite her as he lectured her never-dimming smile.

Brunetti looked for the remote control, but there was none to be found. It was not on the sofa or the table, and there were no other flat surfaces in the room. Nor were there knobs on the television: what you saw was what you got: local channel, fixed volume. How much local news and entertainment could a person stand before going mad?

There were no pictures and no reading material of any sort in the room, no rugs or decorations, and no other furniture. On the table were some plates and glasses, cups and saucers, apparently stacked and pushed aside as days passed. The plate that sat in the line of vision between the screen and the viewer's chair held a dried-out piece of cheese, some prosciutto that had curved in on itself; beside it, pieces had been sliced from a loaf of white bread. The glass beside the plate was half full of red wine; the level had gone down as it evaporated in the overheated room, leaving a reddish stripe above the remaining wine.

Brunetti went into the small kitchen on the right. On the table sat an almost empty two-litre bottle of red wine. He did not bother to open the cabinets or the refrigerator but backed out and went to the door where he had seen the foot.

It was a large foot, wearing a man's shoe, and it was lying on the floor, a grey sock that might once have been white exposed above it. Brunetti leaned forward and into the room. The grey-haired man lay on his left side, his head cushioned on his bent elbow. He could have been taking a nap, one leg stretched out, the other trapped and bent slightly under it. He could have been asleep were it not for the handle of a kitchen knife protruding from the right side of his neck and the pool of dried blood in which he lay. And the smell. Not even the years of smoke, which had discoloured the white door of the refrigerator and darkened the tiles in the kitchen, could cover or disguise that distinctive iron-rich smell, nor could they overpower the smell of rot that Brunetti sensed slowly sinking into his own clothing.

He backed away from the body and left

the apartment and stood on the landing. He dialled Bocchese's *telefonino* number and told the leader of the forensics squad what to prepare for, gave him the address, and told him to get a team there as quickly as he could and to bring a pathologist, if one was free.

'I shouldn't ask this,' Bocchese said, 'but did you touch anything?'

'No,' Brunetti said and broke the connection. He remained on the landing outside the apartment, trying to draw the line that would connect what he had just seen to something else. The dead man had saved Manuela from death, and this had come to the attention of the police. Cavanis had been there when it happened and had always denied — after having described it — that he had seen anyone try to harm Manuela. Nothing necessitated a link; nothing proved cause–effect; no straight line led from Rio San Boldo to Rio Marin.

Cavanis could have interrupted a burglar; one look back at the poverty of the room put an end to that idea. An enemy could have done it, although a man with enemies does not leave his keys with a barman and tell him to give them to whoever asks for them. Random violence? In Venice? The possibility didn't remain in Brunetti's mind long enough for him to find the energy to dismiss it.

Brunetti went downstairs and out into the sunlight to wait for the boat.

It took the crew another quarter of an hour to arrive, but when they did, they came in force. Aside from the pilot and Bocchese, there were two photographers and two technicians. The boat glided up to the side of the canal; Brunetti caught the rope and wrapped it around the bollard, then hauled the first man up to the pavement.

Bocchese came on deck and told the pilot to move the boat ahead fifty metres to a stone staircase leading down to the water: he got out there and walked back to Brunetti, leaving it to the crew to unload and move the equipment.

'Murder?' Bocchese asked. When Brunetti nodded, the technician added, 'Rizzardi is on his way.'

'Where was he?'

'At home,' Bocchese said. 'When I told him you'd called it in, he said he'd come even though that idiot's on duty.'

Brunetti thought it politic to ignore Rizzardi's comment about his colleague, who was considered an idiot by everyone at the Questura.

Bocchese went back to the two technicians

who were carrying their equipment from the boat. Though he was a head shorter than both of them and at least twenty years older, the younger men looked to him for instruction; their very bearing displayed deference.

When they were all on the landing, Brunetti accompanied them to the green door and into the apartment. He realized then that his morning's reluctance to go to the Questura had followed him here. He disliked being at the scene of this crime, disliked watching as the camera was set up and photos were taken of the dead man and everything around him, from every angle. Even more did he find the necessity to avoid the dry puddle of blood grotesque. He didn't want to see the knife, didn't want to see the way the blood had flowed down the dead man's body and seeped into his clothing, nor to start calculating how long he could have lived while the blood was still flowing.

Brunetti retreated to the landing, leaving the others to do their jobs, and tried to push his mind away from the thought of what it must be to know that you were dying, that you were wounded beyond recovery, beyond help or hope, and were going to die. He could wish only that alcohol and shock and sudden loss of blood had dulled Cavanis' mind — for this must be Pietro Cavanis — and lessened his terror.

'Guido?' A voice from the door to the street called him away from these thoughts.

He turned and saw Ettore Rizzardi, the pathologist, come to bear witness to the obvious, as was so often his duty. Tall and thin, Rizzardi managed to convey a sense of energy held in restraint.

Brunetti shook his hand and then led him into the apartment; he could think of nothing to say. Brunetti watched the pathologist gaze around the room, and registered the moment when he saw the foot. Rizzardi closed his eyes for a moment, and had Brunetti not known him better, he would have suspected him of saying a prayer.

One of the technicians offered each of them a pair of plastic gloves, but Rizzardi had brought his own. He opened the package and put them on. Brunetti did the same.

Brunetti followed the pathologist into Cavanis' bedroom and saw the doctor already bent to take the man's pulse. Rizzardi looked at his watch and took out a notebook. He glanced at Bocchese. 'Your people finished in here?'

'Yes.'

'All right, I'll take a look.' He stepped back from the corpse and took a surgical mask from his pocket, ripped off the protective paper, and put it on. He handed one to Brunetti, who was glad to do the same. Rizzardi took a heat-sensitive wand from his pocket and placed the tip on the dead man's temple, then wrote in his notebook. 'Will you help me, Guido?' he asked.

Together, they straightened the man's body and rolled him on to one side. The knife jutted straight into the air.

Brunetti studied the angle of the blade. 'Killed from behind,' he observed.

The pathologist nodded. 'Killer's right-handed.'

Both of them had learned over the years how best to distance at least a part of themselves from what they were doing: view it as a practical problem, akin to figuring out why the bedside lamp wouldn't work. Light bulb? Wall socket? Fuse? Look at the evidence and try to find the cause.

The man had been limp when they moved him, and the smell had grown stronger as they got closer to him. 'A day or two, I'd say,' Rizzardi observed. He set his knee down in a clean place on the floor and looked more closely at the knife and at the quantity of coagulated blood on the man's sweater. 'It must have opened the jugular.'

'Would it have been fast?' Brunetti asked.

'I'd think so, yes,' Rizzardi said and got to his feet. 'I'll be able to tell you more once I take a closer look.'

'When?'

'Later this afternoon, if possible.' He turned back to the dead man and asked, 'Did he drink a lot?'

'Yes,' Brunetti answered. 'How'd you know?' He had detected no scent of alcohol; perhaps it had been covered by the other smell coming from the body, left for who knows how long in a heated room.

Rizzardi led them out to the living room, where the technicians were doing their job: collecting, photographing, putting small bits of things into plastic envelopes. Rizzardi removed his gloves and put them in his pocket. Brunetti wondered how many of them he'd taken home with him over the years.

'If they've been drinking long enough,' Rizzardi said, finally answering Brunetti's question, 'they all take on the same look. You come to see it. Both outside and inside.'

The doctor shook his head as at some private thought and Brunetti asked, 'What are you thinking about?'

'If you know enough about the human body, you come to see it as a miracle. And when you look at the bodies of some of them — like him — who have drunk for years, perhaps all their lives, and you see what the drinking's done to them, and in spite of it all they were still alive, then you know it really is a miracle.'

They shook hands and Rizzardi left, but not before finding Bocchese in the kitchen and saying goodbye to him.

Brunetti stayed behind, watching the technicians work, until the men from the hospital arrived with their plastic coffin. While they waited, one of the technicians went through the dead man's pockets and removed a wallet, a *telefonino,* and a handkerchief much in need of washing. Brunetti watched him place them in separate plastic bags and zip them closed. The technician nodded to the men from the hospital, who put the dead man into the coffin and left the apartment.

The technical squad remained another half-hour, until Bocchese came back and told Brunetti they were finished and he could now move around freely and touch whatever he wanted in the apartment. The two of them shook hands, and Bocchese led his squad down the stairs and out to the waiting boat.

Brunetti, still wearing his plastic gloves, went back into the bedroom, careful where he stepped, and opened the doors of the wardrobe. He saw two jackets, neither of them particularly clean, and a dark grey woollen coat with worn cuffs. Two pairs of shoes rested on the bottom of the closet. The drawers on the bottom held three pullovers and a few polyester shirts. The underwear was grey and unpleasant looking.

Brunetti went through the rest of the apartment. The only printed words he saw were the receipts from Cavanis' monthly pension payment — 662.87 euros, and how was a person meant to live on that? — and a circular from the local parish, inviting all residents to meet the new *parroco*. The refrigerator, at least thirty years old, held another two-litre bottle of wine, this one white, and a packet of petrified cheese.

The shelf above the sink in the bathroom held a grimy glass, a packet of aspirin, and a bar of kitchen soap. The bathtub was disgusting.

Nothing else. For all that his presence was evident in his possessions, Cavanis could have moved in that same day or the day before, yet he had been there long enough for the man in the bar to find his behaviour with the keys normal.

Brunetti left, locking the door behind him,

and went downstairs. He went back to the bridge and to the other side, then along the canal and into the bar.

When the barman saw him, he said, sounding offended, 'You didn't tell me you were a policeman.'

'It wasn't necessary. He hadn't done anything wrong.' He asked for a coffee.

The man shrugged, as though to say he wasn't angry, really: he was just saying it.

He made the coffee and placed it in front of Brunetti, then pushed the bowl of sugar envelopes along the counter towards him.

'Was he really murdered?' the barman couldn't stop himself from asking.

'It would seem so,' Brunetti answered.

'Ah, the poor devil,' he said with real feeling, then surprised Brunetti by saying, 'I hope at least he was drunk when it happened.'

'Why is that?'

The barman had to think a while before he found the words for his answer. 'Because he wouldn't be so afraid. Maybe.' He shook his head again and repeated, 'Poor devil.'

Brunetti sensed another person at his side and turned to see a sandy-haired man a few years older than himself.

'It's really true? Someone killed Pietro?' he asked.

Brunetti nodded, and finished his coffee. 'Did you know him?' he asked the man to his left.

'Well, there's knowing and there's knowing,' the man said and waved towards the place on the bar in front of him. The barman reached for a bottle of white wine and poured him a small glass.

He picked it up and drank it down as though it were water.

'Was he a friend?' Brunetti asked with feigned innocence.

'Sort of,' he said and pushed the glass across the counter.

Brunetti gestured to the barman, and a second glass appeared in front of him. When both were filled, Brunetti tipped it in the direction of the man beside him, then quickly downed half of it. He found it less good than the coffee.

'You're a cop, aren't you?' the man asked.

'Yes. I was supposed to talk to Signor Cavanis this morning. But when I went over there — the way he told me to do — I found him.' Brunetti shook his head and made what he hoped was a resigned gesture with his left hand.

'Did you know him?' the man reversed roles by asking Brunetti.

'No, not really,' Brunetti answered, trying

to sound easy and relaxed. 'But we'd spoken a few times.'

The man finished his wine and held the glass up to the barman. 'He was a good guy. But he drank too much, if you ask me.'

'Ah,' Brunetti sighed. 'I'm sorry to hear that.' Then, quite as if the phenomenon of drinking were a new world to him, he asked, 'Did it change him? The way he behaved, I mean.'

The man nodded his thanks to the barman and left the glass on the counter. 'Yeah, it gave him this feeling that he was important.'

Brunetti took the smallest sip of his wine and set the glass down, then turned to his companion, intent on what he might say next.

'More he drank, more important he thought he was,' his neighbour said and picked up his glass.

'Like knowing about sports and stuff like that?' Brunetti asked, pitching his level of reference to what he thought most men would understand.

'That for one, yes. Hear him talk, he was the only person who ever watched soccer or knew anything about it,' the other man said, but the criticism was coloured by affection. 'But it was more that he kept thinking he'd make a fortune. Ever since I've known him . . .' the man began but then made the grammatical correction and said, '. . . since I knew him, he'd have these great plans for getting rich.' He took another small sip and was surprised to see that the glass was almost empty. 'I guess he thought that would make him important.'

Brunetti finished his glass and waved to the barman, pointing to both their glasses.

'He got the bug again just the other night,' the man continued, nodding his thanks for the wine. 'Big plans. He said he saw something that was going to change his luck, at last, after all these years.' He shook his head at the very idea of it then, seeing the scepticism on Brunetti's face, he turned to the barman and said, 'You heard him, Ruggiero. Saturday night.'

'He was drunk, Nino,' the barman said with a mixture of patience and exasperation. 'You know what he was like: big talk at night, no memory in the morning.'

'But you *heard* him,' the man called Nino insisted.

'Yes, I heard him, but I also *saw* him, and he was drunk. He came in here to get another bottle of wine, didn't he?'

'Was this Saturday?' Brunetti asked.

'The night of *acqua alta,* yes,' the barman

271

answered. Nino nodded to show he agreed but said nothing.

'I've been listening to him for years,' the barman continued. 'So I never paid too much attention to him, not once he started on his big plans. I've heard too many of them over the years; not only from him.' He picked up a clean glass and poured himself some of the white wine and drank it down. 'He said that the time he'd spent watching television was finally going to be worth something. When I asked him what he was talking about, he said he'd remembered something and it was going to make his fortune.'

The other man laughed out loud. 'I can't count how many times something he knew, or remembered, or was told, or read in the paper, or saw on television was going to make his fortune.' He laughed a few more times but then, perhaps recalling that the man was dead, he clapped his hand over his mouth and said, 'Sorry.'

Brunetti and the barman exchanged glances, but neither knew what to say. Both of them took a sip of wine, set their glasses down and looked around the bar, as though waiting for something to distract them and let the moment pass.

Finally the sandy-haired man said, 'Well,

even if he never amounted to much, there was no malice in him, and he couldn't help it if he was a drunk. His father was and his grandfather was, too.' He ran his eyes across the bottles lined up on the mirrored wall of the bar, as if trying to calculate all of the drinking three generations of Cavanis men had done. 'Pity he won't get to change his luck.'

'It didn't get better, did it?' the barman asked of no one in particular.

To break their maudlin descent, Brunetti asked the barman, 'Do you think it really was something he saw on television that made him remember?'

The barman emptied his glass, dipped it into the water in the sink, and began to dry it with a towel. He held it with one hand and rubbed at it, turning and turning long after it was dry.

The other man surprised Brunetti by asking the barman, 'Should we tell him?'

'About his memory?'

'Yes.'

All Brunetti knew was that whatever Cavanis had once seen had vanished in the midst of a bout of drunkenness and not returned. 'Tell me what?'

The two men engaged in a delicate head-ballet, one nodding to the other, that one

273

shaking his head and nodding back at the first. Finally the barman said, 'You tell him, Nino.' To encourage him, he filled his friend's glass, and then, when Brunetti covered the top of his own glass with his hand, his own, forgetting that he'd just cleaned it.

'Pietro's father could do it, too,' the man called Nino began, a remark that confused Brunetti utterly. 'I never met the grandfather, so I don't know if he could do it, but Pietro and his father had memories.'

Brunetti was about to say that most people do, when the man went on, 'I mean very good memories. If you told Pietro something he'd always remember it, or if he met a person or read something. It was like a camera.' To give an example, he said, 'He could remember every move in every game of soccer he ever saw, either live or on television.'

He picked up his glass and held it up towards Brunetti, without drinking. 'Only trouble was this.' He raised the glass and swirled the wine around. 'If he drank too much, it didn't work and he wouldn't remember anything when he was sober again.'

'That's not true,' the bartender broke in to say. 'You know it's not.'

'Let me finish, Ruggiero, would you?' he said impatiently. Then, to Brunetti, 'As I was saying, he wouldn't remember some things if they happened when he was drinking. But then other things came back, and he'd remember them again, but only when he was so drunk he didn't remember new things. Old stuff came back but new stuff didn't go in. Very strange.' He finished his wine, set the glass down, and said, 'Strange guy.' He was beginning to slur words with an 's' in them, Brunetti noticed.

Nino looked at his watch and said, '*Gesù,* if I'm not back at work in ten minutes my boss will kill me.' He held up his glass and asked, 'How much do I owe you, Ruggiero?'

Brunetti placed a restraining hand on Nino's arm and said, 'This is mine, *signori.*'

He took a twenty-euro note from his wallet and set it on the bar, then waved away the barman's attempt to give him change. He looked at his watch, saw that it was after five, and said, 'If I'm not back at work in ten minutes, my boss will kill me, too.'

19

Brunetti knew it was an exaggeration to say that Patta would kill him, but it was not an exaggeration to say that he would view Brunetti's dismissal — reason left undefined — with some relief, for it would remove the major goad in his existence. After which, Brunetti had the fairness to admit, Patta would probably regret his absence. Like any couple that had chugged along for years, he and Patta had developed a way to deal with one another and had learned the precise limits of the acceptable. More importantly, each had learned how to use the skills or contacts of the other for his own purposes. It might not be a recipe for a happy marriage, but Brunetti suspected that many married people would recognize the template.

He got back to the Questura before six and decided that he would wait for Rizzardi's call. He left the door to his office open

so that he would be seen, busy at his desk, should Lieutenant Scarpa pass by, as he often did, especially late in the afternoon. Brunetti read through and initialled some files, went and looked out of his window, then returned to the files, storing their content in abbreviated form in some far reach of his memory that he could sometimes access, sometimes not.

Brunetti's thoughts passed to what the men had said about the effect of drinking on Cavanis' memory. Things came and went, carried on and then carried off on waves of alcohol.

Something 'that was going to change his luck'. Well, his luck certainly had changed, but not in the way Cavanis had hoped or could have imagined. The night of *acqua alta,* which was Saturday. Brunetti remembered only finishing dinner — with no memory of what it had been — and going into the living room to lie comatose on the sofa. He thought they had watched television, but then Paola had changed to something he didn't want to watch, and he had abandoned her and gone to bed.

He turned on his computer, only to ignore it and dial Signorina Elettra's number. When there was no answer, he returned to the computer and sent her an email, asking

her to contact the local television station and ask for a list of the programmes shown on Saturday evening: if possible, to send copies of the programmes themselves, something he thought could be done by means of the computer.

Then he called Griffoni on her *telefonino.* She had already heard about Cavanis, and Brunetti spent some time telling her about the circumstances of his death and the conversation with the men in the bar. He explained that he'd requested the information from the television station and asked if she'd be willing to spend a few hours the next day watching the programmes with him: she might notice something he did not.

'Local television?' she asked. 'An entire evening of it?' She breathed heavily a few times and then said, 'All right, I'll do it, but I expect your first grandchild to be named Claudia.' Then, voice suddenly serious, she asked, 'Anything else?'

'Yes, one thing. I'd like you to go and see Manuela's mother tomorrow and ask if she knew about the sexual violence.'

'If she didn't open the report, then she didn't know,' Griffoni said, surprising Brunetti by how certain she sounded.

'The doctors might have told her.'

'In that case, she would have told you.'

'Perhaps. Or maybe she hoped that if it didn't get talked about, then it hadn't happened.' Brunetti had seen stranger behaviour when parents discovered things they did not want to know about their children.

He gave her as much time as she needed to think about this. He looked out of the window and then at his watch: in a week, it would be even darker at this time, and nothing would improve until springtime.

'All right,' Griffoni conceded, choosing not to argue the point with him, 'I'll talk to her.' Before he could inquire, she added, 'Before movie-time.'

He thanked her and hung up and then, because he had been on the phone, dialled Rizzardi's number. The pathologist answered with his name.

'It's me, Ettore,' Brunetti said. He stopped there, not sure how to ask the doctor if he had done his job.

'As I said, the body is a miracle. Signor Cavanis was proof. He was fifty-four years old, according to his *carta d'identità.* But according to his body, the state it was in, he was at least fifteen years older. He had advanced cirrhosis: I don't know how much longer he would have lived or could have lived. But I don't know, either, how he lived as long as he did. Because of the cirrhosis, blood vessels had grown around his oesophagus, so there was much more bleeding.'

He paused after this, and Brunetti heard a page turning.

'The knife was an ordinary kitchen knife,' the pathologist went on. 'Bocchese has it now to check for fingerprints. He asked me to tell you they'll have them within two days and will run them through the system to see if anyone turns up, but he has to send it out for DNA tests.' Rizzardi paused, but Brunetti knew better than to question Bocchese's work rhythms.

'The person who used it was right-handed,' Rizzardi continued, 'at least the same height as his victim, definitely standing behind him, and was strong enough to drive the blade through the oesophagus. He was stabbed only once and, because of the cirrhosis, more blood vessels were present and enlarged, so the damage was greater. My best guess is that he died some time on Sunday evening.'

Then, changing tack, he added, 'He would have survived no more than a few minutes. He had so much alcohol in his urine — he'd been dead too long for me to get an accurate reading from his blood — that he might not even have been fully conscious of what was happening.'

'Thanks, Ettore,' was all Brunetti could think of to say before he replaced the phone. Suddenly overcome by the awareness of how much of his day he had spent in the company of death, he left the Questura and went home.

Paola had told him that the kids would be out that evening, so Brunetti stayed in the kitchen and told her about the events of the day as she baked slices of *melanzane* in the oven, then fried them with onions and tomatoes to make sauce. He'd told her he wasn't very hungry when he came in, but as he sat and drank a glass of Gewürztraminer and watched her cook, he felt his appetite sharpen, and he suggested she add a second aubergine.

Seeing that it would be some time before dinner was ready, Brunetti said he'd like to go and lie down on the sofa and read for a while, sure in the knowledge that Paola, whose religion was books, would find this a fine and proper thing to do.

He went into the bedroom and retrieved Apollonius of Rhodes, abandoned on his bedside table. What better companions for the darkening evening hours than Jason and the Argonauts? They'd always seemed like pals from *liceo* to Brunetti: no one too serious, no one too adult, all of them out in search of adventure. Before he got to their adventures, however, Brunetti had to read through the expansive genealogies of the characters, major and minor, as well as of the gods and goddesses — the usual cast, the usual weaknesses.

When the genealogies were finished, the women began to wish the soldiers on their way but paused long enough to lament with Jason's mother. And then he read it, 'Would that the dark wave, where the maiden Helle perished . . .' He stopped reading and stared straight ahead. Another drowning girl. His reflections were interrupted by Paola, who came to the door to say that dinner was ready.

'They're so strange, the Greeks,' Brunetti said as he sat down.

He took a few bites of his pasta, nodded in approval, swallowed, and said, 'It's like reading about America in the nineteenth century: so many of them accepted slavery as part of society.'

'And the connection?' Paola asked and set down her fork to sprinkle a bit more cheese on her pasta. It was *pecorino affumicato* and not *parmigiano:* he approved.

'The Greeks saw nothing wrong in going to war over the kidnapping of a woman, yet when a city was conquered, the men were slaughtered, the women enslaved, and no one gave it a thought,' he said.

'Well, no one on the winning side,' Paola said, then added, 'The victors get to write the poetry.'

'I thought that was the history.'

'They write both,' Paola said and got up to get them more pasta.

As they drank their coffee, Paola, holding her cup in the air, asked him with no introduction, 'Do you think she knows?'

Brunetti raised an eyebrow, wanting to make sure he knew what she meant

'This girl. Woman. Manuela. That something's wrong with her.'

Brunetti knew Paola well enough to know how much work she'd put into making the question sound casual. 'Most of the time I think she has no idea,' he answered.

She set down her cup. 'But sometimes?'

'But sometimes her whole face tightens and she looks around, as if she's misplaced something. But then it passes and her face loses all animation.'

Paola picked up both cups and saucers and put them beside the sink. She raised her head and looked out of the window, staring off in the direction of the mountains, invisible now. She stayed that way a long time.

Later, when he was under the covers and reading, he came upon a passage and read it to Paola, about the birds who defended the island of Ares by hurling their pointed wing feathers against the Greeks and wounding 'the left shoulder of goodly Oileus', who 'dropped his hands from his oar at the sudden blow'.

'How very bizarre,' she observed, putting down her book and turning off her light.

Brunetti continued reading until the end of Book Two and then turned off his own light. He feared that his sleep would be troubled, filled with drowning girls, but instead it was peaceful, and he woke to bright sunshine and a sense of optimism.

Brunetti had just finished reading an email from Bocchese when Griffoni knocked on his door and came in. He looked at his watch and saw that it was just after eleven.

'I called her mother at nine and asked if I could stop on my way to work. She said she and Manuela were going to see her mother-in-law, but we could meet on the way.'

'Did you?' Brunetti asked. He didn't know where Griffoni lived, so he had no idea of how convenient it would be for her to get to Santa Maria Mater Domini or to a place between that *campo* and the Contessa's *palazzo.*

'There's a bar near Palazzo Mocenigo: it was the only one I could think of,' Griffoni said. 'We met there and Barbara and I had a coffee, and then I suggested I walk along with them, so that she and I could speak,' she said.

Brunetti noted the use of the first name but said nothing.

'Manuela likes to stop and look in shop windows, so we had the chance to talk. I asked her mother if the doctors had ever told her the full extent of Manuela's injuries.'

Concerned that the use of her first name might have led Griffoni to some sort of all-girls-together delicacy, Brunetti asked, 'Did you ask her explicitly?'

Griffoni's glance was level, and she said, 'I asked her if she'd been told that Manuela very likely had been raped before she went into the water,' she said, then asked, 'Is that sufficiently explicit?'

'Yes,' Brunetti answered. 'What did she say?'

'She said that she might have been told but that, over the years, she's managed to wipe away the memory of the time she spent in the hospital with Manuela.'

'Does she have any idea if her mother-in-

285

law knows about this?'

'I thought to ask,' Griffoni said neutrally. 'She says it's impossible.'

'Why?'

'Because her mother-in-law would have intervened if she'd known.'

Brunetti knew she wasn't finished, so he waited.

'Guido, I don't have kids, so I don't know what it's like to have one of them in a coma. But I believed her when she said she made herself forget it all, and I'd also believe — if you asked me — that even if she had been told at the time, she might not have let herself register what she heard.' After a moment, she added, 'That's all.'

It was only then that Brunetti thought to ask himself if it made any difference whether Manuela's mother had been told or not, had chosen to believe or not.

'Then let's get something to eat before we begin watching television,' he said. He wasn't sure if she was surprised or relieved by his suggestion, saw only that she got to her feet immediately and started towards the door.

While they ate *tramezzini* at the bar down at the bridge, Brunetti told Griffoni what he'd been told by Rizzardi and the little that had been in an email from Bocchese, sent in advance of the final report: 'None of the fingerprints on the knife matches anything on file; the angle of entry suggests the blow was delivered by a person about the same height as the victim, who was 1.75; two more knives like it in the kitchen; lots of DNA traces, but that will take some time to sort out.'

'Do you remember if the doors were double-locked when you went in?'

'No, they weren't, but they lock automatically, so I still needed the keys to open them both. Whoever it was either had the keys, or Cavanis let him in.'

'And our men?' she asked.

'Vianello sent Pucetti and Romani to go door to door to see if anyone noticed anything, but you know the chances of that,' he said.

When Griffoni made no comment, Brunetti sat back and held up his hand. First finger: 'He had keys or Cavanis let him in.' Second finger: 'There was no sign that the apartment had been searched, and I saw that his wallet was still in his back pocket: so we can forget about theft.' Again, Griffoni made no comment, so Brunetti concluded by saying, raising his third finger, 'Either he went there to talk to him and things got out of control, or he went there to kill Cavanis. In that case, he'd take a weapon, I think.'

'Sounds like impulse to me,' Griffoni said.

'There was bread and cheese on a table near the television,' Brunetti said. 'But no knife.'

'*Voilà,*' Griffoni said, but with no sense of pleasure at the fact.

'You're willing to accept that it was a man?' Brunetti asked.

'Women don't use knives,' Griffoni answered, reciting it as though she were Euclid listing another axiom.

Although he agreed with her, Brunetti was curious about the basis for her belief. 'You offering proof of that?'

'Kitchens,' she said laconically.

'Kitchens?'

'The knives are kept in the kitchen, and their husbands pass through there every day, countless times, yet very few of them get stabbed. That's because women don't use knives, and they don't stab people.'

Brunetti toyed with the idea of trying to work this up into a syllogism, but instead he said, 'Shall we go back and look at those programmes?'

Because they had no idea of what they might be looking for, Griffoni and Brunetti had no choice but to watch it all and watch

288

it carefully, even the rerun of *The Robe,* a religious costume meatball that pitted Victor Mature and Richard Burton against Caligula, a fight they were doomed to lose.

Brunetti remembered having seen the film on their old black and white television when he was still a boy, with his father sitting behind him, hooting and laughing at the story and making loud fun of the false piety of the actors while his mother repeatedly asked him to stop mocking her religion. The scene, the one in real life, had ended in tears, and Brunetti had not been able to watch the end of the film.

He watched it now, stony-faced, appalled by the terrible sentimentality, worse acting, and historical nonsense but unable to join in Griffoni's laughter for fear of betraying his mother's memory.

When the last saccharine scene had played itself out, followed by the first in a series of commercials, Griffoni buried her face in her hands and wailed, 'And I thought that was the most wonderful thing I'd ever seen the first time I watched it.'

Brunetti leaned forward and stopped his computer, relieved to see the screen grow black. Signorina Elettra had joined them silently to watch the film and had betrayed her presence only by a series of muffled giggles. Into the silence that followed the darkening of the screen, she said, 'I've never been asked to authorize extra pay for life-threatening service, but I think we all deserve it.'

They talked for a while, then decided to watch one more hour of the programmes before going home. They watched the news, and he saw the vaguely remembered story about the fire in an apartment in Santa Croce. He glanced aside and saw Griffoni shoving back the sleeve of her jacket to see what time it was. 'Only until the end of the news, then I'll buy you both a drink,' he said.

Griffoni turned and smiled. Signorina Elettra did not, for tedium had turned her into a pillar of salt. Next came the strike of the vaporetto ticket sellers, and then the newly clean-shaven Vittori-Ricciardi described his project, and then it was over and they were free for the day.

It came upon Brunetti to spread his hands and tell them, 'Go in peace', but he resisted the temptation and contented himself with renewing his offer of a drink.

20

It was dark when they left the bar, each of them going in a different direction. Brunetti chose to walk home, hoping that the sight of beauty would cleanse his memory of the dead man and the impoverished life he must have led in that apartment. Had he been talking with Paola, he probably would have made some remark about how much more harmful television was to the brain than alcohol, had he not known that this was not true, having seen too many drunks who proved how much worse alcohol was.

His steps took him towards Campo SS Giovanni e Paolo, but he passed the basilica without stopping to go in. Down the bridge into Giacinto Gallina: another bridge, another one and there on the left was the back of the Chiesa dei Miracoli. He crossed the fourth bridge so that he could walk along its side, letting the alabaster walls soothe his spirit. He stopped in the tiny *campo* and studied the façade. He'd once heard of a singer who boasted that her high notes were higher than anyone else's: the church was more perfect than any other perfect church.

His spirit was at peace by the time he reached home. Paola was happy for his kiss of greeting and the children pleased to have his full attention during dinner. As he ate his bean soup, knowing there was only lasagne to come, he wondered why this wasn't enough for so many people. Why did they have to have more? his innocent self asked. No sooner had the thought come than a more mature voice told him not to ask such stupid questions.

Later, when Paola came back to place the deep dish of lasagne on the table, Brunetti looked at her, looked at his children, and said, 'How happy this makes me.' His family smiled their agreement, thinking he meant the food, but it was the last thing on Brunetti's mind at that moment.

After dinner, he continued with Apollonius, who finally approached the story of Jason and Medea. The myth had upset Brunetti from the first time he read it. It was Euripides he'd read then with such chilling effect, when still little more than a boy and reading it in Italian, not yet able to attempt the Greek. He recalled how frightened he had been of Medea's rage as it soared up from every page: 'Hate is a bottomless pit; I will pour and pour.' 'Stronger than lover's love is lover's hate.' Her voice had struck some chord in him; he'd known these things were true, though he had never seen them — not yet — in action. How often, later on, had he heard these confessions in his professional life? Medea had confessed, in a way: 'I know what evil I am about to do, but even my realization of what will come after cannot stop my rage.'

By a conscious act of will, he set the book aside before Jason arrived in Colchis. Not tonight. Not with the memory of Manuela still fresh and not with tomorrow promising to be a day spent examining the life and death of Pietro Cavanis.

When he reached the Questura the next morning, Brunetti called Bocchese to ask when he could check Cavanis' *telefonino* for numbers called and calls received, only to be told that the technicians had not yet checked it for fingerprints, but that should take only a few hours. Brunetti called Griffoni and told her it was movie time again, though it was only a bit after nine.

Together, they spent two hours watching

— to no purpose they could fathom — the last of the programmes from the local television station. As if to counteract the cloying sweetness of *The Robe,* the evening's viewing had closed with a discussion of the problems facing the city. Did people in other cities spend all their time talking about their city? he wondered.

Present were two former mayors, one who fell and one who was pushed. Along with them were a member of the Centre Right, a representative of the Lega Nord, and, no doubt in an attempt to ensure that at least one of the panel would not become violently abusive, a female journalist from the *Corriere del Veneto.*

The presenter asked the politician from the Centre Right party to begin by outlining what he thought were the chief problems facing the city. That was the last time one person spoke alone, for no sooner had the politician begun his answer than he was interrupted by one of the former mayors, who was in his turn interrupted by the man from the Lega Nord, which left the other mayor no choice but to interrupt with his own vision of reality.

Brunetti lowered the volume until they were reduced to whispering, then inaudible — though violently agitated — heads: Francis Bacon might have painted them. The journalist brushed the hair back from her forehead, raised her hand as if trying to hail a cab, and then accepted reality and pulled a book from her bag and began to read.

'Sensible woman,' Brunetti said and then asked rhetorically, 'Do you think it makes any sense for us to watch more of this?'

'Neither for professional nor personal reasons, I'd say,' Griffoni observed. 'If I were to see more of it or to listen to any of them, I'd probably renounce my right to vote.'

Brunetti pressed a key and the participants and moderator went off to cyberspace, leaving a dark screen behind.

Griffoni sat back in her chair, and Brunetti noticed, as he had so many times in the past, just how long her legs were. 'I remember the first time I went to dinner in London,' she said. 'Everyone at the table was English, except me, and after the first course I realized that only one person spoke at a time. When that person finished, someone else said something, and everyone waited until he or she was finished before commenting. Individually.' She smiled, then laughed, at the memory.

'At first I thought they were rehearsing a play or perhaps it was some sort of English party game, but then I realized that this is the way they behave.'

'They wait in queues, too,' Brunetti added.

They allowed the moment to pass in reverent silence and Brunetti said, 'I've been thinking about Cavanis and what we need to know. Who his friends are. Or his enemies. Bocchese will be finished with the *telefonino* in a few hours, and we can check the numbers in the memory and the numbers he'd called recently.'

She nodded in agreement and added, pointing to the screen of the computer on which they had watched the programmes, 'Aside from Victor Mature's flapping nostrils as he accepted the robe, I didn't see anything in those programmes that was interesting, and certainly nothing I could construe as a reason for what happened to him.'

Brunetti checked the time and raised his eyebrows when he saw that it was not yet noon, so endless had the programme seemed.

'I'd like to go over and talk to the man in the bar again,' Brunetti said. 'With Vianello,' he added.

She couldn't disguise her reaction to the Inspector's name, but Brunetti didn't know whether she was offended or surprised.

'It's that kind of bar,' he said in explanation. 'If we walked in together . . .'

'Whereas with Vianello there'll be the glue of testosterone,' she said.

'Exactly.'

She snorted and gave a huff of exasperated acquiescence. 'It's a good thing Manuela's horse is a female or they probably wouldn't let me ride her,' she said.

'Have you?' asked a surprised Brunetti.

'No. This weekend. I'm not on duty, so I'm going out there.'

'Do you miss it?' Brunetti asked.

'Riding?'

'Yes.'

'Would you miss breathing?' she asked.

He called Vianello and arranged to meet at the front door of the bar, then called Foa and asked him to take them over to Rio Marin. The same man was behind the bar and nodded to Brunetti in recognition, then meted out a brief nod to Vianello. They both asked for white wine, which Brunetti didn't much want. The barman poured them without giving in to his evident curiosity.

Brunetti smiled and said, 'I've a few more questions.'

'I've been reading the papers and people in the neighbourhood have been talking about it,' the barman told him.

'They probably make more sense than the reports in the paper,' Vianello said, a comment the barman met with a smile. 'No one from the papers called to ask us for information, and we're the police.'

Brunetti, who had seen a photo of the façade of the apartment in that day's paper, said, 'They must have sent someone over here; that's for sure.'

'Only a photographer, but all he did was take a picture of the house. No one bothered to come in to ask questions.' His displeasure at this injustice was clear.

'Well, we have some,' Vianello said with an amiable smile as he took a small sip of wine.

The barman leaned closer to him.

'Was he a regular customer?' Vianello broke the silence by asking.

The barman grinned. 'Couple of times a day. He came in for coffee about noon and stayed to have a few glasses of wine.'

'Breakfast?' Vianello asked in a knowing way and smiled.

The barman smiled back. 'I suppose you could call it that. Sometimes he'd come back here about four and have another coffee and some more wine.'

Vianello nodded as if this were an entirely normal way for a man to spend his day, as it might well be for some of the barman's clients.

'Once in a while he'd come in about eight for a drink, wait for friends, have a few glasses of wine, then maybe have dinner or keep drinking until he went home.'

'Anyone particular he drank with?' Brunetti asked.

The barman shrugged but didn't answer at first, almost as if he were bound by his sense of professional ethics from discussing a client. Finally he said, but grudgingly, 'Stefano dalla Lana, though he doesn't drink much.' It did not sound like a criticism, but it was hardly meant as a compliment. 'He's a teacher,' he added, as if in exoneration.

While neither Brunetti nor the barman was paying attention to him, Vianello had taken out a notebook and pen. He asked the barman, 'Do you know his address?'

The man gave Vianello a strange look, as if he'd suddenly found himself in a trap he hadn't seen and didn't know how to get out of. 'He lives in San Giacomo dell'Orio, above the ex-Billa,' he said, adding, 'It's still a supermarket, but it has a different name now.' Then, without being asked, he opened a drawer and rooted around in it until he found a much-folded piece of paper and read dalla Lana's telephone number from it.

'Thanks,' Vianello said and shoved his notebook aside, at the sight of which the man's expression relaxed slightly.

'You said Cavanis told you he'd remembered something,' Brunetti began. The barman nodded. 'Did he say anything else about it?'

The barman considered the question and picked up another glass. While he wiped it dry, he said, 'And his luck was going to change. But,' he added with a bittersweet smile that affirmed the vanity of human wishes, 'his luck always was.'

Recalling the keys to the apartment, Brunetti asked, 'Did many people come to get his keys?'

The barman laughed. 'I think Pietro did that for effect, so he could play the vagabond with people. In the last year or so, you're the only one who's come.'

'Did he work?' Brunetti asked, aware that his professional responsibility was to check other possible motives for Cavanis' murder and not only his long-ago act of courage.

'Years ago. He was a baker, worked for that guy in Ruga degli Orefici. They closed last year; take-away food there now.'

'Did he retire? Or quit?'

'No, he had a bad liver, so he had to stop working and take his pension early; couple of years ago. That's what he was living on.'

Vianello put on his slyest expression and asked, 'A real liver problem, or one he and his doctor agreed on?'

'No, no, Pietro liked his job, liked the people there. It was real; all the men in his family got sick: they've all been drinkers.' A thoughtful expression crossed his face and he said, 'He wasn't a bad person; he was never a bad drunk, never loud. Or violent. I don't know how much pension he could have had. Not much. But he was generous with his friends, and he never said bad things about anyone.'

'Sounds as if you liked him,' Vianello said.

'Of course I liked him,' the man said with real feeling. 'You do this job long enough, you learn a lot about people. Some drunks are mean; some are nice people. Pietro was one of those; there was no way he could stop. It would have kil . . .' he began but was unable to finish the sentence.

He reached into the now-cold water in the sink in front of him and pulled out a glass. He took a fresh towel from a drawer and began slowly to wipe the glass. Turning and turning it, he asked Vianello, 'Was it very bad?'

Vianello and Brunetti exchanged a brief glance. Neither spoke, each waiting for the other to do it.

Finally, Brunetti said, 'It was fast.'

Without a word, the barman set the glass on the shelf behind him.

21

Brunetti had sent Foa back to the Questura; now, because San Giacomo dell'Orio wasn't very far from where they were, they decided to pass by the home of this Stefano dalla Lana. Chatting easily and paying no attention to where they were going, they made their way effortlessly to the large *campo,* so different now from what it had been when both of them had begun their police careers. Officers had patrolled it only in pairs then, when it was notorious as a centre for drug dealing, a place where the garbage men routinely complained about the number of used syringes on the pavement every morning. Gentrification had only just begun, but the signs were already evident: a new bar, tables still set outside, and inside everything slick and linear; a good restaurant just over the bridge towards Rialto; and the final proof for local residents of what was coming: three separate buildings wrapped in scaffolding.

'I was down in Santa Giustina a few days ago to meet a friend for a drink,' Vianello said with no introduction. 'Man who runs the bar's closing. They doubled his rent. Same with the guy who sells antiques.' They walked another minute and then the Inspector exclaimed, half angry, half astonished, 'Santa Giustina, for God's sake. Who'd live down there?'

'Foreigners, probably,' Brunetti said as they came into the *campo.* They started to circle around the apse of the church and saw a tall, grey-haired man approaching them. 'Are you the police?' he asked as he drew near. It was a deep voice, speaking Italian clearly but with the give-away Venetian sibilance.

'Yes,' Brunetti said.

'I'm Stefano dalla Lana,' he said but did not extend his hand. 'Ruggiero at the bar called and said you wanted to talk to me and would probably come to find me.' Then, before either of them could ask, he added, 'I thought it would be better to meet you here. My wife's a very nervous person: it would upset her if the police came to the house.' He pointed to one of the benches placed under the trees.

'Of course,' Brunetti said. 'I'm sorry about

your wife.'

'Oh, it's all right,' he said. 'It's just that bad news bothers her more than it should.'

He led them to a bench and sat in the middle, leaving room for them on either side. 'What was it you wanted to know?' dalla Lana asked. He had deep brown eyes from the sides of which radiated the lines that years of strain had left behind.

'We heard that you were a friend of Pietro Cavanis,' Brunetti began.

Though he must have known this was their reason for coming, his face tightened when he heard his friend's name. He looked away, towards the church, and when he looked back at Brunetti, his eyes had grown moist. 'I'd known him all my life. We went to school together,' he said, then began to examine the roots of the tree, resting his elbow on his knee and cupping his hand over his forehead to hide his eyes.

Brunetti let the silence do what it wanted, stay as long as it pleased. A dog ran past, followed by two children, one of them on a scooter.

Dalla Lana looked up. 'Excuse me, please. I still can't get used to it.'

'That he's gone?' Brunetti said.

'I wish it were only that,' dalla Lana said with a sad smile. 'That he'd moved away or gone somewhere for a while. But that he's dead . . .' He broke off and pressed the same hand over his mouth. He shook his head repeatedly, as if the energy of that would be enough to change things.

Knowing that it was not, Brunetti waited a moment and then said, 'The man in the bar told us that Signor Cavanis had been talking about a change in his life that was about to happen. Did he say anything about this to you?' When dalla Lana did not respond, Brunetti continued, 'Since you were his best friend — I wondered if he'd told you about it.'

Dalla Lana grasped his hands together and leaned forward to shove them down between his knees, then in that posture studied the pavement. 'In school, we were the two dreamers. Pietro wanted to do something big in life: become a doctor and cure some terrible disease; become an engineer and invent something that would make life easier; or go into politics and make a difference to people's lives.'

'What did you dream?' Brunetti asked.

Dalla Lana looked at him quickly, as if no one had ever asked him this question. 'I wanted to write poetry.'

'And what happened?' Brunetti asked.

Dalla Lana shook his head again, started

306

to speak but stopped, took a long breath and said, 'Pietro was enrolled at the university to study engineering, but that summer his father died and he had to try to find work.'

'As a baker?'

'How did you know that?' he asked, not attempting to hide his surprise.

'The man in the bar told me.'

'Did he tell you about his father?'

'Only that he died,' Brunetti said, giving half of the truth. 'He said that your friend had to stop working some years ago.'

'His liver.'

'That's what he said.'

'It's what killed his father,' dalla Lana explained, then went on. 'The owner offered him his father's job. It was the only thing he could find. His mother had never worked, and his father's pension wasn't very big.'

'I see,' Brunetti said.

'He had no choice,' dalla Lana said, then, after a long time, 'Bakers have to drink a lot because of the heat and because of the strange hours. That's how it started. But it didn't change him, not really. He was still a dreamer, even till the end. The last time we spoke, he was . . . well, he was dreaming.'

'What do you mean?'

'He called once last week, but I couldn't

answer because I was in class, and then I forgot to call him back. Then he called me again on Saturday night. It was late, and he was drunk. He usually didn't call me when he'd been drinking, but this time he couldn't stop talking. He said he'd found a way to pay me back.'

He saw their failure to understand and said, 'Over the years, I've helped him when I could. Never anything big. To help him pay a bill. Or for the rent.' Seeing their faces, he said quickly, 'That was only once. And it wasn't very much.' He looked down again, as if embarrassed.

'What else did he say?' Brunetti asked softly.

Head still lowered, dalla Lana sighed deeply. 'I didn't understand a lot of what he said. About always being in debt to me.'

He looked up at Brunetti, then at Vianello, then back to Brunetti. 'I didn't want it back. I never asked, never said anything. I wanted to help him. He was my friend.'

Neither Brunetti nor Vianello spoke, and after a time dalla Lana went on. 'He said he saw what would get the money, then he said something about television, but he wasn't making sense. I didn't understand him. I still don't. He said he did one good thing in his life, and now he'd do another because he remembered something, and everything would be all right.'

Dalla Lana stopped and looked back and forth between the two men again.

'Did he tell you what he remembered?'

'No.' Suddenly his mouth contracted in pain and he said, 'I told him to go to sleep and call me the next day. I don't think he understood, but he hung up. And the next I knew, he was dead.' Then, before Brunetti could ask if Cavanis had called again, dalla Lana said, 'When he didn't call, I figured he'd forgotten all about it.'

Out of simple curiosity and to draw dalla Lana away from the thought of his friend's death, Brunetti asked, 'And the poetry?'

'I don't have the talent,' he said, as though Brunetti had asked him the time and he'd said he wasn't wearing a watch.

The three men sat silent after that until Vianello asked, 'If you don't mind telling me, why did you remain such good friends all these years?'

Dalla Lana moved restlessly at that, pulled his jacket tighter around him, making Brunetti conscious that the day had suddenly lost what little warmth it had had. Dalla Lana got to his feet and ran his curved palm up and down the trunk of one of the trees a few times. Then he came back to the bench and looked at them. 'Because he was brave and decent and worked hard when he had a job, until his health betrayed him. And because he read my poetry all these years and told me how good it was, how much it moved him.'

He kicked an empty cigarette packet away. 'Is there anything else you'd like to know, gentlemen?'

Brunetti got to his feet and took dalla Lana's hand. 'No, thank you. You've told us a great deal.'

Vianello stepped up and offered his hand. 'Thank you. I'm sorry for your friend.'

Dalla Lana said goodbye and turned to walk back to where the Billa had been before gentrification had discovered Campo San Giacomo dell'Orio.

22

They stopped on the way to the vaporetto and had a few *tramezzini,* but they were so filled with mayonnaise that they left Brunetti feeling stuffed but not satisfied. As they headed for the stop at Riva di Biasio, he pulled out his *telefonino* and called Signorina Elettra. He'd had enough of going by the official route, so he gave her Cavanis' *telefonino* number and asked if she could somehow obtain a list of the numbers he'd phoned, starting on the Monday before he died.

' "Somehow obtain",' she repeated. 'How elegant, Commissario. Yes, I'm sure I can obtain them. Somehow.' She paused and then asked, 'Is there any need for haste?'

'As in: is there time to wait for a magistrate to authorize the search?' he asked.

'Yes.'

'No.'

'Ah,' she said, dragging out the sound

311

while she, no doubt, considered methods. 'Are you coming back to the Questura?'

'Yes, we're on the way now.'

'I'll have the numbers for you when you get here.'

He and Vianello had fallen into step, and as he walked, Brunetti repeated, silently, 'I do not want to *know*, I do not want to *know*', coming down hard with the step that synchronized with the last word of the phrase. To Vianello, he said, 'She'll have the numbers he called for us when we get there.'

Vianello turned to look at Brunetti and smiled. 'When they fire us all, I wonder if we'll still be eligible for pensions.'

When they arrived half an hour later, they went directly to Signorina Elettra's office. She greeted them with evident pleasure and handed Brunetti a sheet of paper. He took it but kept his thoughts to himself. On it were listed only three phone calls. On Monday and Saturday, Cavanis had called a number belonging to Stefano dalla Lana: the first call went unanswered; the next one, made at 11.11 on Saturday evening, lasted eight minutes. The final call, made at 11.22, was a wrong number, made to the office of the Fine Arts Commission. This call lasted six seconds.

'Too drunk to dial,' Vianello said.

'Strange that he didn't try again with the right number,' Brunetti said.

'Drunks are strange,' Vianello observed.

'He didn't make any calls the day he was killed,' Brunetti said, holding up the paper for both of them to see.

Less than twenty-four hours later, however, Cavanis was lying dead on the floor of his apartment. Brunetti had little faith in coincidence, especially regarding a man who claimed he was going to change his luck and suddenly have lots of money. If there was any truth in what he had said to dalla Lana, he had made no attempt to pursue it, at least not that night and not with his *telefonino*. And then he had been murdered. 'Is there a public phone anywhere near his home?' he surprised Signorina Elettra by asking.

She and Vianello were silent, and Brunetti watched their faces as they tried to picture the *calli* and *campi* in that area of Santa Croce. After a moment Vianello said, 'They're almost all gone, aren't they?'

Signorina Elettra held up her hand in a waiter-hailing gesture. 'Telecom must have a map of where their phones still are,' she said, looking at her computer as though it were the taxi she had hailed and she were impatient to climb into it.

'And then what?' Brunetti asked.

'If I find a map, I'll send one of the uniformed men to get the serial numbers of the phones. With that, it should be easy to find the numbers called from the phones.'

'Ah,' Brunetti whispered, then 'find', as though he were marvelling at some archaic magical formula.

He returned his thoughts to the call that Cavanis might not have wanted to make on his *telefonino,* but it was impossible to enter into the alcoholic mind. Perhaps not reaching the number he wanted had jolted Cavanis into momentary sobriety. Or by the morning he might have realized that he should not use his own phone for the call he wanted to make.

'We'll leave you to look for the map,' Brunetti said, having thought of another possibility.

Before they could leave, however, Signorina Elettra said, 'I found the name of Manuela's family doctor in the medical report you left with me, but he retired soon after the incident and died about five years ago.' Another dead end. Brunetti thanked her, and they left. Outside, they separated, Brunetti to go down to talk to Bocchese, and Vianello back to the squad room.

When Brunetti reached the laboratory

where Bocchese worked, he knocked on the door, didn't bother to wait, and entered. The technician looked up, then returned his attention to a *telefonino* that he appeared to be in the process of reassembling.

'Is that Cavanis'?' Brunetti said before he could stop himself.

'No,' Bocchese answered, then added, 'You can have his phone now.'

Feeling some satisfaction at being able to tell him, Brunetti said, 'We've already got the numbers he called.'

The technician nodded in approval and said, 'She's good,' then picked up a small screwdriver and placed the tip inside the exposed viscera of the phone. He turned it, removed it, put the tip back inside and turned it again. The phone rang, a normal ring like the one made by most landlines. The technician pushed a key, and the noise stopped.

'What are you doing?'

'Fixing the ring signal,' Bocchese said.

'Isn't there an easier way to do that?' Brunetti, a techno Neanderthal, asked.

'Yes. But I dropped it and it wouldn't work. So the only thing to do was fix it by re-establishing the contacts.'

'I see,' Brunetti said, quite as if he understood what Bocchese meant. He counted six long beats before he said, 'Have you finished with the things from Cavanis' apartment?'

'About an hour ago,' Bocchese said, tapping a number into the keyboard of his phone.

An instant later, Brunetti's phone rang, and he reached into his pocket to answer it but removed his hand when he saw Bocchese's face.

'Very funny. Very funny,' Brunetti said in a sour voice, unwilling to reveal his amusement at Bocchese's trick. 'Can I have a look?'

Bocchese pointed with his chin towards a table at the back of the lab, its surface covered with many small items. 'Be my guest,' he said, slipping the back cover of his *telefonino* back on, and starting to insert the tiny screws that held the front in place.

Brunetti walked over to the table and circled it, looking down at the objects exposed on the surface. He recognized some of them. There was a toothbrush, bristles tormented to all four sides, a tube of toothpaste that had been squeezed so tightly that Brunetti would not have been surprised to hear it weep. The meagre contents of the medicine cabinet were laid out in a paltry line. He recognized the bar of kitchen soap.

Further along were pieces of orange peel and a plastic container that had once held food that itself had contained an inordinate amount of tomato sauce. Next to this was a can that had once held tuna fish and two empty two-litre wine bottles.

Flattened on the table were four pieces of paper and two plastic phonecards, both the worse for wear and no doubt discarded because the time on them had been used up. 'All right to touch these things?' Brunetti called over to the technician, who was now talking on his phone. Bocchese nodded and waved his hand, concentrating on his conversation.

Brunetti took out his notebook and set it on the table next to the cards and carefully copied out the long serial number on each card. Big Brother was not only watching us, he reflected; he was also able to trace any call that had been made using these cards.

He turned his attention to the scraps of paper. One was a flyer announcing the appointment of a new pastor to the parish of San Zan Degolà. Another was a wadded tissue which the technicians had decided not to open, and two more were receipts from shops.

Brunetti turned the receipts over; on the back of the second one he saw the familiar

52, the initial digits of a local phone number, followed by five more. He pulled out his phone and dialled the number.

'Soprintendenza di Belle Arti,' a woman's voice answered after six rings. Brunetti ended the call without bothering to speak. So Cavanis had dialled the number he had written down, but why call the Belle Arti? Anyone's guess. Only a fool — or a drunk — would call a city office at eleven at night. Or, for that matter, his cynic's voice added, at eleven in the morning. He thanked Bocchese and said he'd come back to see him if anything ever went wrong with his own phone.

'Most people just throw them away,' the technician said with audible disapproval.

Brunetti nodded and went up to Signorina Elettra's office. She was not there, so he carefully copied the numbers of the phone-cards on a sheet of paper and wrote a note asking her to find the numbers called using both. When he got back to his office, he took out his phone and dialled the number for dalla Lana that Vianello had given him. Because dalla Lana was a teacher, Brunetti was prepared to leave a message, but dalla Lana answered with his name.

'Signor dalla Lana, this is Commissario

Brunetti. There's one thing I forgot to ask you.'

'What's that?' dalla Lana asked in a tired, patient voice.

'Did your friend say anything recently about the Soprintendenza di Belle Arti?'

'I don't understand your question, Commissario,' dalla Lana said, sounding confused. 'What could Pietro have had to do with them?'

'He had their phone number in his home, and he called it after he spoke to you the other night.'

'Saturday?'

'Yes.'

'What would he want with them?' dalla Lana asked. 'At that hour?'

'I've no idea,' Brunetti admitted. 'You're sure he never mentioned them to you?'

'No. Never.' Then, after a moment, dalla Lana added, 'He was very drunk when I spoke to him, Commissario, not really coherent.' Dalla Lana was simply stating a fact and making no attempt to draw conclusions from that.

'Do you know who his other friends were?' Brunetti asked, adding, 'I should have asked you that earlier.'

'There are the men at the bar,' dalla Lana said after a pause, 'but I'm not sure they were really friends. I don't think Pietro saw them anywhere else. And I never met any other friends; I don't know if he had any.'

What did Cavanis do all day? Brunetti asked himself. He visited a bar a few times, watched television, and drank. Is this what's left of life after retirement? Six hundred euros a month didn't permit much else, he had to remember. But still.

'Did he ever mention an incident in Campo San Boldo, when he saved a girl's life?' Brunetti asked.

'Yes, he told me about it when it happened, but he said it wasn't important. He said he dived in and pulled her out without thinking about it.' There was a long silence. 'In fact, he laughed about it, said he was so drunk when it happened that he was lucky he didn't drown himself.'

'Is that all he remembered?' Brunetti asked.

'As far as I know, yes. It's all he ever told me about it, at any rate.'

'Thank you, Signor dalla Lana,' Brunetti said and then, hoping that hearing a compliment for his friend would somehow comfort him, added, 'It was a very brave thing for him to do.'

'Yes,' dalla Lana said and broke the connection.

If Cavanis had told his best friend no more than this about the incident at San Boldo, that would be the end of that. Or it would be, were it not that Cavanis had also said he'd remembered something that was going to make him a lot of money and shortly afterwards had been found lying dead on the floor of his apartment, a knife driven into his neck.

Brunetti found himself thinking of Dante's belief that heresy was a form of intellectual stubbornness, the refusal to abandon a mistaken idea. In Dante's case, this path led to eternal damnation; in his own case, Brunetti reflected, intellectual stubbornness might well be leading him deep into the Dark Wood of Error. Saving part of Manuela from the waters of the canal was hardly the only thing Cavanis had done in his life; it need not have been the cause of his death. Drunks are reckless, thoughtless, rash. They drive off the road or into walls, they start fights they know they cannot win, and they say things that cannot be forgiven or forgotten. They menace and they brag, and very often they push people too hard or too far. Nothing linked his murder to the incident with Manuela Lando-Continui. Nothing linked his murder to anything save Brunetti's own suspicions. This was real life, random and messy and uncontrolled.

His phone rang. He answered with his name.

'Get down here,' came the unconfoundable voice of his superior.

'*Sì, Dottore,*' Brunetti said and got to his feet.

Signorina Elettra was still not at her desk, thus he went into the lion's den with no advance warning and no way to prepare his excuses and prevarications. Even before Brunetti was halfway across the room, Patta demanded, 'Did you put her up to this?'

Patta's wife? Signorina Elettra? Contessa Lando-Continui? Brunetti kept his face motionless.

'I'm afraid I don't know what you're talking about, Vice-Questore,' Brunetti said, for once telling Patta the simple truth.

'This email,' Patta said, slamming his palm down on some sheets of paper at the centre of his desk. 'From the Assistant to the Minister of the Interior, for God's sake. Do you know what this can do to my career?'

'I must repeat, Vice-Questore, that I know nothing about any email sent to you.' He looked Patta in the eye when he said this, hoping that the tactic he used when he lied to his superior would prove equally effective when he told the truth.

'Don't lie to me, Brunetti,' Patta said.

'I'm not lying, Dottore,' Brunetti answered. 'I know nothing about that,' he said, daring to point at the papers in front of his superior.

'Read it before you say that, Brunetti,' Patta said in an ugly voice, slamming his palm flat on the papers again and shoving them in Brunetti's direction.

Once Patta had removed his hand, Brunetti picked up the papers and held them at the correct distance. The cover page bore the letterhead of the Ministry of the Interior. Brunetti reached into the inside pocket of his jacket and took out his glasses. One-handedly he shook them open and put them on. The address jumped into clear focus, as did the text.

Worthy Dottor Patta,

Please note that the Ministry has been informed of — and is about to initiate an investigation of — certain grave irregularities in a number of ongoing investigations currently being conducted by the Questura di Venezia. These irregularities include — but are not limited to:

1. The unauthorized investigation into the

bank records of private citizens and certain public and private organizations.

2. Similarly unauthorized searches of public documents and records.

3. Acquisition and perusal of state documents or reserved information by unauthorized persons or civilian employees.

4. Similar behaviour regarding the reserved medical records of certain individuals.

5. A persistent and deliberate attempt to disguise these actions.

The Ministry expects, by the 14th of the current month, a full and detailed report of any facts bearing upon these irregularities and a list of the persons responsible for these violations as well as an accurate account of the precise nature of their involvement in each.

Attached please find a list of the statute numbers, as well as dates of passage, of the laws being violated by these activities.

The email was signed — there was no polite closing phrase — by someone named Eugenia Viscardi, whose title was 'Assistant to the Minister' and whose illegible signature was placed above her printed name.

Brunetti finished reading, barely glanced at the second page, which contained the relevant numbers of the statutes involved as well as their dates of enactment. He removed his glasses and slipped them back into his pocket. With a gesture that showed just how difficult it was for him to disguise his contempt, Brunetti let the papers fall back on Patta's desk.

'And you believed this, Dottore?' Brunetti asked, making his astonishment audible. 'This?' he repeated, waving a hand at the papers that now lay supine on his superior's desk.

'Of course I believed it,' Patta all but shouted. 'And I believe it. It's from the Ministry of the Interior, for God's sake.'

'Is it?' Brunetti asked lightly, having decided that this scene would be better played as farce than as tragedy. 'Why do you believe that?'

Patta reached over and pulled the papers to him. He lifted them, checked the address of the sender and pounded his forefinger repeatedly upon the letterhead above it: Ministry of the Interior, sure enough.

'Well, that's a credit to the person who sent it, I suppose,' Brunetti said. Should he play this as a scene from Oscar Wilde or from Pirandello? Then, in a much firmer voice, he said, 'May I suggest that, to save ourselves time and effort, and possibly embarrassment, we do one simple thing?'

Caught off balance, Patta asked, 'What?'

'See if there is a Eugenia Viscardi working

325

in the office of the Minister of the Interior.'

'Don't be an idiot, Brunetti. Of course there is.' For emphasis, Patta gave the papers another tap, this time with the back of his fingers. 'She signed this.'

'Someone signed it, Dottore: I don't question that for a moment. But whether that person is Eugenia Viscardi and whether a woman named Eugenia Viscardi works for the Minister of the Interior, those are different matters entirely.'

'That's impossible,' Patta said in an unnecessarily loud voice.

'Then shall we find out?' Brunetti offered.

'How?'

'By asking the person I fear you believe responsible for these excesses to check to see if this woman actually works there.'

'Signorina Elettra?' Patta asked in a softer voice.

'Yes. For her it's as simple as . . .' The simile failed Brunetti and forced him to change to, 'It's very simple for her.'

Unwilling to be a witness to Patta's uncertainty, Brunetti looked out of the window and noticed that the leaves had begun to drop from the vines that had overgrown the wall surrounding the garden on the other side of the canal.

'Why don't you believe it?' Patta asked in

what passed, with him, for a reasonable voice.

'The vagueness of the accusations, for one thing,' Brunetti answered. 'And the failure to name a single person directly. It's a blanket accusation against the entire Questura. And what's the value of a signature that's only scanned and sent? What legal value or credibility does it have?'

Patta pulled the email back towards himself and read through it again. He sighed and read it all a second time, his finger following the lines of the five specific accusations.

He looked at Brunetti and said, 'Sit down, Commissario.' When Brunetti was seated, Patta said, 'There seemed to be something wrong with it on first reading. A certain . . . lack of clarity, especially in the accusations made. And, of course, the tenuous signature.' Brunetti noticed the shift to the passive voice. Signora Viscardi, Assistant to the Minister of the Interior, whose signature was now tenuous, was no longer credited with having made the accusations. Instead, they had been made, requiring no need to attribute the making of them to a specific person. The gears of a Maserati could not be shifted more easily.

Brunetti sat and watched his superior in

deferential silence, wondering how long it would take before the U-turn was complete and the Vice-Questore would reveal that he had smelled a rat from the beginning.

'I smelled a rat from the beginning, you know,' Patta said. 'I'm glad to see that you share my suspicions.' He smiled at Brunetti as at a valued colleague. He pushed himself back in his chair and folded his arms across his chest. 'Any suggestions?'

'Something like this really leaves us only one thing to do, don't you think, Signore?'

Patta nodded sagely but said nothing.

'Once Signorina Elettra checks to see whether this Viscardi woman exists, that is,' Brunetti said, waving towards the papers that lay between them, as if Signora Viscardi were lying there herself, already half exposed to their exacting vision. 'If she does not, then you two can decide how best to respond to this attack.' He was careful to use the plural and keep himself free from any involvement in that decision.

'Exactly,' Patta confirmed. The Vice-Questore picked up his phone and pressed in some numbers. Both of them could hear the phone ringing in the outer office. One, two and then Patta said, 'Signorina, could you step in here for a moment?'

23

Signorina Elettra, whose reaction to the email was even more sceptical than Brunetti's — and whose comments more acerbic — managed to dispel the Vice-Questore's fears in very little time. When a now-scandalized Patta demanded to know who might have done such a thing as to send him a false threat, she had no suggestions to offer. She did say, however, that she might be able to discover the real source within a few days. Patta was pleased with this, as he always was when another person offered to do something for him.

She and Brunetti left their superior's office together, buoyed up by his pleasant farewells. Once the door was closed, Signorina Elettra told Brunetti that her friend Giorgio was out of contact temporarily, so it would be a few days before she would have the information about the calls made from the phonecards. Before he had time to ask why she did not, for once, use official channels to seek this information, she explained that the normal procedure took a minimum of ten days.

The investigation of Cavanis' death thus slowed down: the fingerprints and DNA left on the murder weapon found no match in police records; no one in the neighbourhood remembered having seen anything unusual near Cavanis' building on the day of the murder; the few men who knew him had heard only vague rumours — passed on from the barman — about his expected turn in fortune.

During this period, a young tourist fell to his death from the *altana* of the apartment he and his girlfriend were renting soon after they were involved in an argument in a restaurant. Police attention was diverted for a few days until it was determined that the argument had been between the two of them and a young Italian who had been too forward in his behaviour towards the young woman; further, the girl had been across the street in a café when her boyfriend fell. Their presence in the apartment, it turned out, had not been registered with the appropriate city office, a violation which led to an investigation of the owners of the apartment, a well-known pharmacist and his wife, who worked in the Land Registry Office.

The police soon discovered that they owned and rented to tourists a total of six apartments, none of the income declared to the authorities. They were also the owners of a boutique twenty-three-room hotel which somehow had prospered in a building invisible to the Land Registry Office and the Guardia di Finanza, notwithstanding the fact that they had managed to obtain electricity, gas, telephone, water, and garbage collection services, and employed eleven people, all of whom were registered with the tax authority and paying their taxes.

The Guardia di Finanza soon relieved the police of the need to concern themselves with the pharmacist and his wife. The newspapers, although growing tired of the couple, failed to return the public eye to the murder on Rio Marin, so Pietro Cavanis was replaced by usurers, seven hundred kilos of cocaine in a truck coming off the ferry from Patras, and a band of Moldavian criminals known to be at work in the Veneto.

Brunetti felt obliged to tell the Contessa that they had made little progress in the investigation of what had happened to her granddaughter and decided to do this in person. To his surprise, he found both Griffoni and Manuela there when he arrived late one afternoon, and was even more surprised to learn that Griffoni occasionally brought Manuela to see her grandmother and stayed to have tea with them before taking Manuela back home.

Brunetti met Griffoni on the ground floor the next day and, as they started up towards their offices, asked her about this. She explained that, since the horse that she was going out to Preganziol to ride still legally belonged to the Contessa, the least she could do to thank her was accompany Manuela once a week when she went to see her grandmother.

'What do you talk about with Manuela?' Brunetti asked.

'Oh, about the people we see on the street, or the shop windows, or the dogs that go by, and how nice it is to have tea with her grandmother.'

'Every week?'

'More or less,' Griffoni said. 'It makes Manuela happy.'

'Seeing you?' Brunetti asked.

'Getting out and being with people, seeing life on the streets. Her mother doesn't get on well with her ex-mother-in-law and doesn't like to go there. This way, with me, Manuela gets to see her grandmother, who's very happy to have her visit,' Griffoni said, having failed to answer his question.

'What about the horse?' he asked, pausing when they arrived at the second floor.

'Oh, I go out once in a while and take her out. Petunia's very sweet.'

'Is that enough for you?' Brunetti asked, not at all sure what he meant but thinking of her silver medal and the sort of horse that would be worth transporting to the Olympics.

'At this time of our lives, it is. Both of us have had time to calm down and take things more easily,' Griffoni said, a remark that reminded Brunetti of how very little he knew about her life beyond the Questura.

'Do you ride her in that field?' he asked.

'The first few times, Enrichetta asked me to, and I did. But then we both got bored, and Enrichetta could see that, so she told me to go out on the paths in the woods.' She smiled at that. 'It's much better.'

'I don't remember any woods there,' Brunetti said.

'Well, there's a plantation where trees are grown to be harvested, and there are paths between the trees,' she said, drawing the trees and the paths with her hands. 'Besides, we're not doing anything fancy, just trotting along and getting to know one another.'

'Like a marriage?' he asked.

'A little bit, yes,' Griffoni laughed, but before she could say anything else, Lieutenant Scarpa approached and stopped at the head of the stairs. Brunetti moved so that Scarpa would not have to pass between them.

'Good afternoon, Commissari,' he said, raising his hand and giving Brunetti an uncharacteristic smile.

'Lieutenant,' they both acknowledged and remained silent until his footsteps had disappeared below them. Griffoni said, 'I'll get back to work,' and turned towards her office, while Brunetti continued towards his own.

That same night the temperature plummeted and it rained: buckets, torrents, floods, cascades. The next morning people waited to leave their homes until they could see that the streets had rejected the thin coating of ice that the rain had left behind. The air had been washed clean, and for the first time in months Brunetti could see the Dolomites from the window of the kitchen.

Brunetti put on his thickest-soled shoes, more suitable for the mountains than for the city, and walked to the corner, where he decided to take the vaporetto, conscious that, for the first time in his life, the idea of falling on the street had influenced his behaviour.

When he arrived at the Questura, the officer at the door told him that Signorina Elettra had asked him to go to her office. No, he replied in response to Brunetti's question, the Vice-Questore had not yet arrived.

He could tell, when he entered her office, that she had something unpleasant to tell him. They exchanged greetings, and Brunetti stepped back to lean against the windowsill. No sun to warm his back today. It was Tuesday, and she had been to the flower market, so her office was ablaze, today with tulips: three, no, four different vases of them and no doubt a few more in Dottor Patta's office.

In a bow to autumn, Signorina Elettra was wearing a deep orange woollen dress, with a dark chrysanthemum-red scarf wrapped closely around her neck. Her hair, usually gleaming chestnut, appeared to have more red highlights today. 'You're not going to like this,' she said, not at all to his surprise.

'What?'

'There are two things, Commissario. It's been a week and Giorgio still hasn't been in touch, and he's the only one I can ask to

335

find the calls made with those cards.' She forestalled his question by saying, 'Yes, I sent an official request, but it'll be at least another week before we get any sort of response.'

Brunetti had the feeling that this news was the lesser evil and said, 'Let's hope Giorgio can find the information sooner.' He smiled to show he was neither angry nor impatient.

She gave an uncharacteristic 'Um' before she said, 'And Dottor Gottardi has looked at all the files concerning Manuela and thinks there's nothing to pursue.' She raised both hands in a sign of surrender.

'And?' Brunetti asked, refusing to permit himself to remark that Dottor Gottardi was not proving to be a compliant magistrate.

'He's read your report about the possible link to Cavanis' murder, and he sees no reason to believe the two cases are related. It's not his case, but he says there's not been much progress.'

'And so?' he asked politely. She hadn't yet said anything he particularly disliked, so the surprise no doubt lay in whatever order the magistrate might have for him.

'And so he's suggested you be put in charge of everything that's emerged after that boy fell from the *altana*.'

'I beg your pardon,' Brunetti said. 'I

thought the Guardia di Finanza had taken it over.'

'That case, yes,' she said. 'But he thinks there should be a separate investigation into the private hotels and bed and breakfast places.' She looked at the keyboard of her computer as she told him this.

Suddenly he remembered a picture from a book he'd read to the kids when they were young: a cat on a branch in a tree, slowly disappearing and leaving behind only his menacing smile. And that thought led him to Scarpa's almost cordial smile as he was coming up the stairs.

'It's Scarpa, isn't it?' he asked.

She looked at the screen of her computer and nodded. 'I'd say so. Probably.'

'How did he manage that?' Brunetti asked, sure she would know.

'Do you know Dottor Gottardi?' she asked.

Brunetti had spoken to the magistrate, who had been there only a few months, but had never worked with him on a case before Manuela's.

'He's from Trento, isn't he?' Brunetti asked.

'Yes.'

'And?'

'And his family is involved in local

politics.'

Why was she telling him this? Who cared about the magistrate's family when the only thing that mattered was that he could be such a fool as to believe anything Scarpa told him.

'His father was mayor of their town for thirty years, and now his older brother is.'

'How did you learn all of this?' Brunetti demanded with more force than he should have used.

'My best friend told me,' she said, patting the top of the computer screen.

That stopped Brunetti. 'What else did your friend tell you?'

'The whole family are Separatists,' she said. 'They want to return to being part of Austria.'

'How does this affect Dottor Gottardi?'

She flicked something invisible from the front of her skirt and said, 'Every one of them is to the right of the Lega Nord, especially on the subject of immigration. So Gottardi's chosen to become the family rebel. Everyone's equal, immigrants and southerners must be treated with respect.'

A soft moan escaped Brunetti as he followed this to the logical conclusion. 'So he's got to fall over backwards to show how he treats them with respect? And that means

338

he feels obliged to pay attention to Scarpa because he's a Sicilian.'

'That's a bit of an exaggeration,' Signorina Elettra suggested.

'But no less true for that,' insisted Brunetti. He cast around for a solution, not only because he thought the investigation of the hotels could easily be handled by the uniformed branch — Pucetti was certainly bright enough to do it — but because he refused to become Scarpa's puppet.

He glanced over and asked if she had a suggestion, and her face showed that she had.

Memory led to inspiration and he said, 'The false email from the Ministry of Justice?'

She smiled and nodded.

'Can you prove it was Scarpa?'

'Perhaps not in any way that would stand up legally, but the original sender was not very well disguised in the mail from Signora Viscardi.' She said this last with infinite contempt. 'It can easily be traced back to the Lieutenant.'

A chess player would no doubt have viewed the situation in terms of pawns and rooks being moved about on the board, bestowing advantage here and there. It was now Brunetti's move, but instead of flirting with two forward and one to the right to take the other knight, he wanted to beat Scarpa's head in with a stick.

'What are our options?' he asked.

She smiled at the plural and gave something that resembled a nod. 'He's pushed me beyond options, I'm afraid,' Signorina Elettra said, sounding not unlike an exasperated kindergarten teacher. The time of soft words had ended. 'I think I'll threaten him.'

'How?'

'I'll tell him I'm going to send the email to the actual Assistant of the Minister, who is a friend of mine, and ask her to have the Minister read it.'

'Is she really a friend?' Brunetti asked, marvelling at how wide her net was spread.

'Of course not.' Then, after a moment, she added, 'But at least she exists, unlike Eugenia Viscardi.'

'What will you tell him?'

'That I'm following the trail of the email to its real source.' Her smile was very broad and equally cold. But then her face grew more sober and she said, 'I can't imagine how he could have been so sloppy.' Was that disappointment he heard in her voice?

'He underestimated you,' Brunetti said, meaning it as a compliment.

'Yes,' she agreed. 'How insulting.'

Abandoning all thought of mincing words, Brunetti asked, 'What will you make him do?'

'Tell Dottor Gottardi that he's given the subject further thought and he's seen that he's been rash, and perhaps it would be wise to continue the investigation into what happened to Manuela.'

'For what reason?'

'To avoid the accusation that, by not considering the possibility that she met with foul play, Dottor Gottardi would be discriminating against a handicapped person.' Brunetti's mind reeled. 'I suspect, however, that Dottor Gottardi would call her "differently abled".'

'Will this work with Scarpa?' he asked, filled with a new appreciation of her many talents.

'To a certain degree,' she said. 'He'll become more cautious, I suppose, though I don't think it will help him in the long run. The Lieutenant is clever enough, but I think it's time he realizes just how outclassed he is.'

'You sound very certain of that,' Brunetti said.

'He's a bully, and like most bullies, he lacks the killer instinct. Once he comes up against someone who isn't afraid of him, he retreats.' Then, with absolute conviction, she said, 'He'll do what I tell him to do.'

'And if not?' Brunetti inquired.

'I'll destroy him.'

24

Signorina Elettra had her way. Lieutenant Scarpa found an opportunity to explain his second thoughts to Dottor Gottardi, and the magistrate in his turn suggested to Brunetti that he resume his investigation of that poor handicapped girl and of the the murder of the man who had saved her. The hotel and bed and breakfast investigation was given to another commissario — luckily, not to Claudia Griffoni who, it was feared, might not be sufficiently aware of the many tangled obligations and relationships that existed between and among those requesting and those granting the permits necessary in this expanding business.

Once the case was back in his charge, however, Brunetti made little progress. Cavanis proved to have had few friends. He had used his *telefonino* rarely and within a narrow scope. Aside from the calls made just before his death, he had recently phoned an aunt in Torino, Stefano dalla Lana, the number which gave the forecast of the time and height of *acqua alta,* and the Giorgione movie theatre. Only the aunt and dalla Lana had phoned him in the last four months.

Brunetti was almost relieved when a Chinese-run and staffed bordello was discovered in Lista di Spagna, not far from the train station, and he was asked by another magistrate to look into it. It was banal, really, but the interviews and the follow-up arrests, which led to more interviews and more arrests, all rose upwards on the feeding chain of organized prostitution in the province.

As this investigation mutated and took up more and more of his time, Brunetti thought less often about the dead man and the horror of the first sight of that knife.

In the second week of November, late in the afternoon of the feast of San Martino, Brunetti left the Questura early, hoping to see the children on the street banging their pots and pans and asking passers-by for coins. He had done the same as a boy, though he had never understood the reason for the custom. That had made no difference to him, happy as he had been then to get the money and happy now to be able to give it away.

He saw three or four groups and gave each of them a few euros, delighting them with his generosity. As he turned into Ruga Rialto, he was surprised to see Griffoni and Manuela approaching him. At first he took them for mother and daughter, walking arm in arm, heads together, talking and laughing. Griffoni smiled to see him, and Manuela politely extended her hand as if she had never met him.

'We've just been to visit the Contessa,' Griffoni explained. Turning to the other woman, she said, 'What's the price on those grey shoes in that window, Manuela? Can you see?'

The window was on the other side of the *calle,* so Manuela had to move away from them to go and have a look. In her absence, Griffoni said, 'I suppose I shouldn't tell you this, but the Contessa keeps asking me if we've learned anything.' She kept her voice entirely neutral; there was no hint of reproach.

'How is she?' Brunetti asked.

'Old and weak,' Griffoni said.

'How often do you go to see her?'

'Not as often as she'd like,' Griffoni said. They were interrupted by a group of five boys, who surrounded them and beat their wooden spoons on the bottoms of their pots, chanting the same song about San Martino that Brunetti had shouted out in his own time. He gave them two euros and off they went to encircle an elderly couple, who seemed as delighted by the noise as Brunetti had been.

Turning back to Griffoni, Brunetti said, 'And the . . .' then caught himself just as he was about to refer to Manuela as 'the girl' and changed it to 'Manuela', but it was awkwardly done, and he was embarrassed.

'She loves to be out and walking and see-ing things,' Griffoni said as Manuela came back to her.

'I didn't see a tag,' she told Griffoni, look-ing back and forth between her and Bru-netti. 'Is that all right?' she asked, and he winced at the vulnerability in her voice.

'Of course it is, *Tesoro,*' Griffoni said, linking her arm in hers. 'If they were stupid enough not to put a price on them, then we're not interested, and that's that.'

Manuela smiled and shook her head. 'They're not for us, are they?'

'Not at all,' Griffoni confirmed and patted her arm. Then, in a grown-up voice, the one used for teaching manners, she said, 'Say goodbye to Dottor Brunetti, Manuela.' After the young woman had dutifully done this,

Griffoni said, careful to address the remark to Manuela, 'Maybe we'll see him again at your grandmother's.'

'That would be very nice,' Manuela said pleasantly, proof of how well she had learned her manners.

Griffoni said a polite goodbye and they started down the *calle,* heading towards Manuela's home.

Perhaps prompted by guilt, Brunetti phoned the Contessa the next day. She said she was glad to hear from him and, if the Commissario had time, would be very grateful if he could come and talk to her. It was she who suggested he join Claudia and Manuela for a light lunch on Wednesday, if he didn't mind coming during the working week.

Having seen how adept Claudia was at handling Manuela, Brunetti had no doubt that she would find a way to leave him alone to talk to the Contessa and so agreed, saying he'd speak to Claudia and come along with them.

When he phoned Griffoni, she suggested that he meet them at one at Campo San Giacomo dell'Orio so that she could take Manuela on a different route. 'She doesn't like change, even simple things like which *calle* to take,' Griffoni explained. 'But if I tell her it's because that's where we have to pick you up, she'll agree.'

Brunetti kept back a remark about how important the training of young ladies still seemed to be, but Griffoni must have interpreted his silence differently because she said, 'She can't learn to do multiplication and division, but she has learned to be considerate of other people's convenience.'

'I'll see you there at one,' Brunetti said and hung up.

Because he had promised to go to Rialto with Paola before lunch, Brunetti left the Questura well before lunchtime on Wednesday and met her there. Heavy dark clouds had appeared in the north in the late morning and got worse while Paola and Brunetti were still at Rialto, trying to decide what to have for dinner that night. Cristina, the fishmonger, suggested a *rombo*, but Paola didn't like the look of it and so asked about the branzino, a variety of fish that had Cristina's enthusiastic approval. 'I thought I'd serve it with artichoke,' Paola said tentatively. 'And black rice with peas.'

'The Findus *primavera* are very good,' was Cristina's sibylline reply as she selected a large fish and handed it to her assistant to clean.

By the time they were finished and stopped at Do Mori for a drink, the first rain had begun to fall. As they stepped out under the rain, Paola asked, 'You still planning to go and see her?'

'Yes.'

'Even in this rain?' she asked, pulling her scarf over her hair and taking a collapsible umbrella from her shopping bag.

'Yes. I said I would.'

'Good.' Paola handed him the umbrella. 'Here, you'll need this.'

'What are you going to do?' he asked.

'Run,' she said and did just that, out of reach before he could react.

There were few people on the streets, so he was spared the usual jostle and umbrella-sparring as people tried to pass in the narrow *calli.* Venetians had had ages to develop the technique of tilting the top to the side of the *calle* and slipping along the walls past the oncoming walker. Tourists had two techniques: either they forged ahead in the face of all human obstacles or they stopped and cowered with their backs against the nearest building, the umbrella extended fully open above them, effectively forcing all traffic into the centre of the street.

It had never occurred to Brunetti to try to cancel the appointment with the Contessa.

He did not want to have the conversation, but that was not sufficient reason not to have it. As he entered the *campo,* he saw Manuela and Griffoni sheltering together under the uncertain protection of the awning of a bar. Griffoni wore something that looked like a man's fishing hat, dark blue and wide-brimmed, perfect to cover her head in the rain; the rest of her was enveloped in a voluminous raincoat that fell below her knees.

He slipped under the awning and gave his hand to Manuela and said hello to both of them. 'Lovely day,' he said, which comment sent Manuela off into delighted peals of laughter.

'But it's raining,' she managed to say and broke out in fresh laughter. When she stopped, she turned to Griffoni and said, 'Your friend is very funny, isn't he?'

'Yes, he is,' Griffoni affirmed and patted Brunetti on the arm. Then as a gust of wind lashed at the awning above them, she said, 'Let's go. Your grandmother's waiting.'

'Will the real lovely day begin when we get there?' Manuela asked.

Griffoni stamped her feet, which were protected by a pair of low rubber boots, and said, 'As soon as the door closes behind us, it will.'

With that they set off, Brunetti taking the lead because he knew the way. He cut to the right without having to think about it, over the bridge, dodged a few tourists and turned back to be sure that the women were close behind him. A long, empty patch lay ahead of them, and he picked up speed, just as the rain picked up energy. Another bridge, another short stretch, quick right and then left, another bridge. To protect his back from the rain, he held his umbrella almost at the horizontal, the shaft resting on his shoulder. He heard an occasional whoop of laughter from behind him.

Two men wearing raincoats approached from the opposite direction. Their umbrellas were lowered against the fierce wind coming straight at them, so all he saw of them were their legs and large, thick shoes. The rain had already soaked the front of their trousers, as it had the backs of his own trousers below his raincoat.

Brunetti tilted his umbrella to the side and was quickly past them, when a perverse gust hit him in the face, soaking him and almost yanking the umbrella from his hands. From behind him, he heard a violent snap as an umbrella was torn inside out. There was a noise and then something slid into the back of his left foot. He turned and saw that an errant gust of wind had blown an eviscerated umbrella into him. One of the men came back towards him to pick up his umbrella but, seeing it was broken, kicked it to the side of the street. The other saw his near his own feet and left it there. Both turned and continued on their way.

Brunetti shoved the umbrella out of the way with his foot, then heard a piercing scream like that of an animal in a trap. Manuela and Griffoni had been behind him. He dropped his umbrella at the sound, turned and started in their direction. He saw Manuela backed up against the window of a shop, hands thrust out in front, face mad with terror. 'No,' she screamed, turning the word into a siren. 'No.' She tried to move away, but all she could do was step up on the narrow stone ledge beneath the window of the grocery store and try to push herself flatter against the window.

And again, 'No!' Like the siren for *acqua alta,* the word grew higher with every second. Griffoni was beside her, holding on to her raised arms. Griffoni's head whipped around and she saw the two men, motionless, hair soaked and their wet faces washed clean of emotion by shock.

'Leave me alone. Don't do that. Please.' Again, Manuela's voice grew shriller with every outburst. Brunetti manoeuvred hurriedly around the men and raised his hands to chest height, patting at them and backing them away from the two women.

'Please. Gentlemen. Move back, please,' he said. Only then did he look at their faces and recognize one as Sandro Vittori-Ricciardi, who stood looking at Manuela as if looking at a portrait of his own crucifixion. The second man seemed confused and pained, unable to make sense of anything. But Vittori-Ricciardi could not control the fear on his face as Manuela continued to scream, now past words and returned to her animal noises.

Brunetti put himself between the two men, taking the arm of each. He swivelled them round and started walking them away from the women. The rain continued to pound down; by now all three men were soaked and hardly noticed it.

Speaking to the man he did not recognize, Brunetti said, 'Signore, I'm a police officer, and I'd like to see your identification.' Brunetti pulled out his wallet and showed his warrant card, but it was hardly necessary: the other man was reaching for his own wallet.

'Wait a minute,' Vittori-Ricciardi said. 'Neither of us has done anything. We don't have to identify ourselves to anyone. If you want to do something useful, go back and deal with that crazy woman before she attacks someone.' He turned and started to walk away.

His friend, however, said, 'Hold on, Sandro. There's no reason to cause trouble.' That said, he handed his *carta d'identità* to Brunetti, who took out his notebook and a pen and, hunched over to keep the page dry, wrote down the name. Gianluca Bembo. Born and still resident in Venice.

'*Grazie,* Signor Bembo,' Brunetti said as he handed back his card. 'That's all I need.' Behind him, he could still hear frantic sobbing and turned towards it. The two men walked away.

When he got back to Griffoni, he found her holding the sobbing Manuela against her chest. Griffoni bent down and kissed Manuela on the head, saying, 'That's all right, Manuela. We'll go to your grandmother's now and have something hot to drink.' When Manuela, who had stopped crying, did not move, Griffoni gave her a few gentle shakes and said, 'Come on. It's close by. We'll be there in a few minutes.'

Manuela mumbled something, but her face was pressed against Griffoni's shoulder so it was impossible for Brunetti or Griffoni to make out what she said. 'I can't understand you, *Tesoro,*' Griffoni said, moving slightly away from her to give her space, though still keeping her arm around her shoulder. 'What did you say?'

'He's a bad man,' Manuela said. 'He hurt me.'

Griffoni flashed a glance at Brunetti, who was looking away, seeing not the stout Sandro Vittori-Ricciardi but suddenly remembering the younger, slimmer version in the photo on the wall of Enrichetta degli Specchi's place: the long-haired and clean-shaven young man who had reminded him of someone.

'Do you have a plastic bag?' he asked Griffoni.

She started to answer but thought better of it, opened her purse and pulled out one of the distinctive yellow bags from Mascari.

Not bothering to thank her, Brunetti went back and used his still-dry handkerchief to pick up the broken umbrella that Vittori-Ricciardi had abandoned. He carefully wrapped the handkerchief around the handle and stuffed the umbrella, handle first, inside the plastic bag then closed his hand over the top of the bag in order to keep more water from touching it. He went back to Griffoni, who was now talking to a calmer

Manuela. 'We'll just go and see your grandmother now,' he heard her say.

'And the bad man?' Manuela asked her.

Griffoni looked at Brunetti, who said, 'Don't worry, Manuela. He won't bother you any more.'

25

When they reached the Contessa's home, they gave their coats to the maid, who disappeared with them, then returned to lead them into the warmth of the sitting room, where the Contessa was shocked to see how soaked they were. All three of them had left damp footprints behind them on the floor. She held up her hands when Manuela tried to speak and told her and Griffoni to go and quickly find Gala and ask her to find dry clothing and warm slippers. She insisted that Brunetti remove his jacket, soaked through at the shoulders, and suggested he hang it on the back of a chair. He set the bag holding the umbrella beneath the chair and draped his jacket over the back. She stepped up beside him and moved the chair until the back of the jacket was close to the radiator.

Before she could ask him anything, he told the Contessa he had to make a phone call.

Surprised by his brusqueness, she pointed to a door to a smaller room: Brunetti went in and closed the door. He retrieved his *telefonino* from his back pocket and called Bocchese, told him where he was, and asked him to send a man on a boat to pick up a piece of evidence in the Cavanis murder.

'It can't be the murder weapon,' Bocchese observed drily.

'It might have the same fingerprints,' Brunetti said. 'And the same DNA.'

'My, my, my,' said Bocchese, his admiration audible. 'And just where did you find this piece of evidence?'

'Lying in a puddle on Calle del Tintor.'

'Of course,' Bocchese exclaimed. 'How silly of us not to have thought of going over to look for it there.'

'It's the handle of an umbrella that was lying in the rain,' Brunetti said. 'But I picked it up with my handkerchief — a fresh one — and put it in a plastic bag.'

'When Patta finally fires you, Guido, you can come and work in the lab for me.'

'Thanks,' Brunetti said, then asked, 'How long?'

'Fingerprints by tomorrow: they're easy. DNA not for some time. You know that.'

'Fingerprints should be enough,' Brunetti said.

'I know lawyers,' Bocchese said, 'and his will say the rain changed them.'

'Can it?'

Bocchese laughed, then said, 'If they call me as an expert witness, I'll eat them alive.'

'Send the boat, all right?'

'As soon as we're off the phone.'

Brunetti hung up. When he returned to the other room, he found the Contessa sitting in one of the uncomfortable chairs, her head resting against the back. She glanced at him without speaking, and in the dim light he saw how grey with tiredness she looked.

'Someone's coming to pick that up,' he said, pointing to the destroyed umbrella in its yellow plastic bag.

'If you give it to Gala, she'll see that it's handed over,' she said. He picked up the bag, went out to the corridor and found the maid, small and friendly-looking. When she reached out to take the bag from him, he told her it was police evidence and should be touched only by the man who came to fetch it.

She gave Brunetti a strange look, the bag an even stranger one, then told him he could place it on the floor next to the door. She'd show the man who came for it where it was, she said, and told Brunetti not to worry. Then, from a small table next to her, she took a thick sweater and handed it to him, saying he might want to put it over his shoulders. Brunetti wanted.

He returned to the sitting room, where Griffoni and Manuela were now sitting at a large round table, each wearing an enormous woollen sweater instead of those they had been wearing when they arrived. Griffoni shot him a quick look. Manuela sat quietly, her eyes on her hands, which were clasped tightly together in her lap. She paid no attention to the people around the table or to what sat upon it.

This time, it was covered with mounds of crustless sandwiches, plum cake, biscuits, crème-filled eclairs, and an entire cream cake dappled with fresh strawberries.

The Contessa was sitting behind the cake, and so Brunetti took the last seat, beside her, where, he saw to his relief, there was a short crystal glass and, not far from it, an unopened bottle of the whisky he recalled.

Griffoni poured tea for the Contessa and herself, looked at Brunetti and, in response to his nod, for him as well. Something hot, something hot.

Brunetti turned to the Contessa and noticed how much shorter she seemed, sitting there next to him. Although little more than a month had passed, and her face looked the same, she had grown shorter, and smaller.

'What may I give you, Contessa?' he asked, indicating the food that lay before them.

Before she answered, the old woman looked to her left, where she saw Griffoni speaking to an unresponsive Manuela. 'The truth,' she said softly.

'Let's have something to eat and drink first,' he said.

She reached for the bottle and removed the tax stamp and top.

They ate in relative silence, Griffoni making occasional remarks to the Contessa about the food, then encouraging Manuela to try the cream cake. When they were finished, Griffoni stood and reached to take Manuela's hand. 'Come on, *Stella*, let's go and tell Gala how good everything was. It will make her happy.' This idea seemed to please Manuela, and she got to her feet, leaving her Coca-Cola and part of her cake unfinished.

As soon as the door closed behind them, Brunetti said, 'On the way here, Manuela met a man on the street and lost control of herself. She was terrified of him.'

'What?' the Contessa asked, voice sharp.

'She screamed at him not to hurt her and backed away from him.' Before the Contessa could question him, Brunetti said, 'You know the man.'

'Who is it?'

'Alessandro Vittori-Ricciardi.'

She set her teacup back in the saucer with such force that a wave of tea spilled over the side and flooded the saucer. 'That's impossible. Manuela's never met him.'

'She was terrified of him,' Brunetti repeated, ignoring her last remark, and then asked, 'How did he come to work for you?'

'A mutual friend recommended him.'

'Who?'

'Roberto Severino.'

Brunetti knew him. An architect. An honest man.

'Alessandro has done very good work for us,' she said. 'He's got style and imagination.'

And something to worry about, Brunetti thought.

The Contessa waited to see if he would continue. When he did not, she demanded, 'How could she be terrified of someone she doesn't know?'

'Did Vittori submit a curriculum vitae when he applied for work with you?'

'Of course.'

'Did it say anything about riding?'

'Riding?'

'Horse riding.'

'I don't think so. I would have remembered.'

'Do you still have the curriculum?'

'We must have. In the foundation's office,' she said. Then she asked, 'Why do you ask such a thing?'

'A man looking very much like him appears in a photo at the stable where Manuela's horse was kept.'

'And who saw this photo?' she asked, making no attempt to disguise her scepticism.

'I did. When I went to the stable with Claudia.'

'Are you sure it was he?'

'I haven't had time to speak to the woman who runs the stables.'

The Contessa said nothing.

'Could you tell me how well you know him?' Brunetti asked. When she failed to answer, he rephrased the question. 'How often have you seen him?' He thought of how familiar Vittori-Ricciardi had seemed with the Contessa.

'I see him three or four times a year.'

'That's all?'

'Why should I see more of him?' she asked.

'The way he spoke at dinner made it seem as though you did.'

'That was flattery. I hear it all the time,' she said, as though speaking of the weather report. 'We're in the process of deciding who should get the contract to restore eight new apartments.' She broke off as Claudia and Manuela came back into the room.

'*Nonna*,' Manuela said, 'Gala told me you gave her the recipe for the cake with strawberries.' All her anxiety had been smoothed away, or forgotten, while they were in the kitchen.

The Contessa smiled and held out her hand to Manuela, who came dutifully to her and took it. 'That's an exaggeration, *cara*. A friend served it for dessert, and so I asked her to write down the recipe because I thought you'd like it. I'm happy you do.' When Manuela said nothing, the Contessa tried a direct question. 'Do you like it?'

'Yes, it was very good, *Nonna*. Claudia thinks so, too,' she added, glancing across at her friend, 'don't you, Claudia?'

'Yes, it's wonderful.'

'But you didn't want a second piece,' Manuela said, sounding confused by this.

'I'm invited to dinner tonight, so I have to save a little room,' Griffoni explained, apparently to Manuela's satisfaction. Then, glancing at her watch, she said, 'Come on, Manuela; it's stopped raining and it's time to go home.'

Brunetti got to his feet, leaving half his whisky in the glass, folded the sweater over the arm of his chair, and put on his jacket. As though summoned by telepathy, Gala appeared at the door with their damp coats over her arm. There were kisses and hand-shakes, and soon they were walking back towards Campo Santa Maria Mater Domini. The rain had stopped, yet the day seemed colder, although that might have been the result of their damp clothing.

Manuela broke free of Griffoni's arm and hurried from side to side in the *calli,* looking into windows or avoiding puddles, always only a few steps ahead of them.

'Did she say anything about what happened?' Brunetti asked in a low voice.

Griffoni shook her head. 'By the time we got to the Contessa's, she'd quietened down. She was happy — you saw her — when we had cake, and she was perfectly natural in the kitchen with Gala.' Manuela came back and took Griffoni's arm for a few steps, and then detached herself and walked ahead again.

'You think he was the man who attacked her?' Griffoni asked.

Brunetti raised his eyebrows in an expression that could have meant just about anything. 'I think he worked at the stables, perhaps when she was there. There's a picture on the wall in the office of a man who looks like him. When I first met him, he had a beard, so I didn't recognise him from the photograph. But now he's shaved off his beard I'm sure it's he.' Brunetti slowed his steps and turned to face her when he added, 'You've seen him.'

Griffoni stopped walking. 'What? When?'

'He was in one of those programmes we watched on television, talking about a project he's working on, something about plaques on buildings, historic things.'

When he saw that she understood, he added, 'Cavanis had only one channel working on his television; that's the channel he appeared on.'

Before he could say anything further, Griffoni cut him short. 'That's the Belle Arti.' She grabbed his arm for emphasis. 'They'd be in charge of anything like that.'

'Belle Arti,' Brunetti whispered, thinking of the phone number on the scrap of paper in Cavanis' apartment and that he'd told Griffoni about it.

'What's his name?' she asked in a voice she struggled to keep calm.

'Alessandro Vittori-Ricciardi.'

She shook her head to show she did not recognize it. Then the two of them stood silent, working it out. Manuela came back, and on seeing them still as statues, thought it was a game, and so raised one arm in the air and put the other hand on her hip. She stood motionless like that for a moment until she tired of it and went back to look in another shop window.

'Cavanis recognized him,' Brunetti said slowly, his mind already far ahead of his words.

'And tried to call them because he was drunk and didn't know what time it was,' Griffoni added, a Christe to his Kyrie.

'And then finally did call him,' Brunetti said, closing the litany.

Griffoni's voice suddenly changed and grew sombre. 'It's all circumstantial, Guido. A good defence attorney would hang us out to dry in fifteen minutes.'

'That was his umbrella I picked up,' Brunetti said. 'Bocchese's got it now.'

She said nothing. Manuela hurried back to ask if they were close to home and seemed pleased to be told they were. When she was off again, Griffoni asked, 'Until he's done with it and has or doesn't have a match, what are you going to do?'

Brunetti took out his phone and said, 'Call Enrichetta degli Specchi and see if she has a list of the people who worked at the stables fifteen years ago.'

26

Sandro Vittori, yet to become Vittori-Ricciardi, had indeed worked at the stables during the time Manuela had kept her horse there. His job had been to clean the stables and hold the bridles of the horses ridden by the youngest students as they circled the ring. Enrichetta degli Specchi managed to find his letter of application and the records of his salary for the six months he was there. Then she called Brunetti back to tell him she had also found a copy of a letter her late husband had sent to Vittori, firing him and forbidding him to return to the stables. At Brunetti's request, she promised to fax it to the Questura but read him a few phrases over the phone. ' ". . . will not have a student of mine treated in such a disrespectful manner . . . young girls placed in my trust . . . actions not to be tolerated".'

After reading this to Brunetti, she said, 'My husband was a . . . a private person.

That is, he was very good at keeping secrets. If he knew which girl this man was bothering, he wouldn't have told anyone.'

'Thank you, Signora,' Brunetti said and asked her to fax the letter.

It had arrived by the time they got back to the Questura. It was dated two weeks before Manuela fell into the canal, a description that Brunetti was tired of using. Though the phrases read to him were strong, they left open the exact nature of Vittori's actions. 'Disrespectful manner', 'actions not to be tolerated'. They could mean almost anything, from suggestive speech to attempted rape.

Gottardi, the magistrate, when Brunetti insisted on speaking to him, was both sceptical about and interested in Brunetti's description of Manuela's panicked response when they'd met Vittori on the street, but he insisted that they could do nothing unless the fingerprints or DNA matched.

Brunetti used the skills taught to him by Signorina Elettra — perfectly legal skills — and checked to see if Vittori or Vittori-Ricciardi had a criminal record. Neither name appeared in any city, provincial, or national list of convicted criminals, information he gave to Gottardi.

'This delay gives Vittori time to think of

excuses, construct an alibi if he has to,' Brunetti told the magistrate in a last effort to persuade him to action.

'It gives us time to acquire physical evidence,' Gottardi countered, and that was the end of their conversation. After it, Brunetti paused only long enough to call Griffoni and tell her of Gottardi's decision before he took his dejected and still-damp self home.

The next day, to keep himself busy while waiting for news from Bocchese, he decided to occupy himself with his Chinese prostitutes, only to discover that they seemed to have disappeared, as if swept from the Veneto by some force of nature. It turned out that the women, none of whom had produced identification when arrested, had been released and told to return the following day with their documents. None had done so, and when the police eventually got around to checking the addresses, no one at those addresses — one of which was a vegetable stand, another a tobacco shop — knew what the police were talking about.

The Italian owners of the apartments where the women had been installed were duly shocked to learn that the Chinese gentleman who had rented all three apartments had provided false information and could not be traced. By this time, all of the women and the man who had signed the rental contracts had vanished.

His reflections were interrupted by a call from Bocchese, who said directly, 'Everything — prints, DNA — was compromised by the rain, and there are traces of at least three different people there. I could try to argue that they match the traces on the knife, but a good defence attorney would make a fool of me.'

'Thanks,' Brunetti said, unable to think of anything else to say. More ambiguity. More inconclusive evidence.

He'd lost track of time while reading the files and now saw that the daylight had faded while he was reading, though it was still too early to think of going home.

Perhaps a conversation with Signor Vittori of the added surname might resolve the ambiguity of some of the information they had. He removed the phone directory from his bottom drawer, thinking how such a simple, common action as consulting its pages had become an archaic ritual.

He found the Vs and then, with no trouble at all, an Alessandro Vittori-Ricciardi — there could not be two in the city — at an address in San Marco. He dialled the number and heard a recorded voice asking the

372

caller to leave a message or try calling a second number, which the voice provided.

He dialled that and was answered by, 'Vittori-Ricciardi.'

'Ah, Signore,' Brunetti said at his most pleasant. 'This is Commissario Guido Brunetti. We met yesterday.'

'I beg your pardon,' the man said.

'We met in the rain, in Calle del Tintor. You were with your friend, Signor Bembo. Surely you remember.'

'Ah, of course,' he said in a far more cordial voice. 'In what way can I be useful to you, Commissario?'

'By finding time to have a word with me,' Brunetti said with mirrored cordiality. 'There are a few things I'd like to clarify.'

'I'm afraid I don't understand,' Vittori-Ricciardi said.

Brunetti forged ahead, as if the other man had not spoken. 'It's only a formality, Signore, but I'd like to discuss the reaction of that woman when she saw you.'

'You know there's something wrong with her,' Vittori-Ricciardi said heatedly. 'Certainly you can't treat seriously anything she says.'

'You know her, then?' Brunetti asked mildly.

It took Vittori-Ricciardi a few moments to

respond, but when he did, he came back strongly. 'Of course I know her. She's my employer's granddaughter.'

'Ah,' Brunetti sighed, and then, as though he'd forgotten, 'Of course.' He waited to see if the other man would say anything more.

'That is, I know about her,' Vittori-Ricciardi corrected himself.

'And recognized her?' Brunetti asked innocently.

There followed another pause, this one longer than the last. 'She's been pointed out to me in the past.'

'I see,' Brunetti said calmly. 'Would it be convenient for you to come and have a few words with me, Signor Vittori?' he asked.

'Where?'

'At the Questura. It's where I work,' Brunetti said in his mildest tone.

'When?'

'Perhaps tomorrow morning,' Brunetti suggested amiably.

'What time?'

'Any time that's convenient for you,' Brunetti replied.

'Er,' he began and Brunetti realized he was dealing with a man who, however clever he might be, was not very brave: he could easily have refused Brunetti's request but did not. 'Eleven?'

'Perfect, I'll expect you then,' Brunetti said in his friendliest voice and replaced the phone.

Immediately he called Griffoni, whom he thought should be present at the interview. 'Vittori-Ricciardi's coming in tomorrow morning at eleven,' he said in place of a greeting. 'I'd like you to be here when I talk to him.'

'In what capacity?' she asked, forcing Brunetti to laugh.

'As the attractive woman he can try to impress with his charm and grace.'

'A woman not as intelligent as he is, who will have eyes only for him and think everything he says is wonderful?' she asked.

'Exactly.'

'And whose interest in him will keep him distracted from what he's saying when you question him because he'll be so busy trying to impress this woman?'

'Yes,' Brunetti said.

'And should this woman dress in a particular way?' she asked.

'I leave that entirely to you, Claudia,' he said and told her he'd see her the next morning.

Brunetti went to Griffoni's office shortly after ten the next morning and could not suppress a smile when he saw her. Her hair was a mass of golden ringlets pulled back by a black ribbon so undisciplined as to allow several curls to escape its care. Her sweater was beige, just tight enough to entice the connoisseur's eye to discern the lace on the top of her brassiere. Her skirt, dark brown wool and just short enough, fell above her knees, allowing those perfect calves to show to great advantage.

Her makeup was restrained: pale pink lipstick and only a touch of eyeliner. She might well have been a serious police officer, but there was a strong suggestion of the possibility of something else.

'*Complimenti,*' Brunetti said with open admiration.

'Thank you, Commissario,' she said and batted her eyelids at him. 'It's so encouraging to a woman to know she has male approval.'

'That's enough now, Claudia,' he said and took his place on the simple wooden chair that guests used in her tiny office.

'He recognized Manuela,' he continued, 'and told me I couldn't believe anything she said because there was something wrong with her.'

All expression fled Griffoni's face when she heard this. After a moment, she asked, 'Did he say anything else?'

'No, not really. He said he'd never met her, only that she'd been "pointed out" to him. I asked him to come in to talk to me, and he agreed.'

'Is he that stupid?' Griffoni asked.

'If he shows up without a lawyer, then yes, he is.'

'Why is he coming?' she asked.

'I think it's because it hasn't occurred to him that we might have made a connection to Cavanis,' Brunetti explained.

Griffoni considered this and said, 'You're probably right. We saw him entirely by chance; you'd naturally be interested in a reaction that strong, regardless of the woman it came from. But there's no reason we should connect him to Cavanis.'

Brunetti tried to put himself into the mind

of the younger man, cocky and sure of himself. 'Clever devil: he must know she couldn't testify.'

'Because of the way she is?' Griffoni asked.

'That, yes,' Brunetti agreed. 'And because no decent person would ask her to.'

This time Griffoni nodded. She stared at the wall above his head so intently that he dared not interrupt her. Finally she said, 'None of this makes sense unless he raped her, does it?'

'No. If Cavanis did remember what he saw and told him that he did, then Vittori would have had to commit another crime to cover up the first.' Brunetti balked at hearing himself say 'would have had to' until he thought of the *Macbeth* he and Paola had once seen in London. Macbeth too had convinced himself he'd had no choice.

With a glance at her watch, she asked, 'Should I delay my arrival a few minutes? That would allow me to be surprised and charmed at the same time, wouldn't it?'

'You sound pretty familiar with the scenario,' Brunetti said.

'Customs linger longer in Napoli, Guido. These ideas are still around.'

He got up from the chair and eased himself around it and to the door. 'I'll tell them downstairs to let you know when he arrives.'

'I'll count the minutes.'

Brunetti had thought to aid the scene with props and so had gone down to Signorina Elettra's office earlier and asked for all of the files that he still had to read. He took them back to his office and set four or five to his right, with the rest of them in a pile just in front of him. He opened the first one; it stated the new regulations for the use of official automobiles for work-related travel and ran to five pages. He closed it and set it down, wondering why such a thing had been sent to the police in Venice.

There was a knock at his door. He opened the next file, called out, *'Avanti,'* and looked back at the first page. He counted three long seconds and looked up, noticed Vittori standing in the doorway. He was alone, had actually come without a lawyer: Brunetti could hardly believe it. He smiled.

'Ah, Signor Vittori,' Brunetti said, continuing to drop the second surname. 'Thank you for coming to see me.' He stood but stayed behind his desk, a conscious manifestation of territorial supremacy he was careful to use with visitors who might register it as such, however unconsciously. 'Please,' he said, waving to the two chairs in front of his desk.

Vittori, who was wearing a dark grey suit with a yellow and red striped tie, kept his chin up and his eyes on Brunetti's, but his feet moved reluctantly, and it took him some time to cross the room. The beard had camouflaged the plumpness of his face and covered his double chin: now that it was gone, Brunetti observed, he looked not only younger, but stouter. His mouth, in contrast, seemed thinner than it had been.

Vittori extended his hand across the desk, and Brunetti shook it quickly. His hand-shake was strong but tentatively so, as if he wanted to see if Brunetti would try to win — whatever that meant. Brunetti responded with a firm clasp that he quickly released.

Vittori sat and pulled the legs of his trousers up so as not to stretch the knees. Brunetti gave the lapels and shoulders a quick look and decided the suit was worth the trouble.

He waited a moment, but Vittori remained silent, something he had probably told himself to do. His look was attentive and interested, but also faintly confused, perhaps meant to indicate his perplexity as to why the police would want to talk to him, of all people.

'The Contessa has spoken to me about you,' Brunetti began, smiling amiably while managing to suggest that he and the Contessa were close friends. 'She's very pleased with your work and says you're gifted.'

Vittori looked at his shoes in an affected gesture of modesty. 'It's kind of her to say that,' Vittori said.

'What is it you design for her?' Brunetti asked with genuine interest.

'The apartments that will be rented to young couples. The floors of the *palazzi* are being divided into smaller units, and we try to keep the size of the apartments and the design and fixtures similar.'

'Why is that?' Brunetti asked.

'So that no one will feel cheated if they see the apartment of the person living next to them. There is no conspicuous difference between them.'

'If I might admit to curiosity,' Brunetti began, knowing that it was important to establish the pattern of question and answer early on in an interview, 'what sort of rents do people pay, and how large are the apartments?'

'They're all about a hundred to a hundred and ten square metres,' Vittori said. 'Two bedrooms and two baths. The rent is about five hundred euros a month.'

'But that's nothing,' Brunetti said, not having to pretend to be surprised.

'That's the purpose,' Vittori said, with a proud smile. 'To let young people remain in their city.'

'Well, good for Demetriana,' Brunetti exclaimed, using her first name casually, as though in the habit of doing so. 'I knew the rents were low, but she never told me how low.' That was certainly true enough. Then, with admiration, 'It's a worthy project.'

'It's a shame more people in the city don't do it,' Vittori said.

'I couldn't agree more strongly. 'I think . . .' Brunetti was interrupted by a knocking at the door of his office. *'Avanti,'* he called. The door opened and in walked Griffoni. She had had time to freshen her lipstick, Brunetti noticed, and approved.

Vittori was on his feet and had turned towards her.

'Ah, Signor Vittori,' Brunetti said, 'let me introduce my colleague, Commissario Griffoni.'

Claudia approached, her hand extended. Vittori took it and bent over it; he kissed the air just above it as Griffoni shot Brunetti a blazing smile. Vittori had obviously failed to recognize the hatted and dripping woman he had seen on the street.

'Please have a seat, Claudia,' Brunetti said. Vittori stood behind the second chair and pulled it back a few millimetres. Griffoni swept her skirt under her and sat, feet and knees modestly pressed together.

'Signor Vittori was just telling me about his work,' Brunetti said.

'You're an architect, aren't you, Signore?' Griffoni asked.

'Well,' Vittori said modestly, 'I took a degree in architecture, but I have to confess I prefer working on interiors, using the various elements of space and light to create a setting in which people will feel comfortable and at home while still being aware of the beauty around them.'

'You Venetians have the advantage of living with beauty around you everywhere,' she said with an admiring smile.

Vittori returned her smile. What sort of fool was he, Brunetti asked himself. He's in front of two commissari di polizia and he thinks he's Casanova: if he charms Claudia, she'll help him against me. Well, let him give that a try.

'Yes, that's certainly true,' Brunetti interrupted abruptly. 'But I asked you to come here, Signor Vittori, to talk about the meeting on the street with Manuela Lando-Continui, to which both the Commissario and I were parties.'

'Oh, was that you?' Vittori asked Griffoni. 'I was distracted by the screaming of that woman,' he said and quickly added, 'Or I certainly would have noticed you.'

Griffoni gave him another smile but turned her attention, with visible reluctance, to Brunetti. 'For the sake of correctness, should we be recording this, Commissario?' she asked, careful to use his title, while he had called her by her first name, to show that the men were in charge in this room, and let there be no doubt of it.

With a smile in Vittori's direction, Brunetti said, 'Only if Signor Vittori has no objections.'

In the ensuing silence, Vittori looked from Brunetti's face to Griffoni's encouraging smile. 'No, of course not,' he said, and Brunetti pressed the button on the front of his desk that activated the tape recorder, gave the date, time, and location, adding, 'Conversation among Alessandro Vittori, Commissario Guido Brunetti, and Commissario Claudia Griffoni.'

He moved the pile of papers in front of him to the side, pulled his chair closer to the desk, and gave his attention to Vittori.

'Signor Vittori,' he began, 'yesterday afternoon, in Calle del Tintor, Commissario

Griffoni and I were witnesses to a heated meeting between you and Signorina Manuela Lando-Continui. Could you tell us what happened?'

'Why do you think it was a meeting, Commissario?' Vittori asked with easy curiosity. 'I was walking with a friend, when this woman began — and I think you will have to bear witness that I was at some distance from her when she started — screaming, either at me or at my friend: it was impossible to say.' Vittori sounded genuinely puzzled. 'After all, we were walking side by side.'

'She appeared to be pointing at you,' Brunetti said. 'And she kept looking at you.'

'You sound very certain of that,' Vittori said condescendingly. 'It was raining heavily, both my friend and I were wearing raincoats but were soaked to the skin, so I rather doubt that even our mothers would have been sure which of us was which.'

Griffoni smiled, then pretended that she had not. She looked at Brunetti, who said, 'From where I was standing, she was pointing at you, Signor Vittori. And you say you know her.'

Vittori held up a monitory hand. 'Don't be putting words in my mouth, Commissario. I said I recognized her, not that I knew her. I've seen her on the street a few times, but I've never met her.' He looked to Griffoni, as if asking her to confirm the truth of what he'd just said.

She nodded, held up a hand, palm toward Brunetti in a repetition of Vittori's gesture, then suddenly pulled it back and put it over her mouth. She coughed lightly, then more strongly, and then bent over and started to cough violently, gasping for air. Vittori turned to her and placed a hand on her arm, but she continued to cough, her entire body shaking now. She removed her hand in an effort to breathe, then slapped it back over her mouth but failed to stop coughing.

Vittori, at a loss, did the gentlemanly thing and handed her the handkerchief from his breast pocket. She pressed it to her mouth and continued to cough but managed to give him a few nods and hold up one hand to show him she was all right. Slowly, she stopped and sat in the chair, breathing heavily.

'Are you all right, Signora?' Vittori asked, leaning towards her.

She nodded. 'Thank you. Yes,' she said in a small, rough voice. Brunetti saw that her face was still red, and her voice had grown hoarse.

At a loss for what to do, Brunetti could

only wait until it seemed she was breathing normally, when he asked, 'Would you like some water?'

She waved the offer away and smiled at Vittori, as though he had been the one to speak.

'Then let us accept that the young woman's words were directed at one of you, Signor Vittori,' Brunetti resumed. 'She insisted that you had hurt her in some way,' he said, then, before Vittori could correct him, amended it to, 'that one of you had hurt her. Have you any idea why she might have said that?'

'Maybe I poked her with my umbrella,' Vittori said and turned to Griffoni to share his clever remark.

Brunetti saw the flash of rage in her eyes, but perhaps Vittori saw only a flash and interpreted it as he pleased. His smile remained even after he looked back at Brunetti.

Better to pass over reference to the umbrella for the moment, Brunetti thought.

'Signor Vittori,' Brunetti went on, 'Are you quite sure you never saw her before, perhaps worked with her? Something that would at least allow her to recognize you, no matter how excessive her behaviour?'

'How could someone like that have a job?'

387

Vittori said automatically, apparently pleased to find something to criticize in Brunetti's remarks. 'She's been like that for a long time,' he added.

Brunetti put on a confused smile and asked, ' "Someone like that", Signor Vittori?'

'A retarded woman, if I might use that antiquated phrase,' Vittori said primly. Then, unable to disguise his spite, 'A seven-year-old.'

'Thank you, Signor Vittori. I'll have to ask her grandmother if she's ever done anything like this before,' Brunetti said, interested that Vittori should be sufficiently familiar with Manuela's history as to gauge her mental age.

'I'm surprised you didn't take the trouble to do that before asking me to come in here,' Vittori said with the righteous irritation of the persecuted. Then, turning to Griffoni, he said, 'But it did give me the chance to meet your colleague.' My God, Brunetti thought, do adult men still behave like this?

'If you'd never met Manuela, how is it that you know so much about the nature of her handicap?' Griffoni asked, allowing her Neapolitan accent to appear.

Had she been a puppy that bit his caressing hand, Vittori could have been no more startled. In fact, he pulled away from her at the question, attempting to distance himself from this most unfeminine behaviour.

'Everyone knows,' he said. 'Every Venetian, that is.' Take that, you southerner, he seemed to be saying.

'Knows what, Signor Vittori?' Brunetti inquired.

'That she fell into a canal — was drunk or drugged or tried to kill herself — and was under the water so long that her brain was damaged.'

'And now she's a seven-year-old?' Griffoni asked mildly, then added, 'You do seem to know a lot about a person you've never met, Signore.'

'Everyone in the city knows,' he repeated, and then added, with a self-satisfied smile, 'As I've already told you.' After thoughtful reflection, he said, 'Besides, you just have to look at her to know there's something wrong.'

'You're a very observant man,' she said and smiled.

For a moment, Brunetti watched instinct and habit take over as Vittori smiled at the compliment. But then the smile grew uneasy and forced. 'You just have to look at her face, those vacant eyes.' Brunetti was surprised Griffoni didn't shudder when she heard this.

Griffoni smiled and raised her chin, as if about to engage in some sort of philosophical speculation: and then did just that. 'I wonder what sort of woman she'd be if she hadn't gone into the water? If she were a thirty-year-old instead of a seven-year-old.' She lowered her eyes and looked at Vittori. 'Did you ever wonder about that, Signor Vittori?'

Vittori froze, his face a mask of incomprehension, and Brunetti felt a chill at the realization that Vittori had never posed this question to himself. Fifteen years had passed for him, while Manuela had remained trapped in the amber of immutability. And he had never given it a thought.

The silence expanded. Brunetti felt his mind and heart harden against this man; he looked at Griffoni and saw bleak resolution in her eyes. Vittori sat with his mouth slightly open, as if trying to find some new way to breathe.

Finally he said, 'Why should I think about something like that?'

Rape, attempted murder, murder: Brunetti considered this escalation of crimes. But what appalled him was the fact that Vittori really meant what he said: why should

390

he bother to think about what had been done to Manuela?

Brunetti looked at Vittori and said, 'I've lived here all my life, and I'd never seen her before.' He paused, as though considering a possibility, then went on, forcing a smile, 'Of course, it could be that we live in entirely different parts of the city.'

Vittori sat up straighter in his chair, glanced at Griffoni as though she were a person who'd come to sit next to him on the vaporetto when the rest of the boat was empty, and said, 'I seldom have reason to go to Santa Croce.'

By force of will, Brunetti prevented himself from glancing at Griffoni. He didn't know if she would pounce on Vittori now for admitting he knew where this person he didn't know lived, or would wait until later in the interview.

'My concern here,' Brunetti began, talking man to man, 'is that she might make some sort of official complaint against you. Say something to her mother or her grandmother, either of whom would be sure to ask us what we know about the incident. In that case, I'd be obliged to repeat what I saw and heard her say.'

Vittori threw his hands in the air as a sign of his exasperation. 'How can that be possible, if she's a half-wit? Who'd believe her?'

Brunetti dismissed the possibility. 'I'm thinking about the effect on your reputation. As you said, her grandmother is your employer. I have no way of knowing what her reaction would be.'

'But she wouldn't believe her, would she?' asked a scandalized Vittori.

'Manuela's her granddaughter,' Brunetti said, suggesting that there was no way of calculating the extent to which people would be carried, once the idea of family was involved. Besides, women were so hopelessly sentimental, weren't they?

'All the more reason for her grandmother not to believe her,' Vittori said. 'If the Contessa's been with her all these years, she knows what her granddaughter is.' Vittori sat quietly for a few moments and then said angrily, 'It's not only my reputation, it's my honour that's at stake here.' He took two quick breaths and then burst out, 'The very idea that I'd assault . . . Why, it's ridiculous.'

I will not look at Claudia. I will not look at Claudia. I will not look at Claudia, Brunetti told himself, forcing his eyes to remain fixed on Vittori.

The other man had risen to the role and now demanded, 'How dare she make an accusation like that? How dare she?'

Brunetti allowed time for sweet reason to come to his aid and said, 'The difficult thing here is that people today tend to believe the woman.'

'But she's not a woman. She's just a child,' Vittori said, with no attempt to disguise his anger. 'No one will believe her.'

Brunetti was about to respond when his phone rang. He saw that it was Signorina Elettra's number, so he picked it up with a curt *'Sì.'*

'Giorgio just called me. The last call on one of those cards in Cavanis' garbage was made the morning of the day he was killed to the home number of the man who's with you now. Eight forty-three: it lasted six minutes. It came from a public phone two bridges from Cavanis' home.' And then she was gone.

28

Brunetti folded his hands just in front of him on his desk, the way he could remember the first Questore he worked for doing when he summoned Brunetti for the yearly evaluation of his performance. He allowed himself a quick glance at Griffoni, who sat with her hands folded in her lap. He noticed a small bulge in the sleeve of her sweater, just at the cuff: Vittori's handkerchief, he assumed. Here were traces that would not be compromised by the rain.

'Signor Vittori,' he began in a serious and not particularly friendly voice, 'I'd like to turn your attention away from the vague accusation made on the street yesterday to events in the past.'

'Not when she went into the water, I hope,' Vittori said, trying for irony but coming just short of belligerence.

'No, far closer in time,' Brunetti said easily. 'I refer to the morning on which you received a phone call from Pietro Cavanis.' He looked at Vittori, whose face had been wiped clean of all expression. 'Could you tell me if you remember that, Signor Vittori?'

Vittori tried to look uninterested in the question, but he was no good at it. His head moved backwards a few millimetres, and his mouth contracted in what, in other circumstances, might have been pique or irritation. Had he not shaved his beard, the tiny moue might not have been noticed by either Brunetti or Griffoni.

Brunetti, imitating his Questore, lowered his head and stared at his hands for a moment. When he glanced at Vittori again, he saw that the man was staring at his own hands, clasped in his lap. Brunetti looked at Griffoni, who nodded, face rigid, then indicated to Brunetti that he was in charge and she'd follow his lead.

'That was a Thursday, wasn't it?' Vittori asked in a calm voice, head still lowered.

'No, it was a Sunday,' Brunetti said and gave him the precise date.

'A Sunday . . . I'd probably have been at home.'

'Don't you remember?' Brunetti asked.

After pausing for further reflection, Vittori said, 'I believe I didn't go out that day,' and Brunetti did not call Vittori's attention to the fact that he did not bother to ask who Pietro Cavanis was.

'I've had a lot of work to finish, so I often take it home with me,' Vittori said. Then, in the manner of one overburdened bureaucrat speaking to another, he said, 'You know what it's like.'

Ignoring the question, Brunetti asked, 'Do you remember speaking to Signor Cavanis?'

Vittori stared at him as though Brunetti had somehow gained access to his brain.

'I might have, although I have no clear memory of it,' he answered, with no attempt to hide what he attempted to make look like mild indignation.

'This was a call that lasted six minutes,' Brunetti added, as if hoping to prod his memory.

Vittori studied his hands again, searching for a plausible answer. Brunetti used this opportunity to glance at Griffoni. There could have been a wall between her and Vittori, so little attention did she pay him.

'I might have,' Vittori finally answered. 'People feel free to call me very early.'

'When?' Brunetti inquired.

'Oh,' Vittori exclaimed, 'didn't you say?'

'No, but if it might help you remember, it came at 8.43, which is indeed early,' Brunetti said.

'Yes, yes,' Vittori answered, dragging out the two words. 'It is.' He kept his attention on Brunetti, as if afraid of what would happen to him if he looked at Griffoni.

Brunetti was put in mind of a television programme he had watched ages ago, must be thirty years: *Visitors,* which featured man-sized reptiles disguised as humans. When they were killed, their human carapace fell away, exposing the giant reptile within that was already shrinking into death. Vittori was losing his carapace of casual arrogance and seemed, even as Brunetti observed him, to be growing smaller, as if withering away.

Vittori took a deep breath, started to speak, and then took another. He remained silent for a long time, carefully attentive to his joined hands, which were clasped tight, fingers enmeshed.

When he decided that Vittori was not going to speak, Brunetti changed the subject and said, 'Signor Vittori, we know about your job at the stables, and the letter from Signor degli Specchi.'

Vittori, who had been motionless, froze. Brunetti thought he heard a soft noise, like the sound a man makes when he picks up something heavy.

'People who were working there at the

time,' Brunetti proceeded calmly, 'are sure to remember you and anything . . . peculiar about your behaviour.' He watched these words thud into Vittori.

Vittori continued in close communion with his hands for some time, then looked back at Brunetti. 'Someone saw me on television,' he finally said. 'And he called with some crazy story and said he wanted money from me or he'd call you and tell you.'

'The police?' Brunetti asked. He watched Vittori as he spoke, amazed at how fear could change the face of a person, exaggerating the bones and shrinking the eyes. 'Tell us what?' he prompted.

Brunetti had the feeling that Vittori was working out just how to tell his story. Finally he said, 'He told me if I didn't give him money, he'd call you and say he saw me throw Manuela into the canal.' He waited for Brunetti's response, then added, 'He'd destroy my honour,' and Brunetti heard a small intake of breath from Griffoni, as though she'd touched something nasty in the dark.

'What did you do?' Brunetti asked.

Indignation splashed across Vittori's face. 'What could I do? This was a madman, making a false accusation. I didn't know who he was. His threats were insane.'

Brunetti watched the other man continue to shift the gears of his story until Vittori said, 'I hung up on him.'

Brunetti looked at Vittori, who was again studying his folded hands, then at Griffoni, who shook her head.

'And then?' Brunetti asked.

'And then nothing. He never called back.'

'You didn't try to trace the call?' Brunetti asked. 'Use reverse dialling?'

'No. I was terrified. Accusations like this could destroy my reputation, my career. I'd be dragged through the courts, and that woman would scream her crazy accusations at me. I'd have no chance. Everyone would believe her.'

Brunetti thought it wise not to point out to Vittori that Manuela had not screamed accusations at him, had only screamed. Instead, he asked mildly, 'Should they believe her?'

'Of course not,' Vittori said, throwing his hands into the air. 'She was always following me around, touching me when I helped her into the saddle. She was like one of the mares in heat, begging for it.'

Brunetti glanced quickly at Griffoni, who had grabbed the sides of her chair, as if that were the only way she could keep her hands from reaching for Vittori.

Speaking as though he were a friend of Vittori's, surprised that he had failed to recognize the turn-off to his own street, Brunetti asked, 'But what were you afraid of?'

'A false accusation by a woman who was a minor at the time of the . . .' he drew in his breath and spat out with contempt, 'the supposed attack. Even that would cause me trouble.'

'But no one would get the chance to listen to her,' Brunetti said, careful to avoid Griffoni.

'Of course they would,' Vittori insisted petulantly. 'They always believe the woman.'

'But there's nothing she could do about it or that we could,' Brunetti insisted in the face of Vittori's failure to understand. 'The statute of limitations,' he said. 'It's ten years, and then no accusation can be made. Even if you had done it, you couldn't be charged with it now. It's over. It's gone.'

Vittori's face froze. As Brunetti watched, he struggled to open his mouth, but failed. He broke free of his trance and licked his lips, finally managing to force them open, but he produced nothing more than a bleated 'uh, uh'. The colour had drained from his face, and for a moment Brunetti thought he was going to faint. Time stopped in the room as Vittori tried to force himself back to life.

Brunetti had read that many people, faced with the end of life, see it all pass before them. For Vittori, only the last weeks mattered: Brunetti believed that.

The voice that finally came from Vittori was an old man's. 'That can't be true.' If a desert could have spoken, it would have sounded like this. 'No.'

Griffoni spoke. 'You must be relieved, Signor Vittori. Nothing she says can hurt your honour now. As my colleague has told you: no matter what you might have done to her, it's over. It's gone.'

Had Vittori been standing, he would have reeled from side to side. As it was, he imitated Griffoni's gesture and clasped the seat of his chair. He took one deep breath and then another and then gave an enormous sigh, as at the end of a valiant feat.

Brunetti was tempted to drag this out and give Vittori the chance to say more, but he had never approved of torture, even for someone like the man sitting in front of him, and so he said, 'But the murder of Pietro Cavanis is still with us, Signor Vittori, and I am both accusing you of that crime and arresting you for having commit-

401

ted it.'

At this point in the interview with Signor Vittori, Brunetti was later to testify during Alessandro Vittori's trial for the murder of Pietro Cavanis, Commissario Claudia Griffoni got to her feet and left the room.

During that same trial, Signor Vittori testified that Manuela Lando-Continui had begged him to have sex with her but that he had refused because she was underage and he did not want to endanger his job. Two persons who had kept horses at the stable while Signor Vittori was employed there testified that Signor Vittori had, on the contrary, been almost violent in his attentions to Signorina Lando-Continui, who was both troubled and angered by his behaviour.

In the face of Signor Vittori's repeated protestations of his innocence of the crime of murder, the prosecuting magistrate introduced forensic evidence to the contrary. The DNA sample taken from Vittori's handkerchief matched that found on the knife with which Pietro Cavanis has been killed. Further, the morning of the murder of Signor Cavanis — and shortly after he had received a phone call made with a phonecard found in Pietro Cavanis' possession — Signor Vittori had searched the internet and found newspaper accounts of Manuela Lando-Continui's rescue from the waters of Rio San Boldo, an account which provided the name of Signor Cavanis, who was the only Pietro Cavanis in the phone book and still resident at the address in Santa Croce given in the article.

Unfortunately for him, Signor Vittori had not used the internet to search for the statute of limitations for the crime of rape, which had expired well before Signor Cavanis had phoned him. Had he done so, he might not have been led to murder, for which he was convicted in the first trial, a conviction that is now under appeal.

29

Brunetti, although he knew where they were going, had no idea that they had arrived, so careful had Griffoni been to leave the autostrada well before Preganziol and arrive by a web of small roads well to the northwest of the town, the opposite direction from which one would normally arrive from Venice. Griffoni, who was driving a friend's car, made sure not to be seen from the house and pulled up on the other side of the property, the main building hidden by the new growth on the trees.

She stopped the car a hundred metres from the fence, turned off the engine, and the three people in it sat and listened to the creaks and cracks as the engine cooled and the metal parts contracted. It was springtime, the leaves were on their way back, but still the day was brisk; even the clouds were busy, scuttling to the north.

Brunetti got out first. He looked around

for the dog, but there was no sign of Hector, who was probably assigned to sleep duty that day. Without thinking, he was careful to close the door of the car quietly.

Griffoni was leaning into the front seat to help Manuela unlatch her seat belt, after which the younger woman had no trouble opening the door and getting out. 'Oh, how pretty,' she said, looking around at the fresh green leaves that surrounded them on three sides. 'Everything's new.'

Griffoni turned from her study of the fields and linked her arm in Manuela's. 'Yes, springtime's lovely, isn't it,' she chirped in that voice Brunetti had heard her use with Manuela. It was happy and upbeat and spoke of endless opportunity; it was the voice he had used with his own children but never used any more.

Then, in her real voice, Griffoni said to Brunetti, 'Springtime always makes me think life's decided to give us another chance.'

Manuela turned to look at her. 'I don't understand,' she said.

'It doesn't matter, *Tesoro*. In spingtime, it's green everywhere, and we get to hear the birds. We're in the countryside.' She flung her arms out and spun around, and Manuela imitated her, turning and turning until Griffoni had to take her arm to stop her, pulling her close and holding her until her excitement quietened.

Griffoni turned to Brunetti and asked, 'Shall we take a walk?'

'Yes,' he said. 'Which way?'

'Oh, let's follow that fence and see where it leads,' Griffoni said casually. 'Is that all right with you, Manuela?' she asked, careful not to ask her to decide between more complicated alternatives.

'Yes, yes,' Manuela said and hooked her arm through Griffoni's.

Keeping the wooden fence on their left, they began to walk. Horizontal rails had collapsed here and there along the way: some were propped back in place and held together with twisted lengths of wire. One fence post was entirely covered with the fierce green leaves of a clematis, too early for it to show buds.

Manuela stopped suddenly and Griffoni banged against her side. 'What is it?' Griffoni asked.

'I hear a noise,' Manuela said.

Griffoni stood stock still; so did Brunetti. It took them a few moments to adjust to the silence, but when he did, Brunetti heard the noise, coming from somewhere amidst the trees to their right. Again it came: high low, high low, and then again.

'Is that the noise?' Griffoni asked.

Manuela nodded.

Griffoni released her arm and searched in the pocket of her jeans. She pulled out a five-euro note. Brunetti was busy searching in his trouser pockets.

'What are you doing?' Manuela asked, but, perhaps because she was with Griffoni, she sounded curious, not fearful.

'Do you have any money in your pockets?' Griffoni asked her.

'I don't know,' Manuela said and put her hands in the pockets of her jacket. Her right hand emerged with a few coins. 'I have these,' she said, showing them to Griffoni.

The older woman bent down and used her forefinger to separate the coins on Manuela's extended palm. 'Six euros, twenty-seven,' she said, turning to Brunetti.

'Very good,' Brunetti said and held out his handful of change. 'I've got four euros, twelve.'

Manuela's face showed only confusion. 'I don't understand. I don't understand. Tell me, tell me, tell me.'

'It's a cuckoo,' Griffoni said in her calming voice. 'The first time you hear a cuckoo in springtime, you have to see how much money you have in your pockets. And the more you have, the more money you'll get during the year.'

Manuela looked down at her palm. 'Do I have a lot?'

'Yes, you have more than I do and more than Signor Brunetti.'

'Is that good?'

'Oh yes,' Griffoni said. She folded Manuela's hand around the money, and told her she should put it back in her pocket so she didn't lose it.

'What can I do with it?' Manuela insisted.

'Oh, you could buy yourself ice cream, if you like.'

Manuela thought about this, then asked, 'Is there enough for me to buy some for you and for Signor Brunetti, too?'

Griffoni leaned to her side and kissed Manuela's cheek. 'Of course there is, *Stella,*' she said in an unsteady voice.

'We can stop on the way back to the city,' Brunetti interrupted to say.

Manuela nodded in delight at this thought, then asked, 'Where are we going?'

'Oh, just along the fence a little bit,' Griffoni said.

The cuckoo commented on this, as did a few other birds. They continued to walk, following the fence. At a point where it angled away to the left, Griffoni stopped and turned to look over the fence, putting her right foot up on the first rail.

She put her index fingers under her tongue and gave a piercing whistle, then again. Manuela giggled, and Brunetti looked at Griffoni and then at a flash of motion on the far side of the field.

Something large had started to move in their direction. It seemed to slow, and Griffoni gave another whistle, at the sound of which the motion increased.

It was a horse, catapulting towards them. He knew the names of the different speeds of a horse: walk, trot, canter, gallop. But this was something different: jet-propelled.

As Brunetti watched, the horse thundered towards them, leaping over obstacles the humans couldn't see from where they were, aimed right at them, relentless.

Fifteen metres from them, the horse, began to slow, then slowed again, until it stopped only a metre away and reared up on its back legs. While still in the air, just like a horse in some phony American Western, it threw back its head and let out a high-pitched whinny, then thudded back down on its front hooves and moved up to the railing, head moving up and down, up and down in a frenzy.

During all of this, Manuela had been at

first afraid, then quiet, then stunned. Brunetti turned and watched her, saw her face, for the first time, washed clean of the uncertainty that too often veiled it.

Moving as if spurred by some stronger force, she stood on the bottom rung of the fence and then the second. She leaned forward, arms spread wide.

'Petunia,' she said and wrapped her arms around the horse's neck. 'Petunia.'

ABOUT THE AUTHOR

Donna Leon is the author of the international best-selling Commissario Guido Brunetti series. The winner of the CWA Macallan Silver Dagger for Fiction, among other awards, Leon was born in New Jersey and has lived in Venice for thirty years.